STUDYING FORM

Andy Wheildon

Steve Danby

For giving me Zoë

Friday, 22 March 1991

Nottingham, England

The room was dark except for a shining angle-poise table lamp and a CRT monitor screen hooked up to a computer, both of which were sitting on a desk with a tower computer underneath in the corner. The monitor illuminated Ian's face whilst the lamp shone down on numerous manuals and scribbled notes. The remainder of the darkened room was sparsely furnished: a wardrobe, two chests of drawers and a single bed. The bed was unmade, a quilt hanging half off the bed and one of two pillows lying on the floor.

It was early evening, and as the minutes passed, Ian became more and more agitated. He had been working on a computer program for some days, and it felt like he was no closer to getting it to work than on the day he had been assigned the task.

Outside, the wind was blowing hard, and his bedroom curtains flapped with every gust. A new gust sent a fresh shiver of cold through to his bones. It was impossible to keep warm at this time of year. Sash-chord windows had a lot to answer for during the winter and early spring months. Ian's personal heating system, PAJO, worked only occasionally. It was a cheap heating system and cheap was currently Ian's way of life. Since PAJO stood for 'put another jumper on', there were times when he felt more like the Michelin Man than an undergraduate.

This was Ian's final year at Nottingham Trent Polytechnic. His A-level grades four years earlier had not been good enough to propel him to his first choice, Loughborough University. But he had enjoyed life in Nottingham. He had gained excellent marks over the previous three years and was well on his way to hopefully gaining an honours degree in Computer Technology and Robotics. This evening, however, was proving somewhat troublesome as he battled with his software code. The application under development was supposed to control a robotic arm in performing a simple task of seek, identify, extract and replace. Unfortunately, things were not running smoothly.

Ian had been making constant reference to a printout from his noisy, and somewhat outdated, dot-matrix printer. The computer kept beeping and displaying messages like 'syntax error' and 'unmatched parentheses', and finally, with the advent of a General Protection Fault (which proved fatal to his program), he decided to call it a day since he would have to restart his computer, and he just couldn't be bothered.

He reflected on the fact that he had saved his code to the computer hard disk moments before the computer crashed. Fortunately, therefore, none of his recent work was lost – it just didn't work! He decided the best course of action was to nip downstairs, get a beer from the fridge and relax in front of the telly for the rest of the evening.

Studying Form

*

Meanwhile, Nigel – in the same house but in a different room – was poring over endless books, newspaper articles and video recordings of horse races, making notes, cross-referencing what he'd just read and seen. He watched a video for a third time and got slightly annoyed when a particular horse didn't win. *But that's racing*, he reasoned.

Nigel owned the property the two were living in, and he rented a room out to Ian. To be more precise, Nigel looked after the property which belonged to his parents, fully knowing, eventually, the property would become his by way of inheritance. The dwelling was a three-storey, semi-detached townhouse built in the 1920s on the relatively quiet Mapperley Road. Nigel had lived in Nottingham for most of his life, enjoying primary school in Carlton and hating secondary school in Gedling. Fortunately, he left school with enough O levels to keep many potential employment doors open. However, over the relatively few years that had followed, life had conspired to deal a few bad hands which had led to those doors being swiftly closed and locked, the metaphorical keys thrown away.

*

Ian made his way into the kitchen rubbing the back of his neck and stretching to release the tension in his shoulders. He turned the kitchen light on and looked at the total devastation around the sink and the mess on the worktop. He called out, 'You dirty git,' to his landlord upstairs.

Ian opened the fridge door, licking his lips in anticipation, expecting a cold can of lager. Working at the computer for so long, he deserved a drink.

'Aagh, you bastard!' Ian slammed the fridge door shut, stormed up to Nigel's room and burst in without knocking.

Nigel looked up from his desk and grinned. 'Looks like you need a drink!'

'That's my beer,' Ian exclaimed. 'Why do you always drink my beer when you run out? I've been working in my igloo of a bedroom for two and a half hours with the computer as my only source of heat and *that* can of lager'—Ian gestured to the drink in Nigel's hand—'the only thing to look forward to. And you have to go and bloody pinch it.'

'Don't worry, I'll replace it.'

'Replace it? When? I want it now!'

Nigel passed the half-empty can to Ian.

'I don't want it *now*!'

'But you just said—'

'I know what I said. I want a *drink* now – a full drink, a fresh drink. It's no good offering me a second-hand, half-empty can.' Ian paused to regain his composure. 'And when are you going to do something about the heating? My room is freezing.'

'It's on my to-do list, *as you jolly well know*. It'll soon be at the top,' Nigel said with a smile, 'along with the arrival of the warmth of summer.'

'Trying to be posh doesn't suit you. And another thing.' Ian was now in full stride. 'The kitchen – it's like a bomb has hit it. You live like a slob.'

Studying Form

'For fucks sake! And you constantly whinge. Give me a break. I'll wash up, I'll get the heating fixed, I'll replace your beer – don't worry. Anyway, you're not the only one who's been busy tonight. You know what's happening tomorrow, don't you?' Nigel turned back to his papers.

'A horse race?' Ian speculated. An easy guess really since Nigel's life revolved around horseracing.

'Correct. A horse race. Well done. The first big betting race of the Flat season, and I am going to pick the winner.'

'Of course you are.' Ian's tone was patronising. 'So, what happened to the jumpers? What happened to the National Hunt?'

'The start of the Flat season along with the chance for me to perfect my system, that's what happened to the jumpers. You know, I work too when I'm not at work, just like you do when you're not at school.'

'*Polytechnic* actually.' Ian hated his place of academia being referred to as a school, and Nigel knew it. 'And once I graduate, it's going to get me a decent job. Not a barman, like you. You'll be pulling pints all your life, you will. You'll know the name of every brick in the Arboretum the rate you're going.'

'The Arboretum Public House is an excellent establishment, especially during term time; not that you'd know – you've always got your head in your books. For now, I will pull pints, pull birds, pick winners and make money. I like living for today, thank you very much. Life feels pretty good at the moment. I haven't quite figured what the end's going to be, but I do know that all this is just means to an end.'

'If you keep stealing my beer, the end is nearer than you think, you git.' Ian sighed, his shoulders dropping as he relaxed. 'So, you reckon you've got the winner for a race then? Which race?' He was always fascinated by what Nigel could predict in the racing game, though he tried not to show it too often.

'Nearly, and tomorrow. It will take another half an hour of reading the form and watching a few more races before I know the winner. I've narrowed it down to two.'

'OK, so tell me, how long have you been studying this race?' Ian enquired. He moved round to the back of the desk, where Nigel had his books stacked high, and looked over his shoulder.

'Two days, on and off—' Nigel said.

'Two days!' exclaimed Ian. 'Just for one race. You must be mad.'

'Well, when I say *on* and *off*, it's more off than on, what with the rekindled interest Lucy has been showing me recently. I'd say about fourteen hours' work to cross reference all the relevant races and make the necessary *informed* decisions.'

Ian gave Nigel a look of disbelief. Nigel having an *informed* opinion on anything seemed preposterous. But on reflection, he knew he was being unfair. Nigel did spend a lot of time with his head in his form books, and he was generally successful when he decided to have a bet.

Studying Form

Ian picked up some loose pieces of paper and walked over to a chair on the other side of the room. He tipped the contents of the chair onto the floor.

'Now who's the slob?' Nigel said. Not that he minded untidiness. He only applied attention to detail when working on his horses.

'These notes are meticulous, so neat and detailed.' Ian sat down and started to read what he'd picked up from the table. 'It's amazing to think this has been penned by the same git who pinched my beer, the same slob who lives in a tip. The same, the very same, who doesn't know the meaning of the word 'washing-up'.

'Two words. Washing up is two words.'

'I hyphenated it, smart arse... Yes, truly amazing.' Ian paused for a moment, flicking between bits of paper. 'You know, this has the makings of a database – it's structured just like you structure information in a database. I assume the horses underlined are related in some way to the other horses in the race you are studying?' Without waiting for a response from Nigel, Ian went on, 'Have you ever thought of getting a computer to do all this cross-referencing, filtering and analysing?' Again, without waiting for an answer, Ian decided he'd had enough. He handed back the bits of paper and told Nigel he'd be going for a couple of pints down the local at about half-nine, if he was interested.

Nigel said he would come along if he knew he'd chosen the winner of the race by then.

Andy Wheildon

*

At 9.05 p.m. they were both on the way to their local pub down Forest Road, Nigel very pleased with himself and quietly confident that, by that time tomorrow, he'd be a bit closer to his ultimate goal of being rich.

Once in the pub, Ian made his way to the bar. He usually bought the first round whilst Nigel investigated the situation at the pool table. Ian ordered two pints of Murphy's and watched the first pint pour itself, nice and slowly, whilst the barmaid served someone else.

Ian reached over and flicked off the pump just before the froth started to spill over the side of the glass. The pint sat there unattended for a few moments. He didn't recognise the barmaid and thought she must be new, but he couldn't help noticing how radiant she looked.

She must be pregnant, he thought to himself. According to his mother, women always had an aura of radiance when they were pregnant. Ian smiled to himself as she returned to serve him – no bump. The two had a quick chat whilst she poured the second pint. Nigel walked up to the bar and, as always, tried to undress the girl with his eyes. She noticed and smiled at him, a polite smile rather than anything flirtatious.

'We're on next.' Nigel took his drink from the bar and consumed rather a large mouthful. He moved towards the pool table, telling Ian to be sure to get some change for the table.

Studying Form

Ian paid for the drinks, and the barmaid gave him ample coins in his change, without being asked. The smile Ian received from her was far better than the one doled out to Nigel. Ian was shy when it came to the opposite sex, and he felt himself blush as he turned away. He was going to live off her smile for a couple of days at least. He wished he had the gift of the gab. If he could chat up women, life would be... Ah, well...

Still thinking about the barmaid and women in general, Ian was quickly brought back to the real world when Nigel asked the age-old question, 'Heads or tails?'

'Heads,' Ian replied, as usual. He won the toss and decided to break.

He went to the cue rack and picked one out, looking at its tip and shaking it to ensure the weight in the butt wasn't loose. Then it was a case of find the chalk. Not too difficult – the chalk was where the chalk usually was.

Having prepared his cue, blowing off the excess dust from the tip, Ian bent over the table to break. A firm shot to the right of the pack usually guaranteed a couple of covered pockets and sometimes a ball would drop. Not this time though. The balls split favourably for his opponent, and Nigel grinned like a Cheshire cat. The result seemed a formality.

Ian moved away from the pool table and over to where he'd left his pint. Leaning on his cue, he tried to look cool. Maybe a girl was watching, any girl.

Nigel dispatched a red towards the top right-hand corner pocket and nudged another of his balls towards the top left. The pocket already had one of his balls in close attendance but also a couple of Ian's as well. The cue ball tucked itself on the top cushion, difficult to cue. Ian smiled; Nigel grimaced.

The first few shots were always very competitive, hardly ever was a word spoken whilst they fought for superiority on the table. In truth, they were quite evenly matched, with Nigel being only slightly better. Ian didn't mind losing, but he hated losing without having put up a fight. It looked like, with the cue ball where it was, he might be getting another shot in this sooner than he'd first thought. Nigel took his time deliberating over the shot.

'Anyone would think your life depended on it,' Ian remarked.

Nigel ignored him and, with a very fine cut, pushed the ball he'd previously nudged onto one of Ian's balls and into the top left corner pocket. The cue ball went up the table and stopped close to the centre pocket on the left. It was an excellent shot.

Ian was almost speechless. 'Shot!' he managed to say, whilst Nigel walked round to the next shot, chalking the cue.

Nigel broke the conversational ice, mentioning his evening's work.

'It's a cert., you know, tomorrow. The race I was working on. It's the first big handicap of the Flat season, the William Hill Lincoln Handicap. Would you like a history lesson?' Surprisingly, he missed his next shot.

Studying Form

Ian took a sip of his Murphy's and gave Nigel an emphatic, 'NO.' He returned to the table with relief, as his friend mentioned someone called Ron Hutchinson and the 1969 Lincoln. The balls scattered around the table looked good; he might be able to pot a few. The first into the centre pocket was a formality. It dropped in without touching the sides. Not a difficult shot really, considering he'd drunk less than half a pint.

'You're not listening, are you?' Nigel persisted.

'What?' Ian wasn't listening.

'The horse tomorrow – it's going to win. I'm certain of it, and it's a horse called Amenable, if you are interested.'

Ian got up from leaning over the table and walked round to his drink. 'There is no such thing as a certainty in horse racing. I've heard that from you so many times. The bookies might get inside information; trainers may tell their owners their horse is going to win. But for Joe Public, the likes of you and me, there's no chance.'

'Yes, I know. I don't mean every race. I'm not saying I know the winner of every horse race. Select the race carefully, study the form, the track, the jockeys, and the trainers – all the variables. Then apply the formula, and *voila*, the race is won. If you're unsure or there is something you cannot figure out, then leave that race alone and move on to a different one.'

'Why pick this race, then? What has this one got that's different to all the others?' Ian walked back to the table and stooped to take his next shot. He missed.

'First, it's a handicap, which is the type of race I concentrate on. Second, it's a big handicap with quite a few horses in with a shout of winning. Third, it's a big gambling race – as are most handicap races, incidentally. The odds will be decent.' Nigel also missed his shot; the game had deteriorated, but the conversation was hotting up.

'But you say your horse is a dead cert.,' Ian persisted. 'How can you be so sure?'

Nigel drained the last of his first pint and held the glass up to show he was off to the bar. Ian would have usually sat waiting by the pool table whilst Nigel went for the refills. Tonight, he decided to follow him to the bar – after all, the barmaid was well worth a second look. Also, no-one else seemed interested in a game of pool so their change on the side of the table seemed safe enough.

Nigel smiled. 'You're hoping, aren't you? She's way out of your league.'

Ian was slightly put off by Nigel's comment. Never being confident when meeting women for the first time, he knew he was just going to stand and gawp.

The bar was quiet which meant the barmaid walked over to serve them almost immediately. It was Nigel's turn to buy the drinks, but the barmaid kept smiling at Ian whilst pouring.

'I'm mistaken,' Nigel freely admitted as they wandered back to the pool table. 'I think you're in there!'

Studying Form

'If only. Anyway, tell me more about the horse,' Ian said. 'Why will it win?'

Nigel spent the next fifteen minutes explaining the System he had developed which, given all the right conditions, the right horses, jockeys – if all the right circumstance were in place – would accurately predict the outcome of a race.

At first, Ian was sceptical, but as Nigel set out the rules and the variables and, most of all, the fact his system had already proved successful all five times he'd applied it, Ian began to believe Nigel might be on to something.

The only thing wrong with the System, as far as Nigel was concerned, was the time required to finally make a decision. The volume of information being considered was vast, and Nigel didn't know what horses would run in what race until the night before the race – the overnight declarers. Considering the horses too soon could possibly be a waste of time; the trainers could withdraw their horse at any stage or the going could change overnight. In fact, the going could change during the race meeting itself, if it rained long and hard enough.

After Nigel had finished, Ian was at a loss as to what to say. There were no immediate questions that came to mind; it appeared Nigel's system covered everything.

'Who else knows about this system?' Ian finally asked.

He was relieved to hear he was the only one Nigel had confided in. When asked why, Nigel freely admitted he knew he might be on to something big, if only he could process his data more quickly. Nigel had actually used the words 'figure it all out', but Ian had put him right – a computer could be used to process the volume of data. Nigel had long suspected Ian could be an asset. When Ian had mentioned computers earlier in the evening, Nigel knew he had a chance of getting his fish to bite. And now, Ian was ready to bite.

Nigel wanted Ian's help, Ian's computer expertise and a great deal of Ian's time.

Ian, on the other hand, wanted another drink. He picked up the two pint-pots and walked across to the bar, deep in thought. The barmaid was pleased to see him, which was blatantly obvious from the smooth greeting she gave him. It was a pity Ian didn't notice.

Nigel called over, requesting a packet of pork scratchings.

'Better make it two,' Ian said to the barmaid as she stretched up to reach a packet from the cardboard holder on the back of a door. Seeing her stretch, seeing a few of the contours of her body, reminded him he should be enjoying this bit of the evening, getting served. Maybe it was the two pints he'd already had, or maybe it was the excitement he felt thinking about Nigel's system. Whatever the reason… *In for a penny*, he thought.

'Do you fancy a drink?' he asked.

'I thought you'd forgotten I was here,' she joked. 'You seemed miles away.'

Studying Form

'Yes, sorry about that. I think I *was* miles away. Anyway, I'm back now and the offer still stands, if you fancy a drink. By the way, what's your name?'

She told him her name and, yes, she'd like a drink. She then told him he owed her £5.40 exactly.

Ian gave her a tenner and thanked her for the change, putting it in his pocket. The two packets of pork scratchings were crushed into the same pocket. He took a mouthful out of both pints, on the premise it's better to do that than to spill any whilst walking back.

'That was £5.40!' he gasped as he got back to the table where Nigel had lodged himself. Ian always remembered his first round when, at the age of sixteen, he'd paid 50p for two and a half pints of Batman's Best Bitter from a pub in Scamblesby, near Louth. Nowadays, however, was another story.

'How much? £5.40? You're joking. You've been overcharged, sunshine. That silly lass behind the bar has made a mistake. Go and have a go at her. It's always the same when they get someone new in here.'

'Two pints, two packets of pork scratchings.' He pulled the packets from his pocket and threw one into Nigel's lap. 'And one gin and tonic *for later on.*'

'You mean you bought her a drink? Well, it serves you right.'

'Expensive, isn't she.' They both laughed, and Ian looked over to the bar. She was gorgeous.

As they walked home, each eating large kebabs, they were both deep in thought. Ian thought about the barmaid, wishing he could remember her name, whilst Nigel thought about the amount of chilli sauce on his donner and the problems it would cause him on the loo the following day.

When both the kebabs had been consumed, the conversation began once more.

'What I need is all the past races put on a computer along with all the relevant form,' Nigel said, running a hand through what was left of his hair. If he was anything like his father, he would be totally bald by the time he was thirty-five.

'How much data does this amount to?' Ian was reluctant to ask. He had a good idea the answer was going to be phenomenally large.

'Don't know really. Let's try and work it out. The races I cover are handicaps only, and there are approximately four thousand handicappers in training. Let's say they all race about five times a season, that's about twenty thousand.' Nigel stopped in his tracks. Twenty thousand in a season – it would be impossible... and twenty thousand was a conservative estimate.

'Someone has to have done it already,' Ian reasoned as they approached their home. 'Somebody will have to enter the results somewhere, so all the newspapers, all the form books and all the racing journals can tap into the information. Someone, somewhere, has got the answers you need.'

The two had their obligatory cup of coffee, once Nigel had washed a couple of cups and a teaspoon – the bare minimum. They went their separate ways, Ian wishing Nigel luck for the race the next day.

Studying Form

Considering it was 1.15 a.m., later in the day would have been more accurate.

Saturday, 23 March 1991

The horse, Amenable, won at very generous odds.

It was the first time for a long time Ian had left college early. He'd been unable to concentrate on his lecture in the morning, and he'd done nothing but watch the clock through his afternoon seminars. The fact it was a Saturday had only contributed to his lack of concentration. Teaching on a Saturday was not the usual practice for the polytechnic, but the past few weeks had seen the Friday timetable move to Saturday as a result of staff shortages. A handful of engineering lecturers had been 'called up' for Territorial Army training all at the same time, and the polytechnic had had to react quickly to ensure courses were not interrupted.

Ian was fully aware that Nigel's infectious enthusiasm and confidence of the previous evening had rubbed off on him. He genuinely believed Nigel's choice was going to win.

The final seminar of the afternoon, Artificial Intelligence, usually so spellbinding, had lost its hold to the magnetism of Flemings the bookmakers. *Strong enough magnetism to destroy any microchip*, he thought as he made his way through the late afternoon shoppers.

Studying Form

His heart was thumping as he pushed open the door of the bookmakers, thumping so hard it almost hurt. The first thing that struck him was the smoke. Everyone, or so it seemed, in the betting shop was smoking. Not being a smoker himself, Ian found the smoke noticeable to say the least.

He walked across to be near the counter he had used earlier in the day, where he'd fumbled for a betting slip and nervously filled out the instruction: £10.00 win. He had paused when detailing the stake money – £10 was a lot of money. A few pints at least, a few gin & tonics for thingy – he still couldn't remember the barmaid's name.

'Amenable, £10 win, plus tax,' he had said at the counter, only to be asked by the cashier for a race time and venue.

'It helps the manager sort and settle the bets,' she'd informed him.

Having completely forgotten the race details given to him by Nigel the previous evening, he had to apologise whilst the cashier sighed and looked up the details for him from the racing press. Once the betting slip had been endorsed, the pink returned and the stake paid, Ian had gone on to struggle through his most fidgety day ever. Time had dragged.

Now, however, time was standing still for nobody. The betting shop was a hive of activity. Every cashier was busy; a queue had formed at the pay-out area. Lots of people were picking up winnings.

Ian turned his attention to the screens which were the subject of interest to many of the others in the shop. One screen had a race in progress, some people in the shop shouting encouragement, urging the horses to go faster.

'Hit the bastard,' suggested one punter. 'Use your bloody whip!'

As if the jockey heard him, the whip came out, and the horse got a short, sharp reminder he was in a race. The commentator noted the horse was 'moving up a gear'.

Not surprising, thought Ian, *after having a whip smacked across its backside*. The horse duly obliged, passing the winning post at least three lengths ahead of the rest.

The punter punched the sky in celebration and turned towards the pay-out area. 'Piece of piss – easy money!'

The adjacent screen flashed and caught Ian's attention. Doncaster results.

The race he was interested in was the 3.40, on the next screen. He waited, hoping the rest of the shop couldn't detect his anxiety. He looked round, trying to display an air of confidence.

The second screen flashed up, and there it was. At 22/1, Amenable had beaten the second favourite, St Ninian, into second place; in third place... To hell with third place. He stared, rooted to the spot, his eyes glued to the screen.

He heard someone say, 'Excuse me.' The horse had won, and he had put a *tenner* on it, and he was about to go and collect £220!

Studying Form

'BLOODY SHIFT.' This time the request was issued in his right ear with considerable force. The whole shop went quiet as everyone looked to see what the shouting was all about.

Ian turned to see a man towering over him with a look of menace in his eyes, waiting to get by. Ian moved.

The man walked past, glaring, and Ian followed him towards the pay-out window, fumbling for his betting slip. The man stopped to become part of an orderly queue, whilst Ian continued to search for the slip, oblivious to all around him. He collided with the huge gent, sending him stumbling forwards onto the punter in front, and a domino effect ensued. The man slowly turned and towered over Ian.

'I'm terribly sorry,' said Ian, still looking for his betting slip. 'I can't find my ticket. Ah, here it is.'

The queue shortened by one more, and everyone's attention returned to the pay-out window.

Ian moved up to the counter and passed his pink slip under the bandit screen. The cashier looked at the number at the bottom of the slip and, having found the top copy of the betting slip in one of the many pigeonholes, informed him of his winnings.

'That's £230, luv.'

Ian had expected it to be £220, but then he realised he was getting his stake back too.

The cashier turned to a colleague who watched as she counted the money out and passed it under the bandit screen.

Ian picked it up and bundled it into his back pocket. He didn't have a wallet since he never had enough money on him to warrant carrying one. He turned away and left the shop just in time to catch the 5.15 bus home.

Ian burst through the front door, tossing his college stuff to the floor and throwing his coat towards a hook on the wall. It missed the hook, and he left it where it fell. The radio was on in the kitchen, and at that precise moment, Johnny Mathis and Deniece Williams were telling the world 'Too Much, Too Little, Too Late'. Ian turned the radio down.

Nigel was standing at the sink with his back to Ian, doing the washing-up. The sight of him at the sink startled Ian, but he soon forgot about it when Nigel stopped washing and turned around.

'It won,' Ian exclaimed. 'It bloody won. I'm rich. I won a fortune.'

'So you had a bet, did you? How much?'

'A tenner,' Ian said proudly, walking to the fridge. It was full of beer.

'I told you I'd replace it,' Nigel said. 'Chuck one over for me – let's celebrate.'

They both cracked open a can, Nigel's making a bit of a mess because it had just been thrown the length of the kitchen. 'Let's go to the pub and get plastered,' Ian suggested. 'I'm going to buy the barmaid all the drinks she wants. God, I wish I could remember her name.'

Studying Form

'Try going through the alphabet, it usually works for me,' Nigel suggested, sitting at the table and putting his feet up on the only other chair.

'What? Annabel, Angela, Alison, Andrea, Amanda… It'll take forever. Belinda, Beatrice, Brenda—'

'Yes, but it's the familiar names that'll come to mind first, so if you're struggling then just go on to the next letter. Like I said, it *usually* works. Just hope the name doesn't begin with a Z or you could be there all night.'

'Zoë, that's it. Amazing! Well done.' Ian was elated. *Zoë*.

'Zoë.' Nigel sighed and looked skywards. 'With or without an umlaut?'

'What?'

'It doesn't matter.' Nigel smiled inwardly and stared at his love-struck lodger.

'Zoë. Will I ever forget? I hope not. Anyway, as I was saying, I put a tenner on. Two hundred and thirty quid is now sitting in my back pocket.'

'Not bad, well done. And thanks.'

'Thanks for what?' Ian asked. 'It should be me thanking you.'

'I don't know. Thanks for believing in me and showing a bit of interest and confidence. Maybe we can take this further.'

Ian contemplated for a moment what Nigel might mean. 'By the way, how much did you put on?'

Andy Wheildon

'Hundred and fifty.' Nigel took a long drink from his can, then looking at Ian, he belched and smiled.

Ian just stared, whilst Nigel drank some more. The six o'clock news came on the radio, more casualties in Croatia, more fatal errors in the Health Service and inflation was at five per cent per annum – the lowest for three years. 'Clever bloody Tories,' commented Nigel.

It had taken a few seconds to sink in and a few more to work it out. 'Three thousand three hundred plus your stake – £3,450! Bloody hell, I don't believe it. I hope you paid your tax upfront.'

'Don't swear! I'm sure *Zoë* wouldn't like it. And yes, I did pay tax upfront. So did you, I hope?'

'Three and a half grand! You're going to need massive trouser pockets for that amount of money when you go and pick it up. Three and a half grand! You put £150 on a horse – you're insane.' Ian couldn't believe it.

'I'll probably be given a cheque – that's what happened last time. I insisted.'

'Last time? How much last time?' Ian asked.

'Two thousand six hundred. The System works – I told you last night. The System works. So no celebrating down the pub, no getting plastered. We've got to talk. Three grand, matey. We are talking big money... potentially, very big, regular money. I don't want you sharing this windfall with every Tom, Dick and Zoë.' Nigel's tone was adamant.

Studying Form

Ian held up his hands defensively. 'No problem. In fact, probably a good idea.' He went to the fridge and took out two more cans of beer. Carlsberg. 'Probably the best idea in the world. I've been thinking,' he said, when he'd kicked Nigel's feet off the chair and put the cans of beer on the table. 'The database we need has got to be available already. Like I said last night – someone, somewhere must keep records for all those publications you subscribe to.'

Nigel went into the living room and returned, clutching an armful of magazines. He passed a few to Ian and took one for himself.

'What are we looking for then?' Nigel asked.

'I don't know. Publishers would be a good start. "Data supplied by" would point us in some sort of direction. We might have to make a few phone calls, pretend we want to use the information for a new publication or something. To be honest, I haven't a clue.'

Ian walked across to the noticeboard hanging by the fridge and tore off a piece of paper from the 'Forget-Me-Not' notepad. BEER was written on one piece with the words 'keep the bastard happy' scribbled underneath. He smiled, unpinned the price list for Perfect Pizza and returned to the table.

'Fancy something to eat?' Realising he didn't have a pen, Ian got up again and fumbled for one in a cupboard drawer.

'Yes, please. The usual, I think. Twelve-inch deep pan American Hot…'

'With extra chillies,' they said in unison.

Andy Wheildon

Ian passed the pen and 'Forget-Me-Not' paper, a present from Lucy, across to Nigel and told him to note down anything that might help in their search for information. The next day was Sunday – as good a time as any to start looking into creating a computerised database.

Ian went into the hall, and Nigel heard him ordering the pizza over the phone. 'Twenty-five minutes, that's great.' Ian hung up and came back to the kitchen.

Walking over to the sink, Ian saw Nigel had actually done *all* the washing-up. 'Find the Fairy Liquid, did we? Manage to wrestle the top off it, aye? Hope you had your Marigolds on. We don't want you getting chapped fingers now, do we?'

'Very droll, I don't think. For your information, I find washing up quite relaxing.'

'I wish you'd relax more often!' Ian pulled a couple of plates off the drainer, dried them with a disgusting floral tea towel – another gift from Lucy – and put them on the table. 'Do you want any sauce with the pizza?'

'Tabasco, if there's any left.'

Ian finished setting the table and turned off the radio, replacing the hour-long early evening news with a cassette. Elton John, 'A Single Man'.

Nigel groaned. 'I'm going to throw that away one day. There are more artists than Elton John, you know.'

Studying Form

Ian turned the cassette over and played Madonna. He was pretty certain Nigel was no fan of Madonna either.

The front doorbell rang, and Ian went to get their dinner.

As they ate their pizzas, Nigel explained more about his system: how long it had taken him to develop, how he had grown in confidence as the System had gone five races without failing. Then towards the end of the previous season, how it had all gone horribly wrong. A horse that the System said should have won had come third. He had hoped to place a couple of big bets at the end of the season, once he was confident the System worked. After that unexpected loss, however, the horses Nigel selected continued to win, and now, apart from the one loser, he'd picked eleven winners. Every now and again he had modified the System to further reduce the 'chance' variable. Now he was confident he had a winning formula. 'The horses will win!'

Ian asked if he'd re-applied the data to the race where the chosen horse had lost, just to see if the modified system would have given a different result. Nigel said he had, and it hadn't.

The doorbell rang, and Nigel looked at Ian then put a piece of pizza in his mouth and smiled.

'I'll get it,' said Ian resignedly.

It was Lucy, Nigel's girlfriend. Ian was surprised but tried not to show it. He thought they'd split up a couple of weeks ago. *She's probably come round for the tea towel*, he thought. Some hope.

'Hi,' she said as she walked past him without being invited in. She didn't need to be asked, since she'd been on the scene longer than Ian. He always wondered why the two of them hadn't started living together. He'd have to ask Nigel one day.

'Hi,' he replied, somewhat inadequately. Lucy knew he was nervous around women and sometimes flirted with him quite unashamedly. Nigel didn't seem to mind – as long as he got his 'oats' he was happy. Very noisy oats they were too!

'He's in the kitchen,' Ian called after her. He followed her through. He liked Lucy, despite everything. He thought of Zoë. Zoë… He remembered her name.

There was a bit of small talk between the three of them in the kitchen, but horseracing wasn't mentioned. Lucy didn't like the sport. It was the reason she and Nigel had parted company three months earlier. Lucy had wanted to go to a Ramones concert over in Derby, but Nigel had preferred to go to the races. The situation could easily have been resolved since the race meeting was in the afternoon and the concert was in the evening. But Lucy was stubborn, intransigent and, at the time, quite keen on another bloke. A silly argument had resulted in a parting of the ways and Lucy getting to see her concert with her new man. Nigel got two winners and very drunk.

Anyway, that all seemed to be well in the past, but recent conversations between Nigel and Ian had led Ian to believe Lucy would soon be history once more.

Studying Form

He wasn't sure whether he'd miss Lucy or not. Time would tell.

Once the pizzas were finished and after Madonna turned herself off, Nigel and Lucy made a swift exit, leaving Ian to deal with the dishes.

Ian decided not to wash up. Feeling a little lightheaded, he decided another can of beer was a good idea. Whilst drinking, he flicked through the pages of the magazines almost absentmindedly. Then, as he was finishing the can, tilting his head back but trying to keep the magazine in his vision, he spilt the drink down the side of his face and onto his shirt and the magazine.

He was annoyed at his stupidity but giggled despite himself. The horrid tea towel was sitting next to him, so he used it to dry his face. It smelled a bit, and he made a mental note to find a clean one later. His attention turned to the table where it was apparent he had spilled more than a bit of lager. Whilst mopping up the beery pool on the page of the publication he'd been flicking through, he noticed an acknowledgement to Race Line Data Systems of Newmarket.

Ian made a note of the name on a piece of paper that had other possible sources of information listed on it. He was sure, however, RLDS (as it was referred to in the rest of the article) held the key to his database.

Twenty-five minutes later, coming to the end of the article, he was convinced. The piece of work, scripted by a Mr Justin Livingstone-Smythe, explained how indebted the racing world was to RLDS. Their constant supply of accurate, up-to-date information fed the insatiable appetite of the racing press and public.

Andy Wheildon

From basic one-off requests, such as how often has a five-year-old won the Cheltenham Gold Cup (at the time of the article, a five-year-old was anti-post favourite) to the bread and butter of their existence – namely a full results service for the tabloids and broadsheets forty-five minutes after the final race of the last meeting of the day.

Ian wondered how the information was supplied. For it to be so quick, it could only be done via the telephone network or satellite. Firing a signal 250 miles above the earth from Newmarket for it to drop back to an address just down the road in London seemed a bit excessive. Ian felt, or rather hoped, good old copper wire as laid by British Telecom would be the medium used for getting the 'accurate and up-to-date' information from A to B. *A to me*, Ian thought. He'd always fancied himself as a bit of poet.

Tomorrow, he would try to figure out how to get his hands on the information he required. To be honest, he wasn't quite sure what information he actually required. He'd have to ask Nigel.

He went to the fridge and got another can of beer. Was it his third or his fourth? Definitely his last, so he'd better take two. Ian then made his way into the living room and began to watch *Close Encounters of the Third Kind* for the umpteenth time.

The following day, a Sunday, would see both Ian and Nigel feeling a little worse for wear, both suffering from the alcoholic excesses of the previous night.

Sunday 24 March 1991

Ian surfaced at 11 a.m., and made his way, slowly, to the bathroom. Each step led to a slight movement of his head. Each slight movement of his head led to pain. The agony between his ears was like he'd expect to get from hearing Concorde climbing to 25,000 feet, accelerating at full thrust. The light was also far too bright. *Concorde flying straight into the sun*, he thought. *Thank God tomorrow is only one day away. You always feel better tomorrow.*

Having stared at himself in the mirror and contemplated his tonsils for a moment, he felt ready for the toothbrush. His hands were a bit shaky, but the third squirt of toothpaste stuck to the toothbrush. The water gushing noisily from the tap moved the previous two errant squirts of paste as far as the plug hole. Ian's fingers managed to force the offending bits down the drain and on towards a water treatment plant by the River Trent. By the time his toothbrush reached his mouth, however, the third bit of toothpaste was missing as well.

Unbeknown to Ian, it was now on the rim of the toilet seat. He decided to forego brushing his teeth; a strong coffee seemed a better idea.

He opened the bathroom door and nearly jumped out of his skin when he almost walked into the ghostly white Nigel hovering on the other side.

'What the fuck are you playing at? Standing there like a zombie scarecrow.'

'I need the toilet,' Nigel said. And he pushed his way into the bathroom, locked the door and swore when he got toothpaste all over his bum.

Ian decided Nigel's 'system' could be placed on hold for the day. His head was in no mood to do any constructive thinking. His college work would have to wait until his hangover had abated in the evening. Shopping would be the order of the day. Thank goodness for Sunday trading.

Waiting for the coffee maker to make the coffee and for Nigel to make his way out of the bathroom, Ian thought about how he could ask Zoë out. How on earth was he going to pluck up the courage? How was he going to react to the inevitable rebuff? Humiliation! He stared out of the kitchen window, and his thoughts drifted towards the warmer summer months. A couple of deck chairs, a bottle of wine, Zoë and the sun.

Ian's reverie was broken by the sound of a flushing toilet.

'I wouldn't go in there too soon if I were you,' Nigel said.

'Thanks. I'll bear it in mind. How do you feel?'

'Not good, not good at all. I had a kebab on the way home, just for a change.'

'Chilli sauce?'

'Loads of chilli sauce.' Nigel grinned. Then he remembered how awful he felt at that precise moment and grimaced. 'I could kill a coffee. Pour me one too, would you?'

Studying Form

A couple of minutes later, both were sitting at the table sipping coffee which was far too hot. Nigel got up and got his full-fat milk from the fridge to try and cool his drink down. Ian just blew on his, splashing a bit over the side of the cup. Nigel noticed. 'Animal.'

'Fat git.' Ian's response was meant as a friendly provocation. Nigel was slightly overweight. The fact that he was not very tall as well exaggerated the situation. Nigel was, however, comfy with the way he looked.

'Just because *you* use semi-skimmed milk and fill yourself with lentils. Lucy says you're so skinny, it's unhealthy.'

'You can tell Lucy to mind her own business.'

'No, I can't. Not anymore. Not after last night.'

'Oh dear, not again. What happened this time?' Ian asked.

'I'll tell you later; I'm not in the mood right now. This is it though. I've had it with her. Tonight, laddie, you and I are out on the pull! By the way, have you thought any more about how we get the information we need for the races we're going to cover?'

Ian briefly told him about the article he had read the previous night and suggested there was not much either of them could do about it over the weekend. He would get on to it on Monday and make a few enquiries. Today, he was going to spend some of the £230.

'Buy a CD or something for the car,' Ian said, more to himself than to Nigel.

'I'd buy another car if I were you,' Nigel said.

Ian's red Fiat Panda had, it was fair to say, seen better days. It had probably also seen better drivers. Ian always found it difficult to concentrate whilst driving, especially during the summer months. As the temperature and hem lines rose, his powers of concentration fell, whilst his powers of observation remained pin-sharp. Unfortunately, his observant mind would give precedence to a lovely pair of legs over a red traffic light. It was only a matter of time before Ian's car would make intimate contact with another vehicle. Probably long before Ian made intimate contact with any form of female flesh.

'OK. Here's what we'll do today. Lunch, town, tea, pub.' Nigel, as always, had it all planned out, not that Ian minded. He was easy-going enough to see that the plan included the things he wanted to do – shopping in Derby, and, hopefully, seeing Zoë again. He hoped Nigel had forgotten the interest she had shown him. If Nigel was in one of his infinitely unhelpful moods, Ian could wave goodbye to Zoë from his boat on a sea of embarrassment.

*

After their coffee and a bit of toast, the two went shopping together, Ian driving and Nigel telling him how to drive. Ian treated himself to some cotton trousers from Man at C&A. Nigel commented that it was a little bit early in the year for cotton. Ian accepted there were still a few chill winds around at the end of March. He was, however, an impulsive buyer. If he saw it, liked it and had the money to buy it, he bought it. *Act in haste, repent at leisure*. A motto he often had good reason to reflect upon.

This time, though, the trousers were superb. Even Nigel thought they were a good purchase, though he would never say so.

Ian also bought a CD. Jean-Michel Jarre, *Equinoxe*. He already had the album on vinyl from when it first came out, and he had also copied it to cassette. On reflection, he could see that this purchase had been somewhat rash, but he tried to justify it with the usual quality-of-sound excuses that accompanied any CD purchase, and: 'So I can now have one copy at home and one in my car.'

Nigel, on the other hand, bought two books, both on racing. One was an autobiography of Peter O'Sullivan. Ian recognised the name. The other book was called *One Hundred Great Handicaps*.

'There aren't a hundred great handicaps in this country. But if we can bet on a good few of the ones listed in here, we'll make a packet,' Nigel said.

'If we get it right,' Ian said cautiously.

'*O ye of little faith*. We'll get it right, don't you worry. We are going to be rich, boyo.' Nigel's eyes lit up.

Ian felt a shot of adrenaline course through his veins, the hairs on the back of his neck stand up.

*

The evening saw Ian in the bathroom for longer than usual. It didn't take him too long, as a rule, to have a shower. It didn't take too long to brush his teeth, especially now his co-ordination had returned and he was able to get both toothbrush and toothpaste into his mouth at the same time.

Tonight, however, he had to be sure he looked his best. He had a good look at himself in the mirror and decided against squeezing a spot to the left of his mouth. He knew it would only make it worse.

Spots, the occasional one or two, had always been a part of his features. He had wished many a time they'd go away, but when they persisted, he came to look upon them as champions of his youth. Later in life, the spots would disappear, along with his youth. It may seem perverse, but sometimes he liked having the odd *youthful* zit.

Nigel, on the other hand, hadn't taken very long to get ready. In fact, he was conscious of small wafts of body odour and was beginning to think maybe he should have had a wash. *Too late now*. It was 8 p.m. and serious drinking time was being wasted.

'Hurry up, for Christ's sake. I want a drink and preferably today, if it's all the same to you,' Nigel shouted through the bathroom door. The door swung open, and Ian stepped out into the hall.

Nigel started to cough. 'Too much smelly,' he said.

Ian had to admit he had been a bit heavy-handed with the Rapport aftershave his sister had bought him for Christmas – Christmas three years ago. Ian hoped aftershave didn't go off over time.

Studying Form

*

At 8.20 p.m., the two walked into the smoke-filled lounge at the Falcon, a sea of bodies between them and the bar. Ian's heart sank – he couldn't see Zoë behind the bar.

The jukebox was on, and The Clash were asking 'Should I Stay or Should I Go'. The volume was loud, so Ian had to raise his voice to make himself heard.

'She isn't in,' he called to Nigel.

'What?'

'Zoë. She isn't behind the bar. She can't be working tonight.'

Nigel turned to Ian and saw Zoë directly behind him. She was collecting glasses, and it was obvious from her smile she had heard what Ian had said.

She put her mouth to Ian's ear. 'Hi,' she said. 'You're right. I'm not behind the bar. I'm behind you trying to get past with a load of dirty glasses. I am working though, as you can see. Let me get you a drink when I get back behind the bar. That is, of course, if you have come here for a drink?'

Ian felt a blush begin to rise, then Nigel chipped in with: 'He wants a drink and to ask you for a date!'

There was no suppressing that blush now, and Ian's face duly obliged. Had it suddenly got hot in the pub? It certainly felt like it. This might just be the night Ian decided to kill his landlord.

'A date?' quizzed Zoë. 'No problem. The drink might take a little time though. What would you both like?'

Ian was not sure he had heard right. Was it 'no problem' that he wanted a drink or was the date 'no problem'? He couldn't remember how Nigel had posed the question. Ian wished he could keep up with things. He hadn't had a drink yet, but his senses were already leaving him fast.

Nigel acted as spokesperson again. 'Seems like the cat's got his tongue; he'll have—'

'A pint of Murphy's? Two pints of Murphy's?' Zoë walked off towards the bar with her tray of dirty glasses stacked high. As she went, she turned to Ian and smiled. 'Rapport – my favourite.'

The two of them followed Zoë to the bar. The throng of people parted in front of her as she carried the dirty glasses. Once there, she loaded them into the glass-washer, washed her hands and pulled two pints. Nigel paid for them, and both he and Ian went in search of somewhere to sit. They both knew it would be impossible to get on the pool table. It would be booked up solid.

Eventually, they settled themselves next to the fruit machine, and Ian put his pint on the windowsill next to it. He pulled a couple of pound coins out of his pocket and fed the machine. Nigel frowned and said, as always, 'Mug's game.'

'So what. Let's say it's money I won. Easy come, easy go.'

'Yeah, but you could spend that money on better things. Like Zoë perhaps?

'Tell me,' Ian asked, 'exactly what was the conversation that took place by the door just now?'

Studying Form

Nigel tried to make it as simple as possible for his friend to understand.

'We have established that if you ask her for a date, the answer is going to be yes. So, ask her for a date, next time you're at the bar.'

The fruit machine coughed out two ten pence pieces. 'Not bad for two pounds.' Nigel grinned.

'Yes, you're right. A mug's game. Let's grab that table. I could do with taking the weight off my feet.'

The two slipped onto the seats at a recently vacated table and in doing so received an unfriendly glance from a foursome whom they had just pipped to the post.

'Well, that's racing,' Nigel said. They both laughed, which again didn't go down too well with the four. 'What are the plans for tomorrow, then? What are we going to do about all this information we need?'

Ian described in some detail how he intended to contact the Race Line Data Systems people in Newmarket about the article he had read. How he would also start working on a structured database which would interrogate and manipulate the data in a format which would match Nigel's requirements.

Nigel wasn't sure what was meant by his 'requirements'. So Ian told him. Actually, he started by getting Nigel to fully explain the approach he took in finding his winners. After a little time, it became clear points were awarded to each horse in a certain order when meeting certain criteria.

Andy Wheildon

First of all, the race under scrutiny had to have all its features analysed: what grade of handicap it was, whether the course was left hand or right hand, what the distance was, what the going was likely to be. Over a long, hot summer, the last one was easy. If the weather was changeable, however, then the going could cause problems. The final bit of analysis for the race in question was the weight the horse had to carry, the actual handicap. This was usually easy because the official handicapper would apply the weights according to breeding and past performance. Sometimes, however, it was obvious a horse had not run at its best previously and was thus carrying a lesser weight than expected, giving it a better chance than a horse which had run true to form recently and had been duly penalised with extra weight to carry.

So, that was the easy part over, now they had to deal with the practicalities. When had the horse run before? Where had the horse run before? Who was the jockey in that race? Had the jockey been influential in the outcome of that race (very subjective)? Over what distance and under what conditions had the horse raced? And finally, what opposition had the horse been up against? Had the opposition run since, and if so, how had it done? Had the horse under consideration run against current opposition before, or had previous opposition run against current opposition? All these questions were relevant and had to be answered.

Once answered, once assessed and analysed, the choice would be made: to bet or not to bet – would they have just wasted all that time analysing the race, just to realise there was no way to predict a clear winner.

'Blimey.' Ian was not happy. The calculations, the cross-referencing, were going to be phenomenal.

'That's why I need you and your computer,' said Nigel.

'Yes, a fair conclusion. How long have you been considering me as part of your scheme?' Ian asked.

'Oh, ever since you moved in and I realised you were a bit of a buff with bits and bytes.' Nigel smiled and looked into his empty pint glass, firstly to indicate it was time for Ian to visit the bar, and secondly, to contemplate how he had managed to say 'a bit of a buff with bits and bytes' without his tongue getting tied.

Ian sighed; he hadn't been looking forward to this bit. He was going to have to ask Zoë out when he went up to the bar. There was no doubt he would never forgive himself if he didn't, but he wasn't sure he could.

Nigel could see the distress his pal was in and offered a bit of advice. 'Don't ask her out for a drink, whatever you do. She works in a pub!'

Ian's heart sank. So it would have to be the cinema, or a meal. *What if she hates the flicks and is on a diet?* Ian could feel himself getting increasingly agitated. He took a deep breath; this was silly. It should be pretty straightforward since she had apparently said 'yes' already.

Eventually, he got to the bar and put the two pint glasses on the counter. Whilst he fumbled in his back pocket for some money, a bloke came up to him and picked up the glasses raising his eyebrows as if to say, 'What can I get you?'

'Shit,' Ian exclaimed. It wasn't Zoë serving him.

'Sorry?'

'Oh, nothing. Er, two pints of Murphy's please.'

'And two packets of pork scratchings?' Zoë was standing next to him, on his side of the bar.

'Yes, and two packets of pork scratchings.' Ian smiled and turned to Zoë. 'Three if you fancy a packet?'

'No thanks – I'm not too keen.'

'A drink perhaps?' Ian's mind was racing. What was he going to say next if the answer to that one was a polite no?

'No thanks,' she said. 'A bit busy, isn't it? Is it always like this on a Sunday? I suppose it must be.'

'Usually, more so in the summer when the weather's good.' Ian couldn't believe he was talking about the weather. 'Is this the first Sunday for you then?'

'It's my first, and it'll be my last at this rate if it's up to me. This is the first break I've had for three hours, and I've only been given five minutes. I'm knackered.'

Ian laughed at the word 'knackered', which luckily seemed to go unnoticed. He paid the barman for the drinks.

Studying Form

'And I'm not too keen on some of the punters – they keep badgering me and asking me out and asking if I've got a fella.'

'Well, I wouldn't hold that against them – the thought had crossed my mind once or twice!' Ian tried to say it with an Australian accent.

'*Crocodile Dundee*! Very good. I like that film.' Zoë smiled. 'You could always walk me home after work if you wanted to. Actually, I'd be rather grateful, what with some of the people I've had to put up with tonight. Would you mind?'

'Well...' Ian considered the situation, weighed up the pros and cons, dwelled on the 'ifs' and 'buts'. 'Sure,' he said, with a tad too much enthusiasm.

'Thanks, it would mean hanging around for half an hour after closing whilst I help clear up. You sure you don't mind?' She knew he didn't mind, and he knew she knew. She looked up at the clock behind the bar and her five minutes were up.

'Oh well, only two more hours to go. Two and a half before we get out of here.' She turned, leaving Ian to pick up the pints and packets and return to Nigel who he had no doubt would be spitting feathers by now.

'About bloody time! Well, how did you get on then? I saw you were talking to her. Or rather she was talking to you. I'm wondering if she asked *you* out?'

'Very funny. But actually, yes, she did. I'm walking her home after she's finished work. Apparently, she's not enjoying the attention she's getting from some of the punters.'

Ian went to sit back in his chair only to realise he was on a stool and slightly off balance. He sat upright somewhat abruptly and spilt a bit of his drink on his lap.

'You'll be fine, really. She seems very nice.'

They then returned to the subject of horses.

*

At 10.30 p.m. the final bell rang, and time was called. Ian noted on his watch it was actually 10.25 p.m. 'A bit early, as usual,' he said, more to himself than to Nigel.

Nigel drained the last of his drink and finished off his pork scratchings, turning the empty packet into a neat, tight ball and dropping it into an ashtray. 'Well, I'll be off then. Are you sure you're going to be OK?'

Ian smiled and told him not to wait up and not to lock him out.

Nigel left, and Ian sat alone to finish his drink; he felt very vulnerable. He knew he lacked confidence and wondered whether, during the last couple of hours, someone else had taken Zoë's fancy. Maybe she would come across and say she didn't need walking home, maybe she'd been offered a lift or something like that.

As he drank the last of his beer, he looked into the bottom of his glass which made him go slightly cross-eyed as he followed the last bit of froth up the glass and towards his lips. When he refocused, he saw Zoë walking towards him. He swallowed hard expecting to hear the worst.

'How many of those have you had? I don't want you staggering around so much that it's me having to walk *you* home!' She was moving amongst the tables, collecting glasses and stacking them into a tray which would go straight into the washer. It didn't take long for the tray to fill up. As she turned to go back to the bar, she asked Ian to stack the chairs on the tables when people started to drift out.

The landlord called for the die-hards to drink up and be gone. A few punters mumbled their dissatisfaction at having to leave then left anyway. Every pub, the length and breadth of the country, was currently going through the same routine. Ian knew, in some drinking establishments, the routine would not be running as smoothly as it was here. Someone somewhere would be making a fuss. He'd seen a few skirmishes in his time, especially around the polytechnic.

He got up and walked over to the bar with his glass and an ashtray. Zoë had asked him to 'do the chairs', but he knew the ashtrays had to be collected first and the tables wiped. Occasionally, he too had been one of the die-hards, so he'd seen bar staff clear up before and knew the form. He put the ashtray and a glass on the bar and said to one of the blokes washing up he'd bring the other ashtrays over since he was hanging around for Zoë. The bloke smiled, thanked him for his help and said his name was Peter, by the way.

Ian smiled back and said, 'I'm Ian,' somewhat inadequately. He then said, 'Pleased to meet you,' which wasn't entirely true – he was neither pleased nor displeased. He shrugged and turned towards the tables.

With the ashtrays collected, tables still damp and the chairs on top of the tables, Peter said it was okay for Zoë to go, and he thanked Ian for his sterling work. Ian smiled and the two walked out, the landlord locking the door behind them.

Zoë took a deep breath of fresh air. It had been hot in the pub and very smoky. As the clear air filled Ian's lungs, he felt a little giddy. Maybe he had polished off one too many. He stuck his hands in his pockets and straightened his back, hoping not to sway.

'OK, which way?'

Zoë put her arm through his and guided him in the direction of her home, completely in the opposite direction to his own. She held him close, to keep warm. 'This way. It's not far. Peel Crescent, do you know it?'

'Er, yes, I think so. Quite posh, isn't it? Near to the hypermarket though.'

'We live at the far end of the crescent and don't see too much of the traffic. It can be a bit of a hassle though sometimes.'

They continued with the small talk for the remainder of the journey, about ten minutes. A quick calculation told Ian it would take forty-five minutes for him to get home. Eventually, he decided he'd call a cab, so he kept his eyes peeled for a phone box.

The house was posh. It sat in its own land with tall conifers on the left-hand side. Ian tried to figure out which way was south, wondering if the trees would block the sun. Not that there had been much sun recently. Spring, however, was just around the corner. The driveway led to a double garage, a path broke off from the drive and wound up to the front door. Georgian columns stood each side of the entrance. *A bit tacky*, thought Ian, but he got the distinct impression he was in the company of a young girl with wealthy parents.

Zoë fumbled in her handbag for a set of keys and unlocked the front door. Before opening it, she turned to Ian and told him they'd have to be quiet so as not to wake her parents or Jason.

Ian assumed Jason was a brother and made a point of being quiet.

As the door swung open, Zoë let Ian go in first. He stood in the hallway not able to see much because of the dark. Zoë locked the door behind her and brushed past him, taking hold of his hand as she passed.

She led him into a room with two settees and three easy chairs. She turned on the light and told him to make himself at home whilst she made some coffee. Ian was left alone to nose around. There were pictures on the wall which were not to Ian's taste. One was of an overgrown pond and a wooden bridge whilst another was a grey rectangle inside a black square. There were bookcases heavy with books, and in the corner of the room was an ornate cabinet containing expensive-looking cut glass. The TV, which was mounted on what could best be described as a feature wall, had the biggest screen he'd ever seen.

He wandered over to one of the bookcases and saw someone in the household was interested in the Second World War, whilst someone else had a fascination for house plants and gardening. There were no plants or flowers in the room though. As he looked round to make sure he was right in thinking there were no plants, Zoë came back with a tray, two mugs and a coffee maker. 'No milk?' he asked.

'None left, I'm afraid. Don't worry though, it's quite nice without milk. That's a Monet print – *Water Lilies*. Can you pour? I've just got to go and check on Jason; I won't be long.'

'Check on Jason?'

'My son, he's only ten months old. I'll probably have to give him his feed soon.' Zoë smiled, turned round and left the room. Ian just stood, frozen to the spot. He was aware he had his mouth wide open in shock. He closed his mouth.

He walked over to where she had left the tray and poured the coffee. His hands were shaking whilst he thought about the situation. This very pretty, young woman had a baby? The situation was becoming far too complicated. He picked up a biscuit and his drink and sank into the nearest chair. Quite comfy it was too. The crumbs from his biscuit went everywhere, so he got up, brushed himself down and went and sat on another chair. There couldn't be a husband, he reasoned. But if there was, he wouldn't make an appearance tonight. He felt a little better at that thought. He got up again and made himself at home on one of the settees. Maybe she'd sit next to him.

She did.

'He's fast asleep, thank goodness,' Zoë said as she settled herself down with her coffee. She didn't sit too close, but turned towards Ian, resting her right arm on the back of the settee and lifting her legs up onto the couch to make herself more comfortable. She smiled at Ian, making it clear it was up to him to start the conversation.

'Er, any other children, apart from Jason?' he asked, raising his eyebrows, trying to be matter-of-fact.

Zoë threw her head back and laughed. 'I'm not *that* old, for Christ's sake. No, just the one – a mistake I've learned to live with. Actually, I'm very happy to have Jason; he's a lovely baby. I just wish I'd had him in four- or five-years' time, that's all.'

'What happened?'

'I got pregnant!'

'No kidding. Not planned though?'

'No, as I said, one little mistake. And before you ask me where the father is, don't worry – Australia. Gareth, his wife Sarah and his three lovely children are on the other side of the world, well out of harm's way.'

'Does Gareth know? Does Gareth's wife know?'

'Oh yes. When it happened, everybody knew. My parents were angry and hurt, in a self-indulgent way. You see, Gareth and Sarah had been family friends for ages; we'd known them since they arrived in this country seven years ago. They lived next door.' Zoë looked at Ian, trying to gauge if he was paying attention. He seemed to be genuinely interested in her story, so she went on.

'It's the age-old story, I'm afraid: young adolescent girl has crush on older father figure, and whilst babysitting, gets pregnant.'

Andy Wheildon

'So, some nineteen months ago you were nothing more than an adolescent little girl, were you?'

'Well, no, of course not. We'd been having an affair for a year. I'd just turned seventeen, and I got careless with the pill and Jason was the result. The family moved back to Australia to try patching up their marriage. From what I've heard, it seems to have worked.'

'Did you... do you love—'

'Do I love Gareth? No, most definitely not. I probably did, once. But a long time ago. Towards the end...' Zoë considered the point for a moment. 'Towards the end, it was just convenient, routine, fun. It was still very enjoyable, physically. And basically wrong. The fact that we shouldn't have been doing it kept it sort of fresh, somehow. Do you know what I mean?'

'No, I haven't a clue really. I see how it could be exciting, especially early on. Carrying on behind everyone's back, right on everyone's doorstep. But that couldn't last much more than a year, I'd have thought... Well, like I said, I don't know really. What happened when everyone found out?'

'All hell broke loose, basically. My father told Gareth's wife who threatened to kill Gareth. She also threatened to kill me! All immediate, hot-headed, spur-of-the-moment anger which eventually evaporated.' She paused, reflecting on her actions, once again regretting the whole thing.

'Did the wife not suspect anything?'

Studying Form

'Sarah? She did know something was going on. It's funny – she'd known for a long time and so had my mother. Sarah apparently began to suspect something was wrong soon after it started. She confronted him about it, and he denied it. The affair cooled off for a while, but he never told me that was the reason. I had no cause to care one way or the other, but then we started up again. I never thought anyone knew.'

'What about your mum? You said she knew too?' Ian felt like an interrogator. Too many questions, too many quizzical looks; he'd better slow down. But Zoë seemed to be relaxed in telling him everything. She'd shut up when she was ready, Ian reasoned, so he just went on asking questions and listening to the answers.

'Mums are amazing creatures. We were never particularly close. What with me being an only child, I grew up to be independent, and we always seemed to quarrel. But since Jason was born, we've never been closer. I'd never have got through it without her and Dad. Mum was so strong when, for a while at least, I couldn't seem to cope with anything.' Zoë laughed. 'Very unlike me, but there it is.'

Ian took a drink from his cup and screwed up his face. The coffee was stone-cold. Zoë noticed his expression and chuckled. 'God, it's not that bad, is it?'

'No. Sorry. It's gone cold. I'm not too keen on cold coffee. Anyway'—he looked at his watch—'I should be going; it's getting late.' He stood up and took his cup back to the tray. 'Do you mind if I pinch another biscuit? Shortbread is so more-ish.'

'Help yourself. I'm sorry if I've bored you—'

'No, not at all, don't be silly. I've enjoyed it, honest I have. I'm sorry if I've pried, asked questions when I shouldn't. But I must be getting home. It's late.'

Zoë walked him to the front door and let him out. On the step outside, he turned and found, with Zoë still inside and him down a step, they were both the same height. 'Can we do this again one night?' he asked.

'You sure you want to go out with a girl with a kid?'

'No. I want to go out with a girl who's got shortbread biscuits!'

'I'll introduce you to my mother then! She'll be flattered. Yes, let's do it again. I'll look forward to it. Thank you for walking me home.' She leaned forwards and gave him a kiss.

Ian smiled and thanked her.

'Phone me tomorrow night if you want. I'll be in. We're in the phone book: Richards. Under A for Anthony – my dad's called Tony.'

'Pardon? Oh yes, Anthony. Anthony Richards.' They both laughed. Zoë gave a little wave, said goodbye and closed the door.

Ian turned and, as he walked away, started to whistle. Then, realising it was 1.30 a.m., he stopped whistling and started to hum. The heavens opened and it rained buckets, but ask him if he cared.

Monday, 25 March 1991

Ian had gone straight to bed and slept like a log. He'd gone to sleep with a smile on his face and he'd woken up just the same. Life was good for a change. He knew he'd have to go through all the details of the previous evening to accommodate his friend's insatiable curiosity – Nigel had an appetite for knowing things that were no business of his.

Breakfast began at 8.15 a.m. with Ian cooking himself bacon, egg and a couple of sausages. He'd put an Elton John tape into the cassette player in honour of Elton John's birthday – the same day as his dad's. He made a mental note to give his dad a call later in the day to wish him a happy birthday and to find out if he had appreciated the somewhat rude card Ian had sent.

The smell of the cooking, and the coffee he was brewing, percolated through the house and disturbed Nigel's lie-in. He was down the stairs like a shot and sat himself at the table, his gaze glued to Ian in anticipation. Ian thought he actually saw Nigel lick his lips. Was it the stale dry taste in his mouth from the night before? Was it the fry-up Ian was preparing? More likely the need to know what had happened between him and Zoë the previous evening.

'Morning.' Nigel smiled at Ian. 'Get home all right, did you? I didn't hear you come in so it must have been *pretty* late.' The emphasis on the word 'pretty' was either Nigel suggesting Ian never stayed out late, which was true, or Zoë was pretty, which was also true.

Ian didn't respond; he just carried on preparing his breakfast.

'Well? How did you get on? What happened?'

'I'm going to see her again,' Ian answered. 'But...'

'But what?'

'She's got a baby!'

Nigel was stunned, initially. Then his shock turned to disbelief, then he started to laugh.

'It's not funny.' Ian struggled to keep a straight face. 'Like I said, I'm going to see her again. I don't think I'm going to let a baby called Jason put me off.'

Who was he trying to convince? Nigel or himself?

*

During his lunch break at college Ian had found a phone number for RLDS of Newmarket. After phoning his dad and enjoying a joke regarding the birthday card, Ian got in touch with RLDS to discuss the possibility of obtaining some past racing results for a publication he was working on. He had been told the information he required could either be faxed, posted or, if he had a modem and the correct software to handle it, the information could be transmitted via telecom. The last option, he was informed, was usually reserved for sending large amounts of data on a regular basis to clients who held accounts with the firm. When asked about the publication he was working on, Ian had had to waffle somewhat and say it was only at the idea stage and was a publication that would make up part of his studies at Trent Polytechnic. The lady at the other end of the line seemed satisfied and quizzed him no further. She said she would send details of the services they provided and asked Ian for an address. He gave her a box number used by students at the polytechnic.

Very pleasant, he thought as he crossed the quadrangle to the Computer Science faculty in the Newton Building. He went up to the fourth floor using the staircase – his bit of exercise for the day. Once there, and once his breath had returned, he went into a room which was bursting at the seams with computer hardware. A technician was sitting behind a desk, fiddling about with the insides of a computer. He looked up and smiled when he recognised the intruder. 'Get tae fuck,' he said, in way of a greeting.

'What a pleasure it is to see you too,' Ian said. 'Celtic lose again, did they?' Ian wasn't that interested in football. Malcolm, on the other hand, was extremely keen on the game and his team was Celtic.

'Nae chance, thae wan again, an still three point aheid o th' rest.'

'Excellent news. The mighty Mariners are doing well too. I think they might get promoted this season.' Ian's hometown's team, Grimsby Town, were enjoying a purple patch.

Malcolm wasn't the least bit interested in the east coast team. 'Whit dae ye want the noo, whit are ye efter?' He was in charge of the computer hardware, signing out whatever was taken, signing it back in on its return and mending it if broken. He was always busy which seemed to suggest things got broken all the time. The truth of it was the hardware was getting no younger. In fact, much of it was obsolete, and he had to rebuild and constantly maintain stuff which should probably be written off and replaced.

'A modem.'

'Oh aye, whit fur?'

'To receive and transmit information down a copper wire in digital form, taking advantage of the latest technology our splendid telecommunication systems have to offer,' Ian stated in a matter-of-fact tone.

'Smart erse, eh? *Mind m'ain business*. Ah'll hae a swatch.' He started tapping on a keyboard and pushing his mouse across the table. He then took the rollerball out from the underside of the mouse and blew dust and debris out of its gut. Having reassembled the mouse whilst making reference to belly-button fluff he looked up at Ian and told him he was in luck. 'Aye, ah sh'd hae tae in thon blue cupboard.' He pointed to a cupboard which was most definitely green.

Ian pointed out the mistake with some amusement. 'Why someone who is colour-blind would choose a storage system that relies on colour, I'll never know.'

'Practice big man, practice. If ah git yist tae the shades o grey ah meet jist point tae th' right wan sum day. How long are ye needin it? An' mind gimme the serial number. How's the project yer daein? Artificial Intelligence, ah ken?'

'Yes, that's right, AI. Recently I've been a bit preoccupied with something else.' Ian checked himself to make sure he didn't divulge the subject of his preoccupation. He needn't have worried though.

'A lassie, ah ken?' Malcolm chuckled to himself and asked again for the serial number of the modem Ian had extracted from the blue cupboard adjacent to a whole row of cupboards that were green. The information was fed into Malcolm's PC.

'So, I'll be off hame the noo.' Ian failed with his attempt at a Scottish accent.

The word *bawbag* was still ringing in his ears as he got the bus hame.

*

Ian arrived home in the early evening and got on with the task in hand straight away. He connected the modem to his PC and then realised the telephone was some thirty feet away – out the bedroom door across the landing and down the stairs to the table near the front door. He thought himself a bit of a plonker for not considering this problem earlier. He would have to buy an extension lead.

Nigel was on a shift down the pub, so Ian was on his own to do as he pleased. Telly, a video, phone Zoë? The choices were endless. Phoning Zoë might come over as being a bit too keen. Nigel had told him not to do it so soon, reminding him about the time

Nigel had phoned a girl a bit too often, and she had given him the cold shoulder as a result.

So phoning Zoë was out of the question. Just then the phone rang, and it was Zoë. Three quarters of an hour later he hung up. *Phew. She could talk the hind legs off a donkey,* he thought as he went through to the kitchen to get a beer. The conversation had been fruitful though since they had arranged to meet the following Friday night and go to the movies.

Later in the evening, Nigel got in from work to find Ian working in the kitchen. 'What the hell are you doing up at this hour; it's way past your bedtime.' He was a little drunk, an occupational hazard. He made himself a coffee and a cup of tea for his friend. Sitting down, he pushed some papers away so he could put the cups on the table.

'Careful. They get handed in tomorrow,' Ian exclaimed.

'Oops, sorry!'

'Git!'

Nigel smiled; he was seldom offended. Never by Ian – somehow, he didn't have it in him. 'So, how have we been getting on with our little venture, our little *adventure*?'

Ian explained the situation with the phone being out of reach of the computer and RLDS were sending information through the post on how to open an account or how to obtain one-off data which should be with them soon. He pointed out the data supplied by RLDS would have to be paid for, as would the extension for the telephone, as would the software they needed to allow them to receive the data, as would other odds and sods. He apologised for having to mention it but thought it best to get things straight from the outset.

To Ian's relief, Nigel agreed. In fact, he had already thought about it and been to a bank for some details on opening a business account. Eventually, there would be more than one account: one for expenses, one for the winnings and then a couple of individual ones for the big share out. Nigel told Ian he had every faith in him and in what he decided to buy, but he would like to know in advance before Ian bought anything.

Ian saw no problem with the suggestions his friend had made but wondered how they were going to share out the winnings, if they ever won enough to distribute. Nigel looked skywards, again emphasising a positive attitude should be applied – the System was a winner and he already had literally thousands in the bank to prove it. However, he recognised that the question of sharing out the profits could become a contentious issue, and it could lead to squabbling, greed, dishonesty and a quick parting of the ways. 'Trust and integrity have to be the bedrock of our relationship – the foundation on which we build and the mainstay of reaching our ultimate goal.'

'So?' enquired Ian, when he was sure his literary friend had finished his eloquent speech.

'So, I reckon fifty-fifty, everything down the middle. You need me and I need you. Together, we can make the bookies squirm and the bank managers more than happy for our custom.'

'That's really generous on your part, isn't it? I mean, it's all your creation. You could do it alone if you wanted to. Buy in the knowledge I've got and keep everything for yourself.'

'Don't talk me out of letting you in! There'll be enough in the pot for both of us, as I see it. With you doing the donkey work, I can see success coming a lot quicker than if I did this alone. Plus, I trust you. If I asked someone else to help, they'd be in and out before I could select the winner of one horse race. Fifty-fifty. Take it or take it.'

'Done.'

'The next race is in a few weeks at Newbury, and I would like to put £200 on this time. That means you've got to find £100 plus a tenner tax'

'In two weeks? You're joking,' Ian exclaimed. Nigel just sat there and smiled, raising his eyebrows. 'Er… you couldn't lend me a hundred quid, could you? I'll pay you back in two weeks. Honest.'

Nigel said he would, though he grumbled good-naturedly about how he 'must be mad'; He had never known himself to be so generous in his life. On reflection, however, Ian said he should come up with the money himself. After all, it was only right they should start as they meant to go on. Fifty-fifty.

The following morning, Ian telephoned his parents. And his mam agreed to lend him £100 for a piece of software which was vital for his studies.

Later in the day, as promised, there was a large manila envelope waiting for him at the college. He eagerly opened it and found two small books and a few fly-sheets trying to sell various pieces of software and hardware. As he walked away from the post room, he began to scan the articles on data transmission and reception. A couple of prices caught his eye. This was not going to be cheap. The System had better work!

*

Following a three-hour lecture on relational databases, Ian took himself off in search of an extension lead for the telephone and a software dealer who could supply the necessary applications for capturing the data from RLDS. The extension lead was no problem. It cost £4.95 from Argos and patiently waited for him at collection point B. The reason it had to wait for him was he'd been stood at collection point C for a few minutes before making a polite enquiry as to the reason for the delay.

'You're in the wrong place, luv,' bellowed a more than helpful shop assistant. And as he walked round to the right place, the rest of the shoppers followed him with their unsympathetic stares.

The software shop was more of a problem. Ian knew of three in the centre of Nottingham and one on the outskirts. All three central shops had informed him there would be a delay of about a week, since the software he was after was specialised and had to be ordered direct from the suppliers. None of them even had a copy of the software for 'evaluation' due to there being too much software piracy and too many virus threats to have floppy disks floating about all over the place.

Ian argued the point with one shop assistant, saying no-one would buy a product if they were not sure of its suitability. To which the clever-clogs sales assistant pointed out there was a thirty-day money-back guarantee on all their merchandise. Ian chose not to labour the point about viruses and anti-virus software. He made his excuses and left.

Whilst he drove to the outskirts of the city, his mind turned to Zoë and where they might go on Friday night. It was ages since he'd been to the pictures, and he hadn't a clue what was showing. As he drove, he realised he would be passing a cinema along the route he was taking. He slowed down when he approached it and looked up at the adverts to read what was on. All he could see were eighteen certificates, suggesting the material was for adults only. Whilst he attempted to read one of the titles, he heard the blast of a car horn behind him. *Impatient sod*, he thought as he accelerated away towards his last port of call before home.

Once more, the journey turned out to be fruitless.

The shop assistant at The Software Hub knew what he was talking about when it came to telecommunications and data transmission. He tied Ian in knots without even trying. The software Ian required, given the PC and the modem he had, could be purchased for £145 plus VAT and would take three days to deliver. Ian said he would have to think about it. The assistant was confident he would not get a better price anywhere. He was also confident he could provide excellent after-sales service, should Ian get stuck.

This last point registered with Ian – there was a fair chance he'd need help should the going get rough. However, he maintained he would still have to go away and think about it. Actually, it was more that he had to go away and get permission from Nigel before spending that sort of money. The shop assistant handed Ian a card with the telephone number of the shop on it and informed him they took telephone orders if backed up with a credit card number. Ian thanked him for his patience and time, and set off for home.

*

Nigel was in his room, numerous books littered about the place and the TV showing a recent race. Ian sat on the edge of the bed where Nigel had indicated, keeping quiet, again, just as Nigel had indicated.

'Go on, my son,' Nigel shouted to the horse as it pulled away from the rest of the field. 'That is one excellent horse,' he informed Ian as he picked up a pen and scribbled a few notes on a loose piece of paper. He put the piece of paper to one side then picked it up again and put it to the other side. *Organised chaos*, thought Ian.

'Is there anything I can do?' Ian asked, as he got up from the bed and walked across to the TV to turn the volume down.

'You could get me a beer from the fridge, if there are any left. You could also sort these bits of paper into alphabetical order if you want. They're notes

I've made on individual horses which are, hopefully, going to run in a couple of weeks.' He handed Ian a pile of about thirty pieces of paper.

Ian took the pile and started to sort them as he went down the stairs to the kitchen. He dropped them onto the kitchen table whilst he took two beers from the fridge. Placing the cans on the table, Ian went back to sorting the pages like Nigel had asked. Once done, he sat down and read the notes on the horse at the top of the pile. A horse called Don't Presume.

> *Don't Presume 3-8-8*
> *2nd last time out, 6f,*
> *good, Nmkt, (0-96)* <u>*Sign*</u>
> <u>*Out*</u>

Ian wandered back up the stairs, making sure he did not drop beer or paper. Having handed over one of the beers to Nigel, Ian pushed a bit of paper under Nigel's nose seeking a bit of background information on what was written down.

'Oh, that just means the horse is running against another in the race we're studying, and they've met before.' Nigel paused for a second or two, collecting his thoughts, then went on. 'Take Sign Out for instance. It's running in the race I'm looking at in a couple of weeks – all being well – and so is Don't Presume. So, on the paper detailing previous form for Sign Out, you should find Don't Presume underlined.' Ian recognised Correct Spell as being another of the horses he had just sorted, so he turned to that page.

Sign Out 3-8-8

Studying Form

4th last time out, 7f,
good/soft, Gwd, (0-75)
Super Heights.
1st, 6f, good, Nmkt, (0-96)
Don't Presume.

There were five more entries for Sign Out, and there had been three entries in total for Don't Presume.

'So if they're running against each other now, and they have run against each other before, you underline them?' Ian summarised, making it sound so simple.

'Labouring the point a bit but, in a nutshell, yes. Anyway, I thought you knew all this already because we had a similar conversation last week, remember? The night I pinched your last beer and you threw a tizzy.'

Nigel spent the next twenty minutes explaining in more detail the approach he adopted to analyse each race and the notes he kept on each horse. And whilst drinking his beer, he explained how all this information, and more, was 'scored' and applied to his formula. All calculations being right, he would successfully predict the winner of the fourth race at Newbury on 19 April.

When he had finished his drink and his lecture, Nigel listened to what Ian had to say about events of the day. Ian said if they were willing to fork out £145 plus VAT, the necessary software would be with them within three days, the extension to the phone had already been purchased at a price of £4.95 and the modem was in Ian's bedroom ready and waiting.

'Are you sure, the software will do what we need it to do?' Nigel asked cautiously. He didn't relish the prospect of spending £170 on a product which might not do the job.

Ian reassured Nigel it was, in fact, the best tool for the job, and anyway, if it wasn't, they could get a full refund within thirty days.

'Well, in that case, what are we waiting for? If you and I are going to be rich, we had better start splashing the cash.' As always, Nigel's excitement was infectious, and Ian felt goosebumps on the back of his neck as he went downstairs to phone the computer shop and place his order.

As luck would have it, the software was in stock as a result of somebody returning the product. Ian collected it the following day and was home in no time. He installed it on his PC with the minimum of fuss. Nigel, on the other hand, fussed round, trying to help but being more of a hindrance. The modem was set up and the phone was perched on a stand next to the table. Ian had inwardly digested the manual describing the modem's operation. He had also read a few paragraphs about the database and data transfer from RLDS.

He would have to transmit an instruction to the database. He would then have to wait for the instruction to be verified by RLDS. Once verification was obtained, RLDS would transmit the required information back to him, debit an account set up by RLDS and create a statement to be issued the following working day. The statement would need to be settled within five working days. Failure to do so would result in termination of the service and civil action to recover the debt. Ian had noted the wording on the literature had been very explicit and equally severe – not that they had any intention of defaulting on any payments. It had occurred to both of them that taking a large chunk of the information RLDS held would serve their purposes more than adequately in the short term. It had also occurred to them that the information would become out of date very quickly and would therefore require constant renewal.

Ian had suggested, once their own database was up and running, they could type in each of the new results themselves, only relying on RLDS on a heavy weekend when there were more than a couple of meetings to cover. Having consulted a timetable of meetings, Nigel was able to confirm that there were only two occasions in the racing calendar when there were six Flat meetings on one afternoon. Therefore, the investment with RLDS only needed to be on a short-term basis, and they would, of course, pay for the service.

'OK, let's put this baby to the test.' Ian picked up the phone handset and placed it on the modem. He then decided placing the handset on the modem was somewhat premature since he hadn't fully programmed his PC yet. The manual resting on his lap informed him how to programme his PC with the settings for the remote computer. He handed Nigel the manual from RLDS and told him to read out the values he needed.

'Baud rate?' he asked.

'Quite fast,' Nigel replied.

'What?' exclaimed Ian. He'd expected a figure, 9,600 or something like it. 'What are you on about?'

'The rate at which I am getting bored is, at this moment in time, quite fast. Computers are, in the main, incredibly boring!'

'Very funny. B A U D rate, if you would be so kind. The number of bits transmitted per second in serial communications.' Ian had spelled it out and then showed off by quoting the definition, trying to put Nigel in his place.

'Smart arse! It's 2,400.'

'Oh, *super*.' Ian gave the word a super posh twist, for reasons best known to himself. Nigel just tutted. 'Now, data bits and stop bits, my good man… Don't ask what they are – we just need to know how many there are of each… I think.'

'You're not filling me with much confidence,' Nigel said, scouring the page for the next bits of information. Eventually, he was able to impart the required values – '8' and '1' respectively. And some five minutes later, Ian was satisfied all the programming had been done. They were ready to transmit, or receive. At any rate, they were ready to give it a go.

Ian moved the mouse pointer to a button which had OK written on it. Nothing happened. He clicked on OK. Nothing happened.

'The computer should now be dialling automatically,' he explained to his friend who looked decidedly unimpressed. He then explained how the PC should transmit a signal to the modem which in turn would transmit to the phone which…

Ian placed the phone handset in the cradle of the modem and clicked on OK again.

DIALLING… please wait, flashed up on the screen. Both their faces lit up as, almost immediately, a screen full of text appeared.

Welcome to RLDS, it began. There were a few legal statements and warnings that prompt payment of bills was encouraged. Finally, the user was invited to type in their account number.

'This is it,' Ian said as he nervously entered a nine-character reference number which had come with the literature from RLDS. On pressing the return key, the screen displayed a new welcome message. This time it was personalised to Ian Turner, detailing Trent Polytechnic as the personal address he had quoted over the telephone earlier in the week. The screen also provided an area for a password. After a brief discussion the two agreed on a password neither would forget: 2Both3! They had both turned twenty-three earlier in the year.

The screen changed once more and posed a series of questions that needed answered in order to interrogate the database.

'OK… Horseracing,' Ian said, whilst he typed. 'English…' This option was chosen from a menu that listed five different countries. 'Handicap…' Again chosen from a menu. Ian then turned to his friend and asked the question on the display. 'What grade of handicap?'

Nigel thought for a moment and then said, 'Seventy-five to ninety.'

Ian typed the information and the screen blinked up a message saying, `Incorrect   format…  please re-enter…`

'Try seventy-five, hyphen, ninety,' Nigel suggested.

So Ian typed, `75-90`, and a new question appeared. '`Dates…`'

Again, the two looked at each other, not really knowing the answer to the question. They were both aware the service provided by RLDS was not cheap, but they were not sure of the cost either. The literature quoted a price per 100 characters transmitted. This meant, if costs were to be kept to a minimum, they had to hope the races had few runners and the horses that ran didn't have names as long as your arm.

'In for a penny, in for a pound,' Nigel mused. The two of them opted for a devil-may-care attitude, to hell with the costs. But what were the costs? 'The race that we are preparing for requires form which dates back to March of last year. So, the first date should be 20 March 1990.'

Ian typed excitedly, regularly correcting typos. Things were now beyond his control, but success would bring riches, or at least a moderate income, to keep himself and Zoë happy… and, not forgetting, Jason.

The screen asked for a second date, which both assumed to be the present date. Again, Ian typed in the required information. There was a pause. COMPILING... Eventually, the screen got some sort of digital diarrhoea. Row upon row of characters appeared on the top of screen then proceeded to cascade off the bottom of the screen in a continuous stream.

Nigel was somewhat panic-stricken. 'We're losing it,' he shouted to his colleague, as the information fell from the bottom of screen as quickly as it appeared at the top.

'Don't worry,' Ian reassured his friend. 'The data is filling the computer's memory. When it's done, we'll save the information to the hard disk and play with it later.'

'Oh, really!' It was obvious Nigel was less than convinced, but he settled down, nonetheless.

Eventually, the transmission of data ceased, and the VDU screen suggested the user: Store to new media.

The System then paused as it calculated the price of the service provided.

Characters transmitted: 77,354. Cost per 100 = 10.67p, inclusive of VAT. Total cost: £82.54. Statement to be issued the following working day. Settlement within 5 working days of issue. Thank you for using RLDS. Press any key to disconnect.

Ian looked at Nigel, smiled, and bashed a key at random. 'Straightforward. Phew.'

'Straightforward, maybe. But what was falling off the screen? What have we got seventy-seven thousand of?'

Ian reassured his friend the data had been stored in a text file on the hard disk. That was why they needed to build a coherent database where the races would be detailed in an order which allowed them to interrogate the information properly and easily.

Again, Nigel wasn't fully convinced but, looking at his watch, suggested they had done enough for the day. He was tired, and it was time to turn in.

Ian agreed and turned off the computer.

As he was leaving the room, Nigel turned to Ian. 'Another thing. I've been invited to a wedding on Saturday: a legacy from Lucy. I've bought what I thought would be a nice-looking wedding card. The trouble is it's blank on the inside, which means I've got to think of a sincere, sentimental greeting to write in it. I'm not too good at poems or sincerity. You couldn't help me out, could you?'

'I don't know… Bring the card over, and I'll have a look.'

Nigel went and got the card from his room and passed it to Ian. The picture on the front was of a couple dancing, the man resting his head on the shoulder of the woman. *La Danse à La Ville*, Pierre Auguste Renoir (1841–1919).

Ian wrote on a piece of paper:

As the music plays,
He draws her near.

Studying Form

And then he whispers in
her ear
That happiness is a day
like this,
And an eternity of wedded
bliss.

He passed the piece of paper and the greetings card to Nigel.

'Brilliant,' Nigel said, reading it. 'You've got talent. Thanks.'

Ian took the paper from his friend and began to scribble again:

As the music plays,
He draws her near.
And then he belches in
her ear.
She knees him in the groin
with force,
And begins to
contemplate divorce.

He handed the paper back to Nigel.

'No. I think the first one is more apt. I like these people. Maybe I'll use the second one at another wedding. Lucy's, perhaps.'

Thursday, 28 March 1991

Ian had been particularly nervous for most of the day about going out with Zoë in the evening. He was taking her to the cinema to see either *Sleeping with the Enemy* or *Robin Hood: Prince of Thieves*. His preference would have been a takeaway pizza and a video at home. As far as the two movies at the cinema were concerned... Ian was a fan of Julia Roberts who was starring in *Sleeping with the Enemy* but probably not a good idea to go all fan-boy during a date with Zoë. On the other hand, *Robin Hood: Prince of Thieves* was a big American film, full of American actors trying to be English and, according to one film review, lacking in authenticity. Ian was enjoying student life in Nottingham and many a local had been looking forward to the film being released. The Robin Hood statue, just up the road from the Ye Olde Trip to Jerusalem alehouse was dear to his heart, and he was reluctant to see a bunch of Yankee swashbucklers vaulting from oak to Major Oak with lack of authenticity to the much-loved fable.

The choice of film would, ultimately, be left to Zoë though, so there was little point in him struggling over the decision. He sighed into his coffee as he pondered what to wear. There wasn't much in his wardrobe, so he opted for the time-honoured 'process of elimination' technique.

Studying Form

The first shirt that came to hand had a collar so large he would probably take to the air if a gust of wind got under it. The second, a thick brushed-cotton check shirt, had him singing the Monty Python 'Lumberjack' song – again, totally inappropriate.

Eventually, the choice was made. Denim. So original. He'd been wearing it the first night he'd met Zoë *and* the Saturday night when he walked her home. It was newly laundered, ironed and comfortable to wear. He hoped Zoë wouldn't notice. The choice of trousers was easy: denim jeans.

At 6.30 p.m. he was ready. He had arranged to meet Zoë in town and go for a drink before the film. The agreed rendezvous was the Bell Inn in the centre of town.

Ian shouted cheerio to Nigel and got no response. Opening the front door, he sighed whilst looking at his decidedly old Fiat Panda. *Will it start*, he thought. The car started first time. Maybe this was going to be his lucky night.

By 6.45 p.m. Ian was standing outside the pub, nervously looking up and down the street. His heart missed a beat when he saw Zoë turn the corner and walk towards him. She was with another man. They walked up to Ian, and Zoë gave him one of her smiles which immediately put him at ease.

'Sorry I'm late, work has been hell.' Zoë's apology was unnecessary. Ian was just relieved she'd turned up. 'Oh, and this is Steven, a colleague from work.'

The two shook hands, and Steven went his separate way. 'Drink?' Ian enquired.

'Definitely. And I'll tell you all about my awful day. You're in for a real ear-bashing. I like the shirt, by the way. Do you only have the one?'

Ian cringed, holding open the door to the lounge. Zoë made her way to the bar, turning to ask him what he wanted to drink.

'There's only one drink,' he said, grinning.

'What if they don't sell Murphy's?' she asked.

'Then we find another pub!'

Zoë leaned over the bar so she could see into the public bar to try and find someone to serve her. Ian looked appreciatively at her leaning over the bar. He smiled inwardly and then realised he was beginning to blush. Once served, the two made their way to a table near the window at the front of the pub, from where they could watch the workers making their way home, bodies hunched up in overcoats and raincoats, heads down against the chill wind.

'Bloody cold out there,' Ian observed.

Zoë turned and looked outside. 'It's not surprising you're cold. Why didn't you wear a coat?'

'It's in the car. I didn't think I'd need it.'

Zoë continued to nag. 'By the time we get out of the cinema tonight it'll be freezing, according to the weather forecast.'

'Yes, well, we'll have to walk fast back to the car. Which film do you fancy? *Robin Hood* or *Sleeping with the Enemy*?'

Studying Form

'If any, it'll have to be *Robin Hood*. I'm not a fan of Julia Roberts. She's too pretty!'

Ian detected from her voice and the *if any*, she wasn't too enthusiastic about a movie. Neither was he, to be honest. 'You're not too keen on either of them, are you?'

'Sorry.' Zoë took a sip from her glass. She looked thoughtful. Finally, she asked Ian if he would prefer they went for a meal somewhere. She hadn't eaten all day and was in need of some sustenance.

'Have a Murphy's!' Ian joked. He was stalling, worried what a 'meal' entailed. He wasn't carrying much money. 'Sure, good idea. Where?'

'Indian. Do you like Indian?'

Whilst they drank their drinks, Zoë went into great detail about her 'awful day' at work. It was a good job Ian was a good listener. Zoë had mentioned previously she worked in a bank for her main job, and when Ian discovered it was Lloyds, he was impressed for the simple reason he liked the corporate colour: green.

Zoë had been on a till which, at close of business, had not balanced. It had taken over an hour to sort it out. Identifying that it was a stray cheque for £31.42 that had caused the problem had been straightforward, but it had taken a good forty-five minutes for a manager to suggest removing the till drawer. Only then did they find the cheque in a void between it and the counter.

'Apparently this is the third time it has happened,' Zoë said, with an air of exasperation. 'The other two times were in other branches though.'

It was agreed they would drive to an Indian restaurant near to where Zoë lived. In fact, Zoë suggested they drive back to her place first so Ian could drop off the car, which would allow him to have a drink if he wanted.

How thoughtful, he mused, still worrying about the money.

The meal was fine, if a little too spicy in Ian's case. He should have gone for the bhuna or balti rather than the Madras. He envied Zoë for her selection which he had sampled in an intimate moment when they exchanged forks.

The bill had arrived and been passed automatically to Ian. He had reached for it with, what he had thought was, an air of confidence. His change in facial expression must have given something away because Zoë soon came to the rescue saying the meal was her idea so she should pay.

'No chance,' Ian exclaimed. 'I have this under control. It just means we will have to go straight home, that's all. No stopping off at a pub on the way.'

'Suits me,' Zoë replied, with a teasing grin which wasn't lost on Ian. He took a deep breath and tried to keep his composure.

With the bill paid, they walked home, arm-in-arm, talking of trivialities, which suited Ian fine. He commented on her being a good conversationalist, which was a mistake because Zoë stopped in her tracks and asked what he meant. 'Do you mean I talk too much, or something?'

Having reassured her that she didn't, Zoë carried on talking. In hindsight, Ian decided she did talk too much. *Talk the hind legs off a donkey, this one could*, he thought absentmindedly, just like he had when they had been on the phone a few days earlier.

They got to Zoë's home at just turned midnight, so Ian was surprised to be invited in. He readily accepted the invitation though since he needed to go to the loo. Zoë gave him directions and went to the kitchen to make a drink.

Having made his way back from the bathroom, making sure to be quiet so as not to wake Jason or Zoë's parents, he went into the living room and sat down on the floor in front of a coal fire which was down to its dying embers. A fireguard surrounded it, but the fading glow still gave off warmth.

He dwelled, for a moment, on a memory from his childhood. Every morning during the winter months, he would wake up to the sound of his mother or father cleaning the grate and building up a fresh fire. Every morning, his slumber disturbed, he would think the same thought. *Why don't they buy a gas fire?* He had kept his thoughts to himself in those days, for fear of a thick ear. Now, not having been woken up too early for the fire's preparation, the advantages of a real fire became quite apparent. It was somewhat romantic, late at night, nice and quiet.

Zoë came in with a tray, two coffees and more biscuits. 'Do you drink Scotch?' she asked, as she set the tray on the floor next to him. His eyes nearly popped out of his head when she bent down beside him, her loose blouse revealing she wore no bra.

'Err... Yes, great, fine. Do you have a single malt?'

'I suspect so. Dad loves his whisky, and he usually buys the best.' She walked over to a cupboard and pulled open a couple of doors. A light turned on automatically to illuminate a myriad of bottles, all shapes and sizes. The first one Ian noticed was Bells, hardly a malt. Zoë picked it up and showed it to Ian. 'Dad gives this to the guests he doesn't like, or who he feels aren't worthy of the real thing.'

'Don't knock it, many a party has seen me escorting a bottle of Bells. Bring a bottle, take a Bells – that's my motto.'

'OK. What would you like?' Zoë reeled off eight or nine names before Ian told her to slow down a bit to give him a chance to remember them all. Eventually, he decided on a Cardhu, having decided to pass on an expensive-looking bottle of 1975 Knockando, and received a measure in excess of a 'large'. That much whisky after the two pints he had already consumed would usually put him under the table. It was just as well he was on the floor already.

Zoë had poured herself an equal measure and sat herself next to Ian, very close. 'Cheers,' she said, lifting the glass.

'What? Oh yes, cheers,' he replied.

Zoë laughed and took a sip from her glass before putting it down next to her. 'I've really enjoyed this evening. I relax when I'm with you. I talk to you, talk about things I normally keep to myself. You're a good listener, you know.'

'You mean I don't say much. Are you calling me boring?'

She gave him a friendly dig in the ribs, and Ian grabbed her hand to protect himself. He didn't let go. They laughed and stared into each other's eyes. He loosened his grip on her hand, and she moved it to the top of his shirt, resting two fingers either side of the top press-stud. They kissed, briefly, and then pulled away. Zoë popped open the first press-stud on his shirt and slowly moved her hand inside. Ian's heart was beating nineteen to the dozen, and he was definitely getting hot. He thought it might be the heat was from the fire, but the embers were probably cold by now. Zoë kissed him long and hard.

This is it, he thought.

And it was.

Friday, 29 March 1991
– Good Friday

The next morning, in his own bed, Ian stared up at the ceiling with a contented smile on his face. He felt like he was floating. His memories of the previous night were still fresh in his mind, and he hoped they would stay as vivid for a long time to come.

They had made love in front of the fire. At first, Ian had been reluctant because of the close proximity of Zoë's parents and the baby. He was worried any untoward noises they made could disturb them. Zoë had been very persuasive though, and it hadn't taken long for passion to overcome modesty, lust to overcome discretion.

But what an appetite Zoë had! It had been 3.30 in the morning when Ian had found a reason to warm to baby Jason. At about that time, Zoë had been trying to get Ian to do what they had already done twice already. At about that time, Ian was so consumed with physical exhaustion he knew he was totally incapable of fulfilling Zoë's desire. It was at about that time, just as he was about to admit his impending failure, her son had started to cry.

She had to attend to Jason, and Ian had tried not to look too relieved when they agreed it was about time for him to go home anyway. A quick kiss, and Zoë was gone, leaving Ian to dress himself and make his own way out. He'd driven home carefully, making sure to keep within the speed limit. Even though he hadn't touched any alcohol for three hours and he'd had a strong coffee, he was not sure he should be driving. With his favourite cassette blasting out of his car's speakers, he sang along to 'Down among the Sheltering Palms', a cover by The Bachelors, at the top of his voice. The roads were, fortunately, very quiet.

Ian eventually pulled himself out of bed mid-morning and had a bath before grabbing a light breakfast. Nigel was visiting his parents in northern France over the Easter weekend, so Ian had the house to himself to do whatever he chose. He chose to lock himself away and work on the database.

The information transmitted by RLDS had taken the form of a series of 'strings'. Each string contained a list of characters, numbers and letters, relating to individual horses and grouped as results to particular races. It was Ian's job to decipher the series of characters into meaningful fields which would in turn fit into database tables. With the help of an old paper Nigel had found at the bottom of his wardrobe, Ian was able to recognise the first series of characters as being the result of a race at Doncaster in mid-March 1990, the first race of the Flat season. Apparently, there had been other races over the Flat before the Doncaster meeting, but they had been on all-weather tracks, AWTs, so Nigel wasn't too bothered with those.

Having recognised the venue, date and time of the race, it became apparent the first thirty characters of each string identified the time and place of the race in question. After three quarters of an hour, Ian had unravelled the rest of the gibberish to decipher the complete result of the first few races at Doncaster the previous year, including the result of the Lincoln where a 33/1 outsider called Evichstar had won. He scribbled a few figures on a piece of paper as he worked through these races, noting down the winners, the distance of the races and the going. It was then just a case of writing a small program to disentangle the rest of the characters into a meaningful format which, Ian hoped, would assist Nigel in deciding the next steps: how the database should be laid out, what sort of filters to apply, how the data would be interrogated and whether or not Nigel wanted to add data of his own at this early stage.

Ian spent the next hour and twenty minutes writing and testing his program, tutting at the careless mistakes. He'd always been careless. A teacher had once compared him to a goldfish, unable to maintain concentration for more than eight seconds at a time. It was true to a certain extent – Ian was an Aries through and through, always starting things but not seeing them through to completion, always speaking before fully considering what he was going to say. On the plus side, a considerate chap with a heart of gold, though he wasn't too sure he had the passionate nature of an Arian, especially after the previous night. He wondered what birth sign Zoë was. His mind was wandering – his teacher had been right.

Eventually, he got his program working, and he let it loose on the mountain of data they had purchased only a couple of nights before. As he watched the monitor flash and rewrite and save and flash again, he wondered if the System could really work, if Nigel had really developed a system which would beat the bookies. He wondered if their friendship, which could hardly be described as deep and everlasting since they hadn't known each other very long, would be able to stand up to the temptations, the greed and the mistrust that a successful system might foster. For the first time, he forced himself to think about Nigel objectively, cynically and without compassion.

Ian only knew what Nigel had chosen to tell him about himself. He knew how old he was, how many brothers (one – aged twenty-six) and sisters (one – aged eighteen) he had, and his family was local, though his parents now lived abroad, in northern France. He knew Nigel had been in trouble with the police when he was given a caution for possession of cannabis at a party. The ironic part being it had been Nigel's first (and last) purchase of weed, and the police had swooped on the venue only seconds after he had made the acquisition. Ian knew Nigel was clever, his nine O levels and two A levels were testament to that, but he also knew Nigel could be lazy. He'd been born 28 February 1968, so he was older than Ian by a mere month.

And what would Nigel have to say about Ian? Was there respect? Was there trust? Ian knew himself to be the more talkative of the two, especially over a couple of beers. He also knew himself to be honest and trustworthy. But, on reflection, that might be more a weakness than a strength, something Nigel could take advantage of. Nigel was prone to making fun of Ian, playing on his friend's social awkwardness. It was all harmless fun at the moment, but Ian wondered if it might turn spiteful.

The computer beeped a few times to tell Ian the program had successfully run its course. He saved the files as a matter of habit, knowing full well his program had been saving the files as it went along. His stomach rumbled, and he decided, at 1.15 p.m., it was about time for breakfast.

The phone rang, and Ian trundled downstairs to answer it, an inconvenient detour from the primary goal: getting to the kitchen for something to eat.

'What took you?' Nigel's greeting from northern France was predictably sarcastic.

'Hi there. How's the family?' Ian ignored Nigel's flippant remark, focusing instead on showing an interest in his landlord's trip.

'Yeah, all's fine over here thanks. Look, just thought I'd let you know I am staying a couple of extra days, so you won't be seeing me until Friday. Mum and Dad are taking us all into Paris to see a show on Wednesday.'

'Sounds great! Tell me all about it when you get back.'

'Will do. Bye.'

The line went dead. Ian looked at the telephone receiver somewhat startled at the abruptness of the call ending. Then he replaced the receiver on its cradle and presumed it had something to with international phone calls   being   expensive.

Friday, 19 April 1991

The weeks passed, and the database began to take shape. Nigel was now able to determine which horses had raced against which in a fraction of the time it had taken previously. He was able to see at a glance if it was worth investing time and effort in one race or another, now he knew exactly how many horses were involved. He realised a future development for the database could be a crude time-manager. If he spent, on average, five minutes on each horse, and the database told him there would be forty-five horses to look at then it didn't take a genius to work out how long he'd have to spend on the race. A scrap of paper and a pencil had aided him to estimate three-and-three-quarter hours, give or take a tea break or two, for a scenario such as that.

The expected result for the race in mid-April had taken shape earlier than expected thanks to the success of the database. They had it narrowed down to one of three horses. All that remained was for the actual line-up of horses to be declared for the race at the overnight stage and for the ground conditions to be confirmed. Nigel was adamant the going needed to be 'good' for them to have any certainty of the outcome for this one.

For obvious reasons, Ian had taken a keen interest in the race and reckoned there would be a lot of horses going down to the start. Nigel explained the bigger the field the more generous the odds would be.

On the day, Friday, 19 April, twenty-four horses went to the post. The only things that had been likely to negatively affect the calculations, according to Nigel, were the weather and the going, and since the weather wasn't doing anything untoward and the going wasn't going anywhere, everything was in place. Nigel's confidence and certainty were becoming infectious once again.

The money was ready in £20 notes – Ian's mother having sent five crisp twenties by registered post the previous week and Nigel's local bank branch dispensing five tatty ones the previous day. *Only ten bits of paper for all that money*, Ian had thought. The design was pretty, though. He always marvelled at the way the silver ran in and out of the paper, to make it difficult for the professional forgers to copy and pointless for the amateur forgers to photocopy. It reminded him of his childhood when, at an early age, he'd discovered it was fairly easy to remove the silver strips from £1 notes without doing too much damage. It had always given him a thrill to spend the money knowing the money might now be considered counterfeit and he could be arrested on the spot! For an eight-year-old, the idea of being arrested and having a ride in a police car had had enormous appeal.

Studying Form

Ian had decided to leave a life of crime behind, however, when he'd been caught, aged twelve, with a friend, walking out of Timothy Whites with a toy that had not been paid for. A stern telling off from the shop manager had seen both villains in floods of tears and a dribble of wee in Ian's pants.

Nigel went to the newsagents early to get the morning papers. He had already read the racing pages on Ceefax and Oracle. He had also looked at the weather forecast for the area. Now all he needed was a quick scan of the racing press to ensure there were no untoward happenings at the relevant stables and the jockeys booked had not changed. Over breakfast, he made his decision. Swift Romance was the one.

'Swift Romance. There it is, that's the winner,' exclaimed Nigel. 'Just as I thought a week ago. Rather apt with you and Zoë getting on so well so quickly.'

'Two hundred quid. There it is, that's the outlay,' exclaimed Ian mockingly. 'Just as it was an hour ago.' He pushed the notes over to Nigel's side of the table as he continued with his bowl of Sugar Puffs, draining the milk from each spoonful back into the bowl, keeping it until all the puffs had gone.

'Thank you, and be sure to thank your mam when you next talk to her!' Nigel knew the stake provided by Ian had come from his parents. Not that it mattered; it was soon to grow ten-fold, at the very least, if everything went to plan. Swift Romance was something of an outsider. The morning press SP forecast had found it difficult to put a price on their selection with 20/1 bar being printed on the page Nigel was looking at.

Don't Presume was the horse listed second from Nigel's system, but the scoring his formula came up with did not have the two horses as close as the bookies would have the punters think.

'So, whilst you're at school this afternoon, I'll be in the bookies watching our money grow. Why don't you come with me and forget about the afternoon lectures, just this once,' Nigel suggested.

'The lecture is too important, and I've got to pass this time, I'm afraid. The next few weeks are important too. I've got to decide on a project and get the support of my mentor. He's got to agree it and, more importantly, provide the financial backing for the new equipment I'll need.' Ian launched into an explanation about the needs of an undergraduate wishing to undertake a thesis in robotics and voice recognition. Nigel listened to his friend, his expression disinterested. When Ian eventually took a breath, Nigel sighed and held up his hands in surrender.

*

With Ian on his way to college, Nigel went into Flemings alone with the £220 in his back pocket having remembered to pocket an extra £20 for the tax. In no time at all, he stumbled out of the shop, ashen-faced and close to panic, unable to believe what had just happened.

He had sensed something was wrong soon after entering the shop. As normal, for the time of day, the shop was relatively quiet, just a background commentary and discussion coming over the Satellite Information Service screens scattered around the shop. There were a few punters busily reading the form, filling out betting slips or gazing into space in search of divine inspiration. One old lady, a regular, sat near the counter talking to a cashier. It was amazing how many old folk frequented betting shops purely to keep warm and have a chat. They occasionally had a flutter, but their main reason for being there was to keep the cold at bay without running up huge heating bills at home during the winter months.

Nigel had subconsciously noticed the cashier recognise him, draw herself away from the old lady and wander across to the shop manager who was busy resetting the previous day's winning bets. They had a hushed conversation whilst Nigel filled out his betting slip. With the slip in his hand and fumbling for the wad of notes in his back pocket, he wandered over to the counter. The shop manager, Frank Ryan, got up from his desk and sauntered across to the till to take Nigel's bet. Nigel slipped it under the bandit screen and smiled, purely out of politeness, as the manager picked it up and quickly scanned it.

'You can have £20 at SP, nothing more.'

'What!' exclaimed Nigel. 'You're joking, aren't you? The betting slip says two hundred pounds, and this is a betting shop, and I want to place a bet. What's wrong with that?'

'There's nothing wrong. And you can have a bet. I'm not prepared to take £200 though. So, like I said: £20, not a penny more.'

'A betting organisation the size of yours, with shops all over the country, won't take £200 from one simple punter?' Nigel was exasperated, close to losing his cool.

'£20, and that's it,' the manager repeated.

'How the fuck can you justify that!' Nigel didn't like swearing, but on this occasion, it seemed the only apt response.

'I am the manager of this betting shop, and I must maintain its profitability as a single unit. It's a matter of economics. I don't really have to justify myself to you, but you seem an intelligent chap, so I'll explain. You walked into this shop fourteen months ago and, after a few small unsuccessful bets, have maintained a winning streak which has cost me over five thousand pounds, with only one exception when a horse let you down, and incidentally, I thought it should have won as well. You have had an incredible run of luck which has gouged massive holes in this shop's profitability. If you know something about these horses, if you *know* they are going to win, then good luck to you. I envy you your knowledge. But you are going to have to take your business elsewhere.'

Nigel just stared, flabbergasted, his dream falling apart before it had had a real chance to take off. He scribbled over a zero on the betting slip and handed the manager a single £20 note, fumbling for the £2 tax using small change in his pocket. Once the manager had processed his betting slip and returned the pink, Nigel turned to leave, trying to keep calm. The few customers in the small shop had overheard the conversation, and they all stared at Nigel as he left. As he walked away, the manager called after him. 'Don't bother trying to place the bet at any of our city offices, because they've been warned about you too.'

Nigel's patience snapped. 'Bastard,' he shouted as he slammed the door behind him and stumbled out onto the street. The manager turned to the phone and called the city branches, describing Nigel's appearance and warning them about any large sums of money for a horse called Swift Romance.

Frantic, just how Nigel felt in that moment, was a film starring Harrison Ford, co-starring the wife of Roman Polanski as a beautiful smuggler of nuclear detonators on the streets of Paris.

Funny how irrelevant thoughts cloud the mind in times of adversity, when clarity of thought is of paramount importance, when one error of judgement could be the difference between life and death, just like in the film Top Gun*, starring*—'Come on, snap out of it. Think. Think straight. How am I going to get the bet on now?' Nigel chastised himself aloud, drawing funny looks from people passing him in the street. The only solution he could think of was to get someone else to place the bet, and the only someone he could think of was Ian.

Time was against him, so he decided to get a taxi into the city centre, directing the driver to the Newton Building on Talbot Street, hoping Ian had lectures there today. Whilst the driver crawled through the midday traffic, Nigel had time to reflect on the one-sided conversation in the betting shop. The manager must have been monitoring his bets for quite a while. But had he decided to confront Nigel through his own volition or had it been a directive from higher management? Either way the manager had made it clear Nigel wouldn't be welcome in the two local betting shops on Mansfield Road from now on.

Nigel knew of three other shops within walking distance of the Newton Building. Maybe he should try them himself alone first? He decided against it – the unfriendly manager would have contacted the others in the organisation by now. Anyway, if they refused his £180, it might make it more difficult for Ian. He sighed to himself and muttered, 'I don't believe it,' under his breath.

'Eh?' enquired the taxi driver. 'You talking to me?'

'No. Sorry. I was just dwelling on a bit of a misunderstanding with the local bookie.'

'Oh, them bastards,' the driver observed, in a shrewd tone. Not another word was said until Nigel's destination was reached. He paid the taxi driver and suggested the man keep the change. 'Swift Romance, 3.40 Newbury,' he said to the driver, smiled and walked away towards the Newton Building.

The driver watched Nigel go and shouted, 'No chance, Dunlop's Alsaaybah will 'ammer 'im!'

Nigel rolled his eyes and focused on where he was going – he wasn't at all sure where he was going.

Studying Form

He needed a friendly face with knowledge of the polytechnic's layout and workings. He went into the Newton Building – an imposing white structure which could be seen from many points throughout Nottingham.

The entrance and corridor beyond were deserted. However, there was a great deal of noise coming from one room along the main corridor of the ground floor. Nigel walked into a refectory where numerous students were all eating, drinking and shouting at once. A piece of chicken leg hit him on the shoulder. *Animals*, he thought, as he stood in the doorway, staring at the guy who had thrown the projectile. The room went quiet, everyone realising the joke had been lost on their unexpected visitor.

'Idiot.' Nigel glared at the fool who had thrown the chicken leg. 'Does anyone know where I can find Ian Turner? He's in his final year, doing computing. It's very important.'

'Er, the only fourth years in today are in the lecture theatre, fourth floor; the stairs are down the corridor on your left.'

Nigel turned away without a word of thanks, the smell of chicken accompanying him to the stairs. Taking the stairs two at a time, he climbed to the fourth floor, making a mental note he was very unfit, or rather making a mental note he should try to get fit. He being unfit was a well-known fact, not noteworthy at all.

The lecture theatre was packed, but Nigel was relieved to see his slightly balding friend on a bench seat in a row close to the rear of the hall and near to the door. The lecturer was busy writing on a blackboard with his back to his audience as Nigel slipped surreptitiously in through the door. Heads turned as students, easily distracted from the matter at hand, heard the door open. The only head not to turn was Ian's. *God, what a swot*, Nigel thought when he saw his friend was engrossed in making copious notes whilst most around him daydreamed. He whispered to the nearest student that he needed to speak with Ian urgently. As he stepped back through the door, heads went together and came apart as the Chinese whispers form of communication got into full swing. Eventually, Ian turned to look towards the door to see his friend frantically waving for him to get out of the lecture theatre.

Nigel couldn't believe his eyes when Ian shook his head and mouthed, No, in an exaggerated manner. Nigel saw red, clenched his fist and smacked it into the palm of his other hand. He then, in an exaggerated manner, to ensure Ian understood, signalled a throat-cut and mouthed, You're Dead. Some of the students turned to Ian and told him he was dead and laughed.

The commotion caused the lecturer to turn around. He saw Nigel through the door and registered the anxiety in his face. He suggested whatever the person wanted, the sooner he was satisfied the better for all concerned. Ian stood up and packed away his course notes, apologised to the lecturer, and made his way out of the lecture theatre.

'What the fuck do you think you're playing at? What do you want?'

Studying Form

'There's no time to stand around; I'll explain on the way.' Nigel turned towards the stairs and walked away from Ian who remained rooted to the spot.

'On the way where?' he called out. Nigel didn't answer, so Ian ran after him and, on catching up, repeated his question. 'On the way where?'

Nigel spent the next fifteen minutes relaying the morning's events to Ian, culminating in telling him he would have to place the bet. Nigel also made it clear Ian would have to visit more than one betting office if they were to get all the money on. Any big money for their horse would immediately raise suspicion, especially if the last bookie had kept to his word and tipped off the other branch offices in the town.

Nigel knew where most of the betting shops were – he had used them for gambling, for shelter when it rained, and for just keeping warm when he couldn't afford to heat his house in the winter. Recently, he had nipped into one shop just to write a birthday card and address the envelope – he hadn't had a pen on him, and the card had to be posted promptly. This time, however, he would have to stay outside. It would all be down to Ian.

As they approached the first betting shop, Nigel told Ian to be casual and take his time. It was sure to raise suspicion if he went in and immediately wrote a betting slip with only one horse on it and then presented it to the cashier. It could indicate some prior knowledge, especially if the shop manager saw the name, Swift Romance.

'But hurry up,' Nigel said just before Ian entered the shop.

'What? Do you want me to be slow and unseen, or swift and noticed?'

'Er… Be careful, but be quick. We've got to visit at least three shops… maybe more, and we haven't much time.'

Ian was in and out in no time, clutching his betting slip and grinning. 'A piece of piss.'

Nigel wasn't at all happy but soon cooled down when he learned how busy the shop had been, making it impossible for the staff to suspect anything. Ian had placed £50 on the horse and had taken a price of 25/1, dutifully paying the tax up front too. Nigel was impressed with that since he had forgotten to mention taking a price if the horse was anything better than 16's.

Three quarters of an hour later, £180 had been placed on Swift Romance for a variety of odds ranging from 20/1 to 28/1. Nigel was a little worried the price was drifting but did not let his concern be known to Ian.

The final port of call was one of the Flemings chain, and it was teaming with punters. Ian wondered if it was the size of the shop that led you to believe betting was popular (the small shop was packed) or if the shop was so small because the Sport of Kings wasn't popular enough to warrant a larger space. It didn't take long for Ian to stop pondering such pointless thoughts as time was running out – it was just three minutes to the off.

Studying Form

Ian had entered the shop alone and placed the bet himself as in all the previous shops. Nigel joined him in the shop just before the off, though they sat apart, glued to the TV monitors. The race, a one-mile handicap, had the attention of the whole shop as the commentator announced, 'They're under orders.' Then, following a slight delay, 'They're off.'

The next one minute, forty-one seconds were a blur to Ian. Actually, the first one minute twenty-five seconds were a blur, whilst he watched, breathing on hold, heart on overdrive, fingernails in retreat. The final sixteen seconds were a cacophony of sound as Ian tried his hardest to raise the roof of the bookies and urge Swift Romance to victory by the closest of margins. She won by a neck.

When the horses had passed the finishing post, Ian's celebrations subsided, and a nearby punter gave a sigh of relief and moved further away in case Ian got as excited with the replay. The replay, however, held no interest for him. He walked over to Nigel who had not batted an eyelid throughout.

'You noisy git.' Nigel's greeting was quite polite considering the thoughts that were going through his mind. 'Everyone but everyone was watching you – the cashiers and the manager…in fact the whole bloody shop. They've never seen you before, but now they'll know you forever, you idiot. Give me the betting slip; I'll collect the winnings.'

As they left the shop, Ian commented on how miserable Nigel was, given they had just won a load of money. Nigel stopped and turned to his friend.

'I'm sorry. It's just become really clear that anonymity is going to be vital to us making this work. We're going to be visiting betting shops on a regular basis and making a mint. One shop, possibly two, are already going to be difficult to use since the manager and staff know who we are.'

That afternoon, they had won £6,750.

*

The following morning, Saturday, Nigel went to all the betting shops to pick up the winnings. Even though Ian had placed the bets the previous day, Nigel was confident the two would not be linked since cashiers don't take much notice when taking bets and only pay a little attention when paying out small amounts.

Having deposited most of the money in the bank before it closed at lunchtime, he met Ian for some pub grub and had a chat about the next race and the tactics they would have to adopt to get their money on. Unfortunately, Ian had more Saturday lectures, so he contented himself with orange juice and lemonade whilst Nigel passed a couple of pints of Murphy's down his throat. Ian took consolation in winning their game of pool 3–0, and Nigel paid for the lot. Scampi and chips always tasted a bit better when it was free.

Nigel had decided the next race to go for was one that was due to run in a week's time. It was a race he wouldn't have considered previously, because there wouldn't have been enough time to study all the form, but now, with the aid of the database and the computerised system, he was confident they could

Studying Form

manage it. He was also confident the time was right to increase the stake on the horse. Previous results for the race in question had brought some long prices, last year's winner having started at a price of 15/2.

Ian was reluctant to ask, but he knew Nigel was waiting for the question. 'So how much do you think we should throw at the bookies next time?'

Head down, contemplating the dregs of his second pint, Nigel paused purely for dramatic effect. He lifted his head and stared at Ian. 'One thousand pounds.'

Ian was aghast. *Far too much*, he thought. 'Does this proposed wager come inclusive or exclusive of the betting levy, which is currently 10 per cent. I think I ought to remind you of that.'

'OK, £1,100.'

'You're mad. This is big money… Surely, it's too big. I'll probably get mugged putting on the bet. My pockets don't hold £1,100. I'll look like the Michelin Man with that sort of money stuffed down my trousers.'

'Good point… Good point, well made! No-one will mug you if they'd have to put their hands down your trousers to get hold of your valuables. Got any cycle clips? Seriously though, I started this venture with one goal in mind: to make money. Now, thanks to you, we have a System which works, and we have a race in one week's time which will bring us approximately seven grand. That's why we need anonymity. We have to put the money on bit by bit, in small amounts. Your bloody celebrations in the bookies yesterday mean they'll probably be reluctant to take our money in the future. Soon all the shops in town will be watching out for us. Believe me, it's how they operate. They monitor their successful punters and make it difficult for them to gamble.

'Furthermore, and completely changing tack, I reckon sooner rather than later we will have to go further afield to go about our business. And if you think I'm going to be driven the length and breadth of Britain in your rust bucket, you've got another thing coming. We are going to have to get a new car. And that, my son, will cost a lot of money if we do it properly – *with style*!'

'Good idea, £1,000 bet sounds perfect. What sort of car?' At the prospect of buying a new car, Ian suddenly became more enthusiastic.

'Well, if we pocket seven grand from the next race, it'll have to be a brand-new one, preferably red.'

Ian drifted off into a personal reverie, wondering what £7,000 would buy, hardly believing how events were taking him over. Only three weeks ago, he had been an impoverished student, forfeiting four years of his life to further his education in the hope it might lead to a better than average chance in obtaining work at the end of it. He was always short of money. He was always tired. He was always studying – his head in books or his eyes glued to a computer screen. He had been lonely in a sea of people. But now things were different. He was busy doing things he actually enjoyed, with agreeable company. His mind turned to Zoë whom he hadn't seen for a couple of days.

Studying Form

Nigel got up from the table with an abruptness that brought Ian back into the real world. 'Right, I'm off. I'll catch up with you later.'

'What are you going to do this afternoon? You're not at work till six,' Ian enquired. He should have guessed.

'I'll be in the bookies... Bye.' Nigel drained the last of his pint, picked up his *Racing Post* and stuffed it into his back pocket. Ian watched him go and wondered how long this 'honeymoon' period would last. It was all new, exciting and successful, but for how long? When would the bubble burst? Pessimism reared its ugly head, as it usually did when things were going well for him. He sighed, drained his glass and followed Nigel out onto the street.

*

Nigel had no real interest in any of the races that afternoon but enjoyed being in the environment all the same. He knew there was a single Flat meeting, so he made his way to the bookies hoping to catch the first race – the 2.15 at Thirsk. Fortunately, there had been a delay to the start of the race, due to a horse losing one of its shoes, 'spreading a plate' as they said in the industry. Flemings betting shop was half empty, or half full depending on your view of life, so there was no problem finding somewhere to sit. Nigel perched himself in front of the TV screens and in full view of the manager who had noticed him entering the shop.

Nigel looked over to the people behind the bandit screen and saw the shop manager and one of the cashiers were looking right at him. *Not again*, he thought, casting his mind back just over twenty-four hours to when he'd been turned away at the other Flemings shop about half a mile up the road. He decided to test the water and have a bet. He had only intended watching the race then going home. Now he knew he'd have to find out if betting in this particular shop was going to be denied to him, along with the other one.

He wrote out a betting slip on a horse he thought had a good chance, but he also knew he was probably throwing money down the drain. If the horse duly obliged, then the manager might make future bets difficult. If the horse lost, then he'd be £30 out of pocket. *Better make it £20 and no tax!* he decided at the last minute. He jumped off his perch (the stools always seemed too high for his short legs) and walked up to the counter, passing the betting slip under the bandit screen along with a crisp new £20 note. The cashier smiled and put the bet through the till without delay – she was obviously pleased to have something to do.

As Nigel walked away, he wondered if the cashier thought he was a mug or not. He used to think punters were mugs, including himself at times, so why not her – seeing so many people spend their afternoons passing their hard-earned cash across the counter, with scant hope of any return. The bet was on, however, and the manager, David Jones, had watched him, saying nothing.

Studying Form

Let's hope it loses, Nigel thought philosophically. The horse, High Principles, lost, or rather it didn't win – second, by a country mile.

Nigel made his way out of Flemings, and Jones, the manager, took a file from a drawer at his desk to make a note of the losing bet on a page entitled 'Shorty' – referring to Nigel's lack of inches in the height department. The betting shop on Mansfield Road, where Nigel's betting activities had started to be monitored, had decided upon the alias. The two shops on Mansfield Road now knew Nigel's identity, having compared betting slips and agreeing the writing to be the same and belonging to a rather short gentleman with a distinct lack of hair. Shorty was costing them money.

Now, something was being done about Shorty.

Thursday, 25 April 1991

On Thursday morning, seventeen betting shop managers from the Flemings chain of bookmakers sat around a long oak table. At its head sat the district manager, James Price. This was a regular meeting, scheduled so that all the managers could discuss forthcoming national campaigns, and any general or specific issues. It also gave Price the chance to discuss local directives at length.

James Price had been in the industry for nearly thirty years. He had been there when it all began. In the early sixties, the sign of a good day was a drawer full of money at the end of racing. A sign of a bad day was a drawer with less money in it than you had at the start of the day.

Price knew the industry inside-out, and he loved it. He accepted there was right and wrong in his business, and he was no angel himself, having exploited weaknesses in the industry in the past. He knew every fiddle his staff could attempt. He'd done them all himself when a young betting shop manager. As for horses, he knew nearly every stable, the length and breadth of the country. He knew the trainers who could be trusted. He also knew of trainers who sometimes instructed jockeys to hold their horses back. James Price, unbeknownst to his employers, made a fair amount of money from gambling. His inside knowledge, his communication channels and his numerous discreet contacts assured his occasional substantial success. James Price was good at his job as a district manager. He also knew his district had started making less money, and he didn't like it at all.

'It's got to stop,' he informed his managers. 'These losses will not be tolerated. It's far too early in the season to have head office breathing down my neck already, so I'm passing on the favour and breathing down yours. We discussed this punter towards the end of last season, and his good fortune seems to be continuing. Well, as far as we are concerned, he can take his good fortune and celebrate it elsewhere. You've got to get him out of our shops. Let the other firms subsidise this joker, Shorty – isn't that what we call him?'

'That's right.' Simon Ryan had known he was in for a roasting when Shorty had taken £3,450 out of his shop when Amenable won the Lincoln. 'I've made it clear to him that he's not welcome. His last attempt at a bet'—Ryan referred to some notes—'would have earned him approximately £6,000.'

'Yes, but he's not out of our hair yet. He's local, and he's got a friend, and he doesn't back losers.'

'He did last Saturday,' remarked David Jones.

'Oh really? I'm pleased to hear it. A bit out of character though, isn't it? The fact he's gone eight straight wins, and now, all of a sudden, he's backed a loser? How much did he lose?'

All heads turned to Jones. When he told his colleagues of the afternoon's events the previous

Saturday, the ensuing discussion concluded Shorty had intended to lose the money, testing the water to see if his money was still good.

'Well, it isn't!' Price was adamant. 'If I hear of Shorty laying bets on my patch again, heads will roll. And I mean gross misconduct. I cannot allow this sort of betting activity to continue from the same punter.'

'But what if he knows something?' Lesley asked. Lesley Lister had been a betting shop manager for three years. It had taken her about three seconds to suss out Price when she first met him. For the first couple of minutes of their first meeting, Price had talked directly to her chest. At one stage, he had actually licked his lips. 'I'm up here,' she had had to say to get his attention away from below the neckline. Price was a flirt and a chauvinist. Lesley Lister had no trouble at all handling Price.

'Go on,' Price said, as all eyes turned towards her. 'Talk to me.'

'Well, this guy is either very lucky or very knowledgeable. If it's luck, then it will run out, in time. If it's knowledge, then it might be a good idea for us to get to know about it. If he has a source, then we could do with knowing what that source is. If he has a system, then we could definitely do with getting hold of it.'

'I just want this pair out of my shops. They're costing us too much money. Let them be someone else's problem.'

Lesley wouldn't let it go. She took it as a personal challenge now. *I'll get this bastard to agree with me*, she thought and continued. 'Look, if they move on, they might move to another one of our shops. I don't know Shorty from Adam. Every time we take a bet from a balding bloke less than five feet six inches in height, we are going to get nervous because it might be him. It's not fair on the staff or the short punters. And anyway, we're not losing too much money on this guy, all things considered. Takings are down because we lost a lot of meetings due to the frost during January and February. There's no way we're going to make that money back if the punters can't gamble, is there?'

'Don't lecture me, young lady. There is a difference between a reduction in takings and taking bets which cost us money. Give me solutions; don't waste my time by restating what I already know. I know it's been cold. I know meetings have been abandoned. I also know our competitors haven't had a Shorty on their patch... because he's been on ours, damn it.'

Lesley changed tack, softening the tone of her voice. 'Look, all I'm saying is we *all* need to know who Shorty is, and his side-kick, not just the city shops, and I think we need to establish if they've got a system.'

'I'd put my money on them having a system,' Simon Ryan interjected. 'I've been watching the types of race they bet on, and it's always the same. Handicap – 0 to 120. I don't know how they decide on which 0 to 120's to choose, but I would hazard a guess they pick the races with the best odds. There is no other constant in the equation: the trainers differ from race to race, and the jockeys range from the champion down to Henderson who's a 7lb claimer. The courses differ: left hand, right hand. The distances differ as well. They've picked winners over a mile and once over two miles one furlong. So, it can't be an insider from one stable. I'm sure it's a system. The only thing which niggles me is the one time they lost.' Ryan opened his file and turned a few sheets of A4. 'Tapestry, Shorty's third bet, lost. Like I've said before, it would have been eleven out of eleven if that one had won.'

Price asked the table, 'Who trains Tapestry?'

Lesley raised her hand slightly, as if back at school, which brought sniggers from a few of the others. She had developed an encyclopaedic knowledge of horses in training. '*Trained* – past tense. Tapestry was destroyed; he broke a leg in a horsebox, so the papers said. The trainer, however, was Collier.'

'*Lambourn* Collier? Well, I never.' Price looked skywards and contemplated the ceiling for a moment.

Lambourn Collier was known to most of the betting shop managers around the table. His actual name was James Frederick Collier, and he'd been training thoroughbred horses out of stables in Lambourn for a considerable number of years. In this, the early nineties, there were three trainers called Collier and each had been given a nickname by the sporting press, relating to the location of their stables. Unfortunately for one Collier, David Collier, who had stables just west of Glossop, Derbyshire, this gave him a rather unfortunate nickname. David Collier did not take too kindly to being referred to as Broadbottom Collier.

Studying Form

'Well now. I have it on good authority – though it is not well known - James Frederick "Lambourn" Collier is not averse to occasionally bending the rules,' Price mused. 'He is known to stop a horse if he has to. I don't know if you can remember the scandal that hit our industry back in '86? Collier had three good handicap horses who never quite found winning ways. At the time, it was said the horses weren't genuine, weren't willing to put their noses in front during a race. Then, over a period of two weeks, the three horses won at generous odds. There was an investigation into suspicious gambling patterns, but nothing was ever proven. Collier got away with it, and I am sure he has done it since.' Everyone remained quiet, absorbing the weight of Price's information, letting it sink in.

'Getting back to Shorty and a potential system – it's as good as eleven out of eleven. Eleven winners! The poor sods – fancy picking one of Collier's horses… OK. So here's what we're going to do. I'm still not happy with the losses, so I'll send a report to head office to tell them what I'm about to tell you, so I'm covered. We'll give this Shorty fellow another bet. We'll get a photograph of him, and then we'll warn him off our patch. It will be up to head office then to decide what to do if he goes somewhere else in our chain of shops.'

'How do we get a picture of him?' Lesley asked. 'The quality of the security cameras is useless. Do you expect me to point a little Kodak Instamatic at him and ask him to smile?'

Lesley's sarcastic remark surprised everyone, including herself. Price laughed, and there was a collective sigh of relief.

'Very funny, but no. I know the cameras in the shops are useless. We all know those cameras are there as a deterrent, nothing more. No, if he makes an appearance in your shop'—he looked towards Ryan and Jones—'then you get on the telephone to me straight away. You've got my office telephone number. You then take his bet, phone it through to head office and contact all the other shops through the pyramid. Then you wait and see if he wins. When you phone me, I'll need a description of what he's wearing.' Price was enjoying this. He was going to get Shorty's photograph, his address and that of his friend. Price had an acquaintance, an acquaintance well known for his investigative prowess, having been a detective for some fourteen years.

The meeting then continued along a similar vein to all other meetings – reasons for slippage, fewer bets than usual, plans for imminent marketing campaigns and the like. Within three quarters of an hour, the meeting was closed, and the managers were returning to their shops.

Frank Ryan, however, nipped to the pub first to grab himself a quick pint and some lunch. He had about fifty minutes before the first race and was confident his cashiers could handle the morning business. He watched a couple playing darts whilst he struggled with a cheddar ploughman's, the biscuits he'd eaten at the morning meeting sitting heavy on top of his trouser belt. His mind turned to Shorty, and then it dawned on him a similar handicap race was on the cards that afternoon at Beverly.

'Shit,' he exclaimed under his breath. If Shorty had placed a bet during the morning, Ryan would be in the clear from Price because they'd all been at the meeting together. If Shorty had placed a bet whilst Ryan was in the pub, Price would pick up on the fact Ryan had been absent from his station, and he'd be in serious trouble. He downed the last of his pint and walked swiftly towards the exit chewing on a pickled onion.

At his shop, Ryan scanned the betting slips which had been taken for the particular races he knew to look out for and was happy to see nothing resembling Shorty's handwriting.

*

The letter Price eventually wrote to head office contained a full rundown of the successful and unsuccessful wagers Shorty had placed. It also detailed Price's own wishes that a final bet be allowed in order to establish the full identity of Shorty and his accomplice, thus enabling them to rid themselves of this most unwanted custom.

In the final paragraph of the letter, Price speculated on the existence of a system. A system which, if widely known (and if it existed at all), could undermine the profitable existence of the company and totally undermine the racing industry.

Andy Wheildon

Once delivered to head office, the final paragraph of the letter had the three most senior members of the security department deep in conversation.

Sunday, 28 April 1991

The information supplied by RLDS was proving invaluable. It was possible to analyse all the races which best matched the System's criteria, with only a minimum of manual intervention by Ian on Nigel's instruction to refine some of the characteristics which may have changed or some of the data which was proving inaccurate. It would now be possible to gamble on every handicap race, provided the odds were to their liking. Neither Nigel nor Ian had anticipated how easy it was all going to be. As Sunday evening drew to a close and the warm computer monitor in Ian's bedroom detailed yet another list of plausible winners, Nigel laughed and let himself flop onto Ian's bed.

'We are going to make so much money, it'll be embarrassing!' Nigel said, more to the ceiling than to Ian who was busy getting a printout of the latest forecast result. He pulled himself up and rested on one arm. 'What'll we do if the bookies stop us from placing a bet? They can, you know.'

'I suppose we'll have to make use of the brand-new car you promised me. We buy a car, we pack our bags and we visit different towns and bet there. Simple.'

'Simple?' Nigel queried. 'I've got a job; you've got college. We can't neglect those in case the bubble bursts. But then again...' Nigel began to reason with himself. 'We won't be betting every day, so a trip to a different town wouldn't be too much of a hardship. We wouldn't have the first idea where the betting shops were though; we'd be running around like blue-arsed flies going nowhere fast.' Nigel paused. 'What do you reckon?'

'I reckon the past few weeks have seen my college work go down the toilet. I'm behind in every subject, my tutors are getting agitated, and frankly, at the moment, I couldn't give a toss! We seem to be sitting on a goldmine. Actually... you're sitting on my shirt – shift!' Nigel moved to one side whilst Ian recovered his, now creased, once beautifully ironed, shirt. 'You git! I was going to wear that tonight. Anyway, as I was saying – I want to concentrate on the horses, on our system. If there's a chance the bubble is going to burst, we'll have to take full advantage of it whilst we still can.'

'Excellent, I was just testing.' Nigel jumped to his feet, moving swiftly to the door. 'I'll get us both a beer.'

*

Three days later, they were ready to place their next bet. The agreement was for Nigel to try placing the money in the betting shop close to the station in the centre of Nottingham. If he failed to get his money on then he would phone Ian at home, and the two of them would visit six betting shops each with the aim of putting on £55 at each shop, a total of £600 with £60 tax. The idea of putting £1,100 on the race, discussed a few days earlier, was no longer being entertained since it would involve visiting too many betting shops if large sums of money were refused. The horse in question, Sky Cloud, was running at Ascot and, with Willie Carson on board, would start at a price of about 8/1.

On the morning of the race, Nigel walked into Flemings on Carrington Street.

He filled out his betting slip, took it over to the counter and slid it towards the cashier. The manager wandered over, took one look at the betting slip then moved to the telephone. It was inevitable: any bet on a single horse over £500, or any bet on a single horse with a possible return of £1,000 or more, had to be phoned through to head office.

The shop manager cleared his throat and began the phone call, aware the notorious punter was within hearing distance…

'Six hundred, tax paid, on Sky Cloud.'

Is the customer known to you?

'Yes.'

Can you identify him over the phone?

'No.'

Is he being monitored by your shop?

'Yes, all of them.'

Hold the line.

'Sorry about this,' he said to the punter, and then returned to the phone. 'Hello?'

Is it Shorty?

'Spot on.'

Okay £600 at SP

'Hang on.' Again, the shop manager turned to Shorty. 'We'll give you the bet, starting price only?'

'Fine,' replied Shorty with an air of resignation.

The manager returned to the phone. 'Yes,' he said, and hung up.

*

Nigel passed the fourteen crisp £50 notes to the shop manager under the bandit screen, Sir Christopher Wren staring back at him whilst the bet was put through the till. Once the notes had been counted and checked to ensure they were genuine, the counterfoil and £40 change were returned to Nigel.

When he had left the shop, the manager phoned Price who in turn phoned his ex-police contact.

*

The Ascot race meeting was being televised by Channel 4, so Nigel and Ian settled themselves down to an afternoon of McCririck and the *Channel 4 Racing* team. Nigel had phoned Ian after placing the bet to tell him all was well. Ian had asked Nigel if it was OK for Zoë to come round. Nigel had agreed, and now she stood in their kitchen watching Ian make two teas and a coffee before the race began.

'Who do you think will win?' she asked Nigel. Out of necessity, Zoë had no idea at all about the System Nigel had developed.

'Oh, Sky Cloud has got a good chance on the form book,' Nigel replied, with an air of indifference.

Studying Form

'Willie Carson, I've heard of him. He's quite famous, isn't he?' Zoë observed, when McCririck mentioned the jockey's name.

A few minutes of small talk between the three of them was abruptly ended at 3.43 p.m. when the horses were brought under orders.

'And they're off,' Nigel and Ian said in unison

The horses were running. With eyes glued to the television, the next one and a half minutes saw a myriad of emotions from all three. As the horses left the stalls it was obvious Sky Cloud had got a dreadful start.

'He's last,' Zoë exclaimed, somewhat needlessly.

'Don't worry, there's another six and a half furlongs yet,' Ian pointed out.

'Another what?' went unanswered.

'Oh, I've heard of him too,' Zoë said as the race commentator told his audience Lester Piggott was trying to get his horse, Nicholas, to go up a gear.

Nigel knew the race was won after the first half mile. He could see Sky Cloud was being held up by Carson, and it was only a matter of time before the jockey would give the gelding his head and allow him to accelerate past Piggott's horse.

With only two furlongs remaining, Carson began to work on his horse, and the gelding lengthened his stride. Within 100 yards, Sky Cloud was in second place with the early front-runner, Nicholas, one-paced. The new leader was Band on the Run who was now going away from the field.

Ian shouted to the jockey to use his whip.

Zoë found herself bouncing up and down on the settee shouting, 'Come on, come on.'

Nigel couldn't believe his eyes. His horse was going to be beaten, his system was going to fail, and his confidence began to drain. The commentator raised both the pitch and the volume of his voice as if to compensate for the noise both Ian and Zoë were making.

In the last fifty yards, however, Sky Cloud pulled alongside and then passed Band on the Run with ease.

'Gee, how exciting,' exclaimed Zoë. Then, after a moment's reflection, 'That means your horse won.'

The television commentator began to assess the slow-motion replay, freezing the action on the line.

Sky Cloud had won at a starting price of 7/1.

'Four grand!' exclaimed Ian.

Zoë turned to Ian and stared at him, her mouth open, aghast. Ian immediately knew he'd made a mistake. Nigel shook his head, saying absolutely nothing.

'You're joking? Have you just won £4,000?'

'£4,200 to be exact,' Nigel murmured. 'We had a bet of £600, and it has just won us £4,200.'

Zoë just stared and, after a few seconds, said, 'You're insane.'

'You're right, we're insane. Fancy another coffee?' Ian tried to defuse the situation, hoping Zoë wouldn't dwell on the subject. But she followed him into the kitchen.

Studying Form

'How can you afford to put £600 on a horse? You always plead poverty when we go out. Are you hiding something from me?'

Ian looked her straight in the eyes and suggested she sit down whilst he put the kettle on. Nigel walked into the kitchen and placed himself next to Zoë. 'Oh, yes. Do tell,' he said mockingly.

There would be no guidance from Nigel's corner then. Ian took a deep breath and told Zoë about the System.

Nigel looked at Zoë. 'Now you know our secret, we're going to have to kill you.' His statement was followed by a stunned silence from both Zoë and Ian. 'Only joking!' said Nigel, quickly jumping in to reassure them. 'I just hope you can keep a secret. Your boyfriend here has been dying to tell you for a while. And now I know you a bit… well, I think you're OK.'

'Er, thanks, I think.' Zoë wasn't sure whether she'd just been complimented or insulted. She was still amazed at the scale of the wager and the size of the resultant winnings though.

The afternoon turned into early evening, and the conversation soon turned to food, drink and a night on the town. Zoë was wined and dined by the two most eligible of bachelors, though, truth be known, she only fancied Ian.

*

The following morning, Nigel had to drag himself out of bed, dress quite slowly and delicately and wander down to the betting shop to pick up a cheque for

Andy Wheildon

£4,800. Ian, on the other hand, had to stay in bed, nurse a hangover in the horizontal position and think about Zoë whilst she slept soundly next to him. Eventually, when Zoë woke up, he had to talk to her as well – not that he minded.

'Let's have a day by the seaside, sometime soon,' Zoë suggested. 'Mum will look after Jason, and we can set off really early to make a day of it. What do you think?'

'Sounds like a good idea. When and where do you have in mind?'

'Well, to be honest, I've been thinking about it for a while, and I'd love to go to the south coast. I know it's miles away, but if we set off really early and don't hit too much traffic, we could be there by lunchtime. I'm thinking either Brighton or Bournemouth.'

Ian thought for a while, trying to picture in his mind the relative locations of Brighton and Bournemouth on the south coast. Eventually, he turned to Zoë and suggested they toss a coin.

Zoë got out of bed, allowing Ian to stretch and reclaim some of the sheets Zoë had commandeered overnight. He watched her walking over to her handbag and smiled to himself. She looked gorgeous from every angle.

Once she had found a coin in her purse, she turned round and looked at Ian. 'Heads, it's Brighton; tails, it's Bournemouth.'

Studying Form

Ian smiled and lay back on the bed, putting his hands behind his head and grinning. 'Oh, give me head...s.'

Zoë shook her head in mock disgust and tossed the coin onto the bed. It landed heads up, so it was agreed their destination would be Brighton – 'London by the Sea'. The 'when' was also quickly decided.

'Bank Holiday Monday, and let's hope it's a nice day.'

*

Whilst Ian and Zoë were agreeing on what to do the following Monday, Nigel arrived at the betting shop. As he rounded the corner, he saw the manager was outside talking to someone on the street. On seeing Nigel though, he hurried back into the shop. *That's not good*, thought Nigel.

He pushed open the betting-shop door and was comforted to see the shop was as deserted as it usually was at that time of day. Walking up to the counter, he passed his counterfoil to the manager, who had not so casually pushed the cashier out of the way.

'Nice one to end on,' the manager said as he took the counterfoil and matched it with the original.

'Pardon?' Nigel's mind had been on the flustered cashier, and he wasn't sure he'd heard the manager right.

'This is the last time Flemings will be paying this sort of money to you. You are no longer welcome in Flemings here in Nottingham or any other part of the country. You're too good, and Flemings can't afford your custom. I'm not barring you. But I do know your face, I also know your friend's too. I'm only going to allow you bets of £25 or less at SP. You are going to have to take these kinds of bet'—he waved Nigel's betting slip towards him—'elsewhere. And when I say elsewhere, I mean another town, another firm.'

This response wasn't unexpected, especially after they'd made it so difficult for him earlier in the month. 'Can I have my money, please?' Nigel wasn't going to let a shop manager ruffle his feathers.

The cheque was already waiting for him, and in no time at all, Nigel was out of the shop and on his way to the bank. Hot on his heels was an ex-cop, his job to get photographs of both Nigel and Ian and to find out where they lived. The simple task was accomplished within the space of two hours. The ex-cop found where Shorty banked, where he lived and, when Nigel and Ian left their house together, he got a photo of them both.

Midway through the evening, after far too many beers, Ian asked Nigel what their next step would be to ensure the future success of their little scheme.

'Well, I've been thinking about that one, long and hard.' Nigel was being precise with his diction and slow in his delivery. He was drunk. 'We travel. We go to a different town, and we hit all the bookies we can find. We keep going to the same town and get to know where the bookies are, and when they suss us out, we move on.' He smiled, closed his eyes and lost his balance, falling sideways onto the sofa.

Ian looked at his beer glass and saw it was empty. He got up, turned off the fire and went to bed.

Studying Form

He knew Nigel would wake up in the early hours, feeling cold, and make his own way to bed.

*

The following morning, the ex-cop, Frank Griffiths, sat impatiently outside Price's office. He hated being kept waiting, and he hated Price. He had known Price for years, back to the bad years when depression – the result of the death of his wife – drink and gambling had taken hold of him with a relentless, overwhelming power. Price had saved him from himself, but Griffiths had been repaying the debt ever since. He was tired of being at Price's beck and call, but Price had information that could put this ex-cop behind bars, and like all ex-cops, Griffiths hated the thought of jail.

'He'll see you now,' said Price's secretary. She had been kind enough to offer a drink whilst Griffiths waited. She did not, as far as Griffiths was concerned, seem very busy though. 'It's the third door to the left, down the corridor. His name's on the door.'

'You've been too kind.' He walked down the corridor, opened the door to the office without knocking and walked over to the large desk where Price sat, feet on table, phone against his ear.

'Look, I'll have to go. Someone's just come into the office. I'll speak to you later.' Price put the phone down and took his feet from the table, sitting upright in his executive chair. 'Knock next time, all right.'

'Your secretary said to go straight in,' Griffiths lied, knowing Price would have a stern word with her later.

'Really? Anyway, what have you got for me?' Price leaned forwards and took an envelope from Griffiths, wasting no time in opening it and tipping the contents onto his desk. There was an assortment of photographs of both Nigel and Ian and a written report covering two sides of A4. The report gave details of Nigel's job and Ian's college education, where they lived and who they had been seen with the previous evening. It also provided information on three bank accounts in Nigel's name with current balances for each. After a couple of minutes of close scrutiny, Price looked up at Griffiths.

'Not bad, my son. Not bad at all. Where did you get the banking details from?'

'The bank.'

'No kidding. Excellent.' He took an envelope from a drawer and threw it into Griffiths' lap.

'Well done. You've earned that.'

'If there's ever anything else, be sure to let me know, won't you.' Griffiths didn't mean it, but he had to say it anyway. He had to keep Price sweet at all costs. 'Why are you so interested in these two youngsters anyway?'

Price moved to the office window and looked out over a park full of pigeons. He didn't answer immediately, losing himself for a moment in his own little world, contemplating what the two *youngsters* could be capable of.

'One of those bank accounts currently has a balance, if your sources are correct, of fifteen thousand, six hundred and forty-three pounds. It's my money!

Studying Form

Those bastards are betting on horses that win.' Price picked up a picture of Ian and pushed it towards Griffiths. 'He'll have a bank account somewhere, eventually, with a similar amount in it. I think these two have got a system, a system that predicts the outcome of certain races, a system that works, a system that could have cost me my job if I hadn't done something about it. A system that has already taken over fifteen thousand pounds from my shops. I'm thinking I want that system.'

Griffiths couldn't believe what he was hearing. He'd been in the game as long as Price, and he had heard of many 'systems'. 'Come off it. There's no such thing as a system, not a perfect system. You know as well as I do. They must be getting tips, inside information. Or they might be just lucky.'

'Yes, I know. I'm just rabbiting on. They've had eleven wins though, eight on the bounce. It would have been twelve straight wins, only they backed one of Collier's horses,' Price informed his guest.

'What, Lambourn Collier? But he's...'

'Yes, occasionally dishonest. I know. Like I said, it would have been twelve out of twelve.'

The phone rang on Price's desk which gave Griffiths the perfect opportunity to leave. He stood up and walked out the door. As he walked past the secretary, his mind was racing and his heart was pounding. If Price was right, and these two *had* developed a system that worked, he was going to get his hands on it.

Monday, 27 May 1991
Bank Holiday Monday

The Fiat had never sounded worse. There was a constant tapping from the engine and a sound like bagpipes being warmed up coming from the exhaust. Outside, it was pouring with rain, and the extremely noisy windscreen wipers were finding it difficult to cope on a dirty windscreen. As a consequence, Ian was finding it difficult to see where he was going.

'Take the next on the left,' Zoë instructed, having noticed the sign to Brighton Seafront at the last moment.

'Left?' Ian hadn't seen the signpost and was sure the seafront would be straight on.

'Don't worry; it's a one-way system, by the looks of things. I've got you this far, haven't I? London was easy, so Brighton should be a breeze.'

The two had been looking forward to a bit of serious sunbathing all week, so it was a pity about the rain. They had decided to still visit 'London by the Sea' regardless of the weather. The boot was laden, heavy with the cold box, swimwear, beach towels and books to read. No need for a bucket and spade at Brighton – too many pebbles and not enough sand.

Eventually, they found the seafront and drove along Kings Road towards Hove. The East Pier disappeared behind them as the West Pier – what was left of it after years of neglect and storm damage – approached. Zoë hadn't been to Brighton before, so she was excited and didn't want to miss a thing.

'Look, the Grand Hotel.' She nudged Ian quite violently and pointed to a large, white fascia with a doorman at the entrance. 'That's the place that got bombed, isn't it?'

'Indeed,' Ian replied. 'I remember it all too well – it happened three days after my mum's fortieth birthday, twelfth of October 1984. We had a party for Mum in the evening the following day, and it was all everyone talked about.'

As they drove past, Zoë looked at the hotel in awe and wondered how much it cost to stay the night. They pulled up at some traffic lights and Ian laughed. 'Are they sure it was a bomb and not cannon fire?' he asked whilst he waited for the lights to turn green. Zoë looked at him quizzically, and he pointed to the pub, right next to the Grand Hotel. 'The Cannon.'

They drove a little further and parked in an underground car park. Ian couldn't believe the prices for parking. He had noticed quite a few NCP signs along the route through Brighton, so it seemed as though National Car Parks had something of a monopoly in the town.

They were both hungry and in need of a walk. Being cooped-up for three and a half hours was no fun in Ian's old car. He really needed to replace it soon with something better, especially now he and Nigel were going to have to travel so they could place their bets.

Zoë had a weakness for pizza whilst Ian wasn't fussed either way, so they went in search of a pizza restaurant and found a Pizza Hut without too much trouble. Having been seated almost immediately, it wasn't long before they were both sipping a cold lager in eager anticipation of a twelve-inch deep pan to share.

'You know, I reckon you're making a mistake with this gambling strategy of yours. If you travel for three and a half hours, like we have today, to a town you know nothing about...' She took a sip of her lager, pausing to make sure Ian was listening.

'Go on,' Ian prompted.

'Well, you're going to spend all your time running up and down every street, looking for betting shops. And with the kind of money you want to put on a horse, you're going to have to find several betting shops, or they'll become suspicious too quickly – just like at home.'

'So, what do you suggest?'

'Go to the racecourse where the horse is running. I've watched a few races with you; I've listened to your conversations with Nigel, and it seems the only realistic option. Listen, the bookies are queuing up, quite literally, to take your money on a racecourse. You've mentioned different areas at each venue, and you've told me about the Tote. There would be loads of opportunities to spread your bets around different bookies, and you've a better chance of remaining anonymous.'

'Yes, but what if the horse is running at Perth or Hamilton Park, way up north in Scotland? What if the next horse is due to run at Salisbury the next day?' Ian paused and reflected on what he'd just said. 'Actually, I don't think they run on the Flat at Perth.'

'You can choose any horse, in any race, on any course with your computerised system. Granted, when Nigel did the work himself, from books, papers, videos and the telly, then he couldn't be so choosy. But now you've developed something on your computer, it's much easier and quicker to choose a viable horse.'

The pizza arrived, and the couple sat back in their chairs, watching the waitress struggle with elastic cheese as she tried to separate two portions of pizza onto separate plates. A knife and fork found their way into Zoë's hands with a fair amount of speed, and Ian knew he'd have to keep himself amused with his thoughts and his half of the meal for the next ten to fifteen minutes.

'And anyway.' Zoë interrupted Ian's deep thoughts. 'If you two are going to make money out of this, you're going to have to treat it as a business. It should become your profession. Overnight stays at hotels or B & Bs, moving from one town to another if you decide to stick with the betting shop option, or moving from one racecourse to another if you take on my idea.'

'I reckon you're right, you know. I've been thinking about what you said and trying to put it into practice in my mind. If we travelled and stayed away from home overnight, we'd need access to the home computer whilst we're away, which means buying a portable computer and then downloading information, buying yet another computer with a modem.' Ian was talking to himself rather than to Zoë.

'I don't know what you're on about with "download" and "modem", but I'm sure you'd be able to do it.'

'I'll have to speak to Nigel. But I think you're right.'

By 3.30 p.m. the rain had stopped, the clouds had drifted away, and the temperature had risen considerably. The couple were now on the beach, sharing an oversized towel. They were not alone. It appeared Brightonians too enjoyed a bank holiday afternoon on the beach. For Ian, it was paradise, since everyone seemed to be topless. Having spent a good six minutes applying suntan lotion to his left arm, Zoë suggested he stop staring and lie down. So he did.

Looking skywards, he asked Zoë if she had liked what she'd seen of Brighton so far, wondering if they might come back one day for a weekend or longer. She told him she had and leaned over to kiss him. She suggested they should stay in the Grand if they ever came back. Ian suggested she should get back to sunbathing.

*

As Ian and Zoë were making the return journey from Brighton to Nottingham, Griffiths was letting himself into Nigel and Ian's house, having just seen Nigel leave in a taxi. Nigel had been well-dressed, suggesting he was going to be away for some time. *You don't wear a suit to the takeaway*, Griffiths had reasoned.

Studying Form

He was right. Nigel had been invited to a dinner and dance by one of his regulars at the pub. It was an office celebration which usually meant a higher ratio of women to men, or so he had been told. Nigel was ever hopeful – hopeful of not being home too early.

Griffiths' main concern was Ian and his girlfriend. He had seen them load their car at 6.45 that morning. Anyone going out on a day trip tries to get to their destination before lunch; they also try to get back before eleven at night. Outside of those timeframes, there is either no point in going or you risk being too tired when you're coming home. Anyway, Griffiths was only going in to have a quick look. If he found anything worth taking, that would be a bonus. His intention was to be in and out within seven minutes.

The back door was easy. It might as well have been left unlocked from the perspective of the professional burglar. The kitchen was a kitchen and nothing else. There was no point in hanging around there. The living room was a mess. Griffiths smiled at the dirty plates and beer cans on the floor. 'Bloody slobs!'

The phone wasn't on the phone table at the bottom of the stairs. There was a table, and there were telephone directories. There was also a square of dust, or rather a square lacking the same amount of dust as the rest of the table. The telephone had obviously been moved. Griffiths ran up the stairs following the cable which took him straight into Ian's room and led him to the computer. Griffiths knew nothing about computers except they were clever beasts that never forgot to send him bills. He looked at his watch, noting he'd been in the house forty-five seconds. He turned on the computer and then, after staring at a black screen for a little while, the monitor too. Whilst they both warmed up, he moved across the landing and opened another door – the bathroom. Closing it and turning to the next door, he heard a beep from the computer. He went back into Ian's room and looked at the screen.

Enter Password :>

Griffiths cursed and turned the machine and screen off again. He made his way back to the unopened door and let himself in. There he found stacks of books, papers and videos. All of them to do with horseracing. He flicked through some of the papers then replaced them, making sure everything looked untouched. He checked his watch again and decided he'd seen enough. He left Nigel's room, closing the door behind him, and made his way downstairs and back outside through the kitchen door.

*

The following day, over breakfast, Nigel and Ian discussed the idea Zoë had proposed the day before. Nigel was initially amazed at Zoë having given it so much thought. All things considered though, he had to agree it was a good idea. 'Obvious, really, when you think about it,' he'd said in the end.

'So we need a reliable car and a few more bits for the computer, so we can link into it when we're away,' said Ian, full of enthusiasm.

Studying Form

'Hang on. Hang on. It's a good idea. But it doesn't mean we're going all over the country living it up in hotels the length and breadth of this fertile land. I want to make money for me to keep, not for a landlord of a B & B or Travellers Rest to line his pockets.'

'We need a new car though. Something you mentioned last month,' Ian persisted. 'My car has just about had it. It'll never get through its next MOT which is due quite soon.'

Nigel sighed. 'A new car it is then. I must be mad. Will you teach me to drive one day? On second thoughts, I'll get someone who can drive to teach me to drive.'

'Bollocks! I'm a good driver.'

The two talked about what car to buy and therefore how much to spend. One of the sticking points was the colour. Ian was adamant it shouldn't be red. 'Red fades, just look at my heap outside,' he said. 'If you want a car that looks old and shabby before its time, then buy a red one.'

Nigel liked red.

Eventually, they decided on a Vauxhall Calibra, something with a bit of power without drawing attention to itself. The asking price was going to be in the region of ten grand. The road to a fortune was going to cost a lot of money. However, it would be money well spent. And it would be a fun thing to do, everything   considered.

Sunday, 9 June 1991

Within two weeks, Ian had taken delivery of a brand-new (for some reason the option to buy a second-hand car never entered into the discussion) Vauxhall Calibra. And it was yellow.

'It was the only one left in the showroom. If we'd gone for a different colour, we would have had to wait another two weeks,' Ian explained to Zoë before she'd even had the chance to comment. To be honest, Ian wasn't too keen on the colour either, but he was as excited as Nigel to be getting it so soon.

'Smells a bit though,' Zoë observed, as she got into the passenger seat.

Ian leaned on the side of the car and spoke through the open sunroof, taking in an eyeful of cleavage. 'It's the seats. We'll get one of those air fresheners from Halfords tomorrow, along with a load of other bits and bobs. Nigel's determined to keep the car in pristine condition at all costs. He went deathly white when he wrote out the cheque on Monday night. I must admit I have been pretty nervous about the whole thing too. But here it is.' He patted the car and opened the door, getting in behind the wheel. 'Come on, let's go and show it off to your folks.'

Studying Form

Zoë's parents were impressed, if not a little surprised. Zoë's father had warmed to Ian, looking upon him as a *genuine* young man who, whilst liking Zoë, had shown enough affection towards Jason to assure them he was not just using her. Not so, Zoë's mother.

They were both surprised at Ian's apparent wealth. Zoë had, of course, talked about Ian, and as her parents, they were keen to know all they could about their daughter's new boyfriend. They had seen their daughter hurt by Jason's father, and they didn't want her to be hurt again. The affair Zoë had had with their next-door neighbour had been difficult for everyone to come to terms with. They had all been hurt and betrayed in one way or another. Ian seemed genuine enough, but how on earth could a student afford to buy a brand-new car?

'You'll stay for dinner, of course?' Zoë's mother posed the question in the form of a direct order, making it difficult for Ian to refuse.

'Love to.' Ian hoped his sarcasm hadn't been noticed. Zoë glared at him whilst Mr Richards grinned. It had been noticed.

'Good. Zoë, you nip and get Jason, and Anthony'—turning to her husband—'can you serve the garlic bread? Make sure you turn the oven down to one-eighty when you get the bread out. Ian come through to the dining room; let me pour you a drink. Squash?'

Ian took a deep breath and followed Zoë's mother to the dining room. He sat down at the table on the chair she indicated. 'Thanks, Marlene. Squash sounds perfect.' He felt uneasy calling Zoë's mother by her first name. It seemed a bit too informal and lacking in respect, but it was how they had been introduced, so he just had to go with it.

Zoë and her dad returned from their errands and took their seats. Here was Ian, sitting at a table with a beautiful young woman, mother of a baby boy a mere eleven months old in his high chair, and the child's grandparents. He was facing mortal combat with the female grandparent, and he relished the challenge. Nothing too dramatic, though, he hoped.

'So, how long have you been at college?' Marlene asked.

'I'm in my final year of a four-year course. I started back in September '87. I've enjoyed it here – both the studying and the city life. Nottingham is quite lively.'

'Forest are doing well,' Anthony interjected. 'Do you like football?'

'I watch *Match of the Day* if I'm not too busy, and I will try to watch any live game on TV, but I don't get to matches very often. I must admit I lost interest in the game for a while following Hillsborough, Bradford and Heysel. All those deaths kind of took the fun out of the sport. I do like Brian Clough though. He plays a fair game and talks the talk. It was a pity Forest got beat in the Cup recently. It would have been nice to see Cloughie win the FA Cup. What is it with Tottenham winning something every time there's a one in the year?'

'Do you like children?' Mrs Richards asked.

Studying Form

Mr Richards looked at his wife in disbelief and shook his head. There was a moment of silence whilst Mrs Richards gazed at Ian, waiting for an answer.

'It depends on the child, I suppose,' Ian said, staring back at Zoë's mother. He glanced towards Jason, who was busy making a mess with some mashed carrots. 'I like pleasant children, and I dislike unpleasant children. I don't think children are born unpleasant though. I tend to subscribe to the adage, "blame the parents". I look forward to getting to know Jason though. He's a nice little chap. You should be proud.'

Zoë squeezed Ian's knee under the table, and he noticed a little smile in her eyes.

'We love our daughter and our grandson in equal measure, and yes, we are proud, even if his arrival wasn't planned. "Blame the parents"? I hope you don't think we are to blame?'

'Mum! That's not fair and not necessary.'

'I'm sorry, dear. Your dad and I love you very much. I get a little too protective at times – I know I shouldn't. Ian, more squash? By the way, how can a college student afford such an expensive car?' She went straight for the jugular once again.

'Mother!' exclaimed Zoë.

'Well.' Ian smiled. 'To be perfectly honest, it isn't entirely my car. Only half of it is. The other half belongs to my flat-mate. His half was paid for by him. My half was paid for by my mum.' Ian wasn't going to expand on that nugget of truth and tell Zoë's parents about the betting system.

Andy Wheildon

Zoë's mother seemed satisfied and cleared the table of the starter dishes whilst her husband busied himself with serving the main meal: steak, roast potatoes and two veg. Zoë took the opportunity to apologise for her mum, placing a hand on Ian's inner thigh, moving it provocatively in an upwards direction.

'Don't mention it, and don't stop!' Ian said, taking hold of her wandering hand. 'A girl with WHT, just what I like.'

Zoë looked at Ian quizzically, but at that moment, her parents returned to the dining room. Ian smiled and winked. 'I'll tell you later.'

The meal progressed without further interrogation from Zoë's mother. In fact, her whole attitude had changed, and she was being quite pleasant. Unbeknownst to Ian, Zoë's father had had a stern word with his wife in the kitchen whilst serving up the dinner. He had seen his daughter happy, truly happy, for the first time in a long time, and he wasn't going to allow his wife's prying to ruin that. 'She's an adult now; all we can do is listen and support. Zoë will ask for our help and advice as and when she wants it. Be patient, and above all, try to be understanding. Be nice.'

'These carrots are to die for,' Ian enthused. This brought a huge grin from Mr Richards and Zoë. They both loved carrots, especially those grown by Mr Richards on his allotment.

'Thank you,' said Mr Richards.

'Indeed,' Mrs Richards chipped in. 'Anthony grows most of our vegetables on his allotment. And his carrots are his pride and joy.'

Studying Form

For the next few minutes, they all enjoyed a conversation featuring brassica, tubers, onions and blight. The conversation petered out though as the meal finished, and Zoë suggested the two of them nip down to the allotment to have a look around.

'There won't be much to see,' Mr Richards warned. 'I am planning to go down there this weekend to plant out some cauliflowers and sow my peas and finish off planting some runner beans. It's a bit early in the season for much to be on show.'

'Not a problem, I'm looking forward to seeing it,' Ian said.

'Don't worry about the dishes,' Mrs Richards said. 'You run along and we'll wash up. I'll see if Jason wants a nap too.'

Zoë and Ian got their coats with Zoë saying they wouldn't be long, and she'd feed Jason as soon as they got back.

It was only a ten-minute walk to the allotment. 'Dad usually walks too, but he drives round when he has a load of stuff like compost, or when he takes his plants from the greenhouse at home.' Zoë pointed to an area where her dad would park.

'Your mum is a bit of a diamond, isn't she? Her and your dad look after Jason quite a lot.'

'I know. I think I have said before, having Jason has bought us closer together. My parents are allowing me to live a little.' It put Zoë into a reflective mood.

When they arrived at the allotment gate, Zoë turned the combination lock to the necessary numbers and opened the gate to let them both in. The padlock was returned to the latch and the combination was randomised to ensure there were no tailgaters.

'Very secure,' Ian observed.

'Yeah, there was some anti-social behaviour in the dim-and-distant past. The perimeter fence is a necessity. There's a lot of equipment and tools on the allotment, and a lot of time and effort goes into growing fruit and veg, if my dad is anything to go by.'

'Yeah, good point. Where's your dad's plot then?'

'Plot number 33, this way.' Zoë grabbed hold of Ian's hand and led the way, snuggling into his shoulder as they walked. The allotment was, apart from them, deserted.

Plot 33 was huge, and Ian noticed how the area was split up into distinct areas. 'Crop rotation?' he ventured.

'Very good. You must have paid attention in science class at school,' Zoë quipped.

'I did, *actually*,' Ian said, giving her a playful punch. He remembered: 'Crop rotation – it confuses the bugs.' A quote from someone in the class all those years ago which had had a load of eleven-year-olds and their teacher in fits of laughter.

Zoë smiled. 'Come with me.' She grabbed Ian's hand and there was a glint in her eye and a cheeky grin.

'Where are we going?'

'You'll see,' Zoë said.

She led him to a tool shed and opened the door, pulling Ian in with a laugh.

Studying Form

'What are you doing?' Ian exclaimed, as Zoë reached for his trouser belt.

'Just shut up and kiss me,' Zoë ordered.

Their kiss was both passionate and urgent. Hands fumbled with items of clothing and giggles took over when the kissing stopped.

Zoë turned round and Ian got the message, entering her from behind as she pressed back towards him. They both gasped as Ian slowly slid deeper inside her. They moved in unison, breathing getting heavier. Ian stroked Zoë's back and deftly unclipped her bra. As they continued to make love, Ian fondled her breasts and knew he was in Heaven. Zoë thrust against him, looking back and smiling encouragement. After a few minutes, Zoë said, 'Harder.' Ian responded.

'Faster.' Zoë sighed, holding his hand tight against one of her breasts.

Ian picked up the rhythm, beads of sweat forming on his forehead. He was close.

'Oh, someone's coming,' said Zoë.

'No shit, Sherlock,' Ian replied. 'Nohhh… shit…. Sherlock… Aaghhhh.' Ian sighed, his eyes tight shut as he experienced the best orgasm he'd ever had. He then noticed the allotment gate. 'Oh dear, someone's coming!'

Zoë was already adjusting her clothes, laughing. 'No shit, Sherlock!'

Ian tidied himself up as they both watched a fellow plot-holder walking towards the shed.

'Quick,' Zoë said, still laughing. She opened the shed door and said hello to a somewhat surprised Mr Sheffield.

'Hello, Zoë,' Mr Sheffield replied. 'How's your dad?'

'Oh, he's fine thanks. You too, I hope?'

'Yes, I'm fine, thanks,' Mr Sheffield looked a bit perturbed when, all of a sudden, someone else emerged from the shed.

'I've just been showing my boyfriend all the tools,' Zoë said, grabbing Ian's hand and pulling him towards the gate. 'See you later, Mr Sheffield,' she called over her shoulder.

'Say hi to your dad for me.'

'Will do.'

That night, Ian explained the meaning of WHT (Wandering-Hand-Trouble) to Zoë in graphic detail as the two went on to christen the car.

Friday, 14 June 1991
Goodwood

Nigel was in full agreement with Ian and Zoë, the answer to visiting as many bookies as possible in a short space of time was to visit the racecourse itself. The bigger the meeting, the more bookies there would be and the less likely it would be that the success of their system would be noticed. On the other hand, if they visited a small provincial racecourse and placed a bet with only a handful of bookmakers in attendance, it was very likely they would soon bring attention to themselves. With this in mind, the size of the bet would depend on the size and prestige of the race meeting they attended.

The next race Nigel wanted to cover was being run at an evening meeting at Goodwood, Sussex, on the second Friday in June. There were a couple of horses he was interested in, running in the same race. Both had recent good form and had been caught by the handicapper. Their weights had both risen, the result of wins against decent opposition. The race was a step up in class, but from the information supplied to and subsequently gleaned from his system, Nigel knew *his* two horses would provide the eventual winner.

So it was agreed, a trip to good old 'Sussex by the Seaside' – actually slightly inland if truth be known – was in order. Ian would be driving down the same roads to the south of England he'd driven not three weeks earlier. He was pleased with the choice of venue – somewhere a long way away, requiring a full day for the round trip. It made buying the car worthwhile. It made the whole business of betting on horses as a *profession* more realistic. It was better than polytechnic.

The weather forecast that morning had been determined from the local met. office, the information being passed on to anyone who was interested via Radio One and Simon Mayo, and the two were on their way.

'The overnight rain won't affect the going,' Nigel said, more to himself than Ian who was desperately trying to ensure they ended up on the southbound carriageway of the M1 rather than the Sheffield/Leeds, up-the-country, northbound carriageway – something which had happened on a couple of occasions in the past.

'London,' Ian said with relief, as he accelerated down a slip road towards the stream of traffic heading south. 'How long do you reckon it'll take us?'

'With no hold-ups or delays, I think it'll be about four by the time we get down there.'

The journey to Goodwood proved uneventful in the main, apart from a heated discussion about motorways in general and the M1 in particular.

'We need to keep an eye on the car mileage for the next few days. The car requires a service at around 1,500 miles. Today will be around 500 miles, I reckon.

Studying Form

By the way, you do realise the M1 was not the first,' said Ian with an air of authority.

'The first what?' asked Nigel.

'The first motorway. The M1 was not the first motorway to be built in this fair land.'

'Really,' said Nigel, in a condescending tone. 'I suppose you will now share with me which motorway *was* the first.'

'Indeed I will. The first motorway ever to be built in this country was… Damn! I can't remember. Hold on. I'm going to have to go through the alphabet; I can't believe I've forgotten this. It's on the way to Blackpool—'

Nigel started to sing 'M1-M1-M1' in an attempt to put Ian off.

'Preston.'

'Rubbish.'

'The first motorway in the UK was the Preston Bypass, no idea when though.'

'I'm not convinced, but I would have thought the M1 was the first!' Nigel decided to leave it alone and changed the subject. 'My folks might be heading to the USA.'

'Really. How come?'

'My dad's parents are not getting any younger apparently, and he feels he should be near them. He's in France, and they are in the States. They're too far apart.'

'Does it change anything with you and your house?'

'No, don't worry – nothing like that. In fact, I think dad will ask me to look after the property in France too.'

'Does your mum like the idea?'

'Yes, she's fine with it. Both her parents are gone, so she doesn't have any tie to England or France, since she is an only child… apart from me, and my brother and sister, obviously. She quite likes the idea of America. She has absolutely no idea about the weather though! They have visited dad's parents in the past but only during the summer months. North Dakota can get very cold in the winter.'

'America is not my strong point when it comes to geography, I'm afraid. Ask me anything about glaciation or viticulture, and Mr Prescott would be pleased to know I can discuss either in detail. But ask me about the states of America, and I'm a bit lost.'

'Mr Prescott?'

'He was my geography teacher at school. Anyway, North Dakota – educate me.'

'North Dakota is in the middle of the States but to the north, believe it or not. It borders Canada and gets really cold in the winter. My grandparents live in a town called Minot which is about forty miles south of the Canadian border, a hundred miles north of Bismarck.'

'And why do you mention Bismarck?'

'It's the capital city of North Dakota, and it's where my dad went to college.'

'When are your folks planning on leaving?'

Studying Form

'Dunno yet. They are just at the talking-about-it stage. I was speaking to Mum last night, and she thinks it will happen but she's not sure when.'

'Wow, North Dakota. Let's see, is it next door to Iowa?'

'No, Iowa is to the east and down a bit. Are you thinking of Idaho? Idaho is one of the states which borders with Canada.'

'No idea.' Ian concentrated on the road ahead, and Nigel turned to stare out of the window for a few miles, lost in his thoughts about what it might mean to have both his parents on the other side of the world.

The long, unexciting journey came to an abrupt halt outside Singleton, midway between Chichester and Midhurst. It appeared the majority of Sussex and Hampshire had decided on a day at the races. Ian commented as such, and Nigel immediately corrected him.

'It will be an *evening* at the races, to be precise. Not that it matters. The sign says two miles to the racecourse, and at least the traffic's moving. Our race is the fourth on the card, so it doesn't matter if we're a bit late. It would be nice to have a look round first, though, soak up the atmosphere.'

'What about the bet, then?' Ian said, deciding to talk tactics. 'Are we going to spread the bet or try to find the best odds and put it all with one bookie?'

'I'm not really sure. As far as some of these bookies are concerned, our stake will be small potatoes to them. But I'm not too keen on the idea of queuing up for the winnings and having half of Sussex watch thousands of pounds being counted out.

'Could you just imagine it? Some sort of mad man watching, following us to the car park, a baseball bat swinging towards your head, then he's running off with our loot. No, I prefer to spread the bets and then return to each bookie and collect the cash throughout the evening. That way, no-one gets suspicious, and we get paid.'

The traffic began to ease, and the RAC signposts pointed them in the general direction of the spectators' car park. The place was packed. The weather was balmy warm, and the crowds were in good spirits. An evening at Goodwood clearly came highly recommended.

The queues to get through the turnstiles were horrendous, but progress was swift. Once inside the racecourse, all were greeted by a steel band which would then go on to wander through the crowds, playing for the duration of the meeting.

When Ian stepped round the corner of the main stand to get to the arena where the bookies pitched their boards, he was taken aback by the sheer beauty of the view. The course was built on a hill, beyond and below was rolling countryside, a sea of green lightly covered by a sandy-coloured patchwork of corn and wheat. It was the first time Ian had been to a race meeting, but having seen them on the television, he had known to expect the multitude of bookies he now saw before him. However, the magnificent view was a secret the TV had guarded jealously from the armchair punters. The early evening sun setting in the distance, warm against his face, made a pleasant change after the five hours of driving to get there.

'Nice here, isn't it?' Nigel observed. 'You don't realise it on the telly. They're not all like this though. When you drive into Pontefract, you pass a great slag heap. The course itself is pretty though, with a very punishing uphill finish.' He laughed at himself, knowing he was showing off. 'Fancy a pint?'

The two friends made their way to a beer tent, passing the steel band as they went. Fifteen minutes later, they emerged with their liquid refreshment, resolving not to try again. It was just far too busy in there.

'Well, I reckon we should split up and have a wander round for the first couple of races,' Nigel suggested. 'Go along the bookies' pitches and watch them chalk up the prices. You'll soon see the generosity of the bookies can vary by quite a bit from pitch to pitch. When we come to have a bet, we'll probably get on at a few different prices. I'm going to have a bet the moment the first chalks up his prices and then wait a while to see what happens. It's up to you what you do. Just make sure you get all your £300 on. Either six bets scattered all over the place or three £100 bets if you can get them on.'

'I know – let's have a competition. We're both starting with £300, so let's see who makes the most. Loser buys dinner tonight. Deal?'

'Deal,' Ian replied reluctantly. He turned away to mingle with the crowd. 'I'll see you back at the car, straight after the race.'

As they separated, Griffiths swore under his breath whilst keeping his binoculars trained on Nigel. Griffiths had followed the two young men down to the meeting, nearly losing them as they approached Goodwood. He had decided to take what Price had told him seriously. He was going to prove or disprove the existence of a system. If a system existed, Griffiths wanted to get hold of it. Thinking back to when he had worked his way round their house, he knew he would soon be stealing that computer if the System proved to be real. He could sell it to the highest bidder, or he could use it himself. If there was no system, then he would tell Price in the hope the man would leave him alone once and for all.

Nigel went in search of some food, so Griffiths missed the first couple of races to keep some twenty-five yards between the two of them. But once Nigel returned to the front of the stands and went amongst the bookies with an air of determination, it told Griffiths this would be the race where the money went on. Griffiths got closer and tried to see which horse Nigel was interested in. The field of runners listed on the boards detailed no less than thirteen horses. Griffiths smiled to himself and began to relax – there was no system on earth which could forecast the outcome of a race such as that. Griffiths knew his horses; he knew there were four or five in with a shout. He began to think he was on a wild goose chase.

Studying Form

Nigel stopped abruptly and pointed to one of the horses. 'Fifty on Northern Flyer,' he said to the old man holding the tickets.

'Nine hundred to fifty, number two four seven.' The old man immediately rubbed the figure eighteen off the board and then gave Nigel his ticket.

As Nigel walked away, he turned to see what price the old man would chalk up in its place. Unfortunately, a man who was looking directly at him obscured his view. Nigel thought nothing of it as the man ducked his head and walked past. The board now displayed 16/1.

Other bookies still carried 18/1, so he wasn't too concerned.

Griffiths, greed had been his downfall and greed was still his trait, went to an adjacent pitch and put £20 on the same horse. He then made his way to the back of the stands and again trained his binoculars on Nigel who had placed himself centrally so as to be able to scan as many bookmaker boards as possible.

As the start to the race approached, the activity amongst the bookies reached fever pitch. Nigel laid five more bets of £50 at prices ranging from 18/1 to 14/1. He was annoyed with himself at the 14/1. It had been his last £50, and the bookie marked the horse down just as Nigel approached.

Ian, on the other hand, had been more fortunate. All his money was on at 18/1 apart from £50 which he placed with the Tote. No-one would know the return on the bet until after the race was run and the dividends returned.

Andy Wheildon

Without knowing it, the two friends were stood quite close to each other when they found their places to watch the race. The fact was not, however, lost on Griffiths. He now had them both within his field of view and was watching them like a hawk. It must have looked strange – fifteen thousand people watching and shouting on the outcome of a horse race, whilst one person watched the crowd showing no interest whatsoever in what was going on inside the final furlong. Whilst Griffiths watched his quarry, he was convinced he had just thrown away £20 on a rank outsider.

It was a very close race with three different leaders in the final three furlongs. Whilst Icanseeformiles and Keen Vision were one-paced in the run-in, Northern Flyer had enough in the tank to pull clear. The horse quickened inside the last two hundred yards, in a manner suggesting the rest of the field was standing still, and won by half a length.

Griffiths had bet when the horse was at 16/1 so, with his stake, was £340 richer. Nigel and Ian made a beeline to their respective bookies to collect, in total, £11,670.

Thirty-five minutes later, the bright yellow Vauxhall Calibra made its way out of the car park, the two occupants quiet but grinning like Cheshire cats. As the racecourse disappeared behind them, Nigel began to laugh which set Ian off. 'Easy-peasy, lemon-squeezy!'

Ian couldn't agree more. 'Next one, please!'

Nigel began to empty his pockets into the footwell of the car; there were bank notes everywhere.

Studying Form

'Right, let's see who's buying dinner.' He started to count the notes and then realised there was an easier way. Reaching into the glove compartment, he pulled out a piece of paper and a pen. 'What odds did you get?' he asked Ian, who was slightly unsure of his directions, having reached a poorly signposted T-junction. 'Just take a left and tell me your prices.'

'Five bookies at 18/1, and the Tote which paid a whopping £32.40.'

'Well done, my son – it looks like you win, and I buy the dinner. Hang on a mo' whilst I do the necessary and work it all out.' Less than half a minute later, Nigel confirmed the amount which Ian should have in his pockets – £6,370 exactly.

'Right, I was all over the place with my betting. I enjoyed it though. Three at 18/1, two at 16/1 and one at 14/1 – boo, hiss.' Nigel put his head down and made the necessary calculations once more, but this time he took a bit longer, firstly because of the different odds and secondly to check his calculations for both himself and Ian. The outcome of their side bet was easy to predict since Ian had equalled or bettered Nigel's odds on all six bets.

He began to laugh and said, 'You win by a country mile, and I definitely pay for dinner.' He looked towards Ian who, for a moment, took his eyes off the road.

'Go on?'

'Yes, you win. We have picked up, in total and including the stake, £11,670. I picked up, including stake, £1,070 less than you.'

Andy Wheildon

'OK, well done, me. You buy dinner, and let's say money no object!' Ian smiled as they turned towards the outskirts of London on the way back up north. 'By the way, that's the car paid for! Oh, and another thing I've been meaning to ask you.'

'Go on?'

'The horse, Icanseeformiles? Why are there no spaces between the words on the race card or in the papers? I assume they are just trying to save space or something. But why?'

'To be honest, I've no idea. But what I do know is all racehorses have to subscribe to an eighteen-character rule. A horse cannot have a name longer than eighteen characters. No idea about the reason but, for some reason, I know the rule.'

'Interesting, thanks.' Ian drove on and tried to work out how many characters were in Icanseeformiles with and without spaces. He failed on both counts, deciding instead to concentrate on his driving and, more importantly, Nigel's navigation.

Griffiths was also pleased with the day's events. He watched the yellow Calibra disappear over the brow of a hill then pulled off the road and into a Harvesters pub for a well-deserved meal and a chance to give his good fortune a little bit of thought.

Monday, 17 June 1991

Three days later, Griffiths sat in the company of Price's secretary once more, whilst she busied herself with a letter. She typed it at phenomenal speed, but also used a phenomenal amount of liquid paper to correct a multitude of errors. Griffiths thought about passing a sarcastic comment in her direction, something along the lines of 'wouldn't it be easier to phone' or 'you'll soon need another bottle'. He decided against it – she appeared to be in a bad mood.

Her telephone buzzed, indicating Price was free. She turned her attention to Griffiths. 'He's free now. You know where his office is. Knock first, though – it's only polite.'

'Thank you so much.' Griffiths was annoyed since he'd been waiting thirty-five minutes.

'In!' came the reply to Griffiths' courteous rat-a-tat-tat on the door. 'What do you want? I'm very busy today. Next time make an appointment.' Price motioned for Griffiths to sit down and took a sip from a cup of coffee.

'No, thanks, I've just had one,' Griffiths said, knowing Price had no intention of offering him a drink. 'Those two jokers who have been taking money from your shops; they've stopped. I don't think you'll be seeing them again.'

'I know they've stopped. If any of my managers accepts a bet of more than £25 from them, they're *totes Fleisch*!'

'What?' Griffiths wasn't too hot on gobbledygook.

'*Totes Fleisch*, it's German for dead meat. Out on their arse, fired. If any manager accepts a bet like the ones we've had recently from those two, they are out. Anyway, why have you come here to tell me something I already know? What makes you so sure they've stopped betting?'

'No, they've not stopped betting, just stopped visiting your shops. You've forced them up a league.' Griffiths then went on to tell Price about the trip to Goodwood and the money they put down on Northern Flyer. He finished by saying he was sure the lads were working a successful system, and he wondered if Price would like to get his hands on it… for a price.

'What would I want with their system? I'd be in abuse of my position if I were to obtain such a thing, let alone use it. I'd be out of a job faster than a jack rabbit with a prairie fire at its back.'

'Wot?'

'Nothing.' Price smiled.

'I'd have thought, if you were to get hold of a proven system and give it to your superiors, not only would they hold you in the highest esteem, but they could also use it to undermine the profitability of all their competitors, big or small.' Griffiths stared at Price, watching him digest what he'd just heard.

Studying Form

'Do you think the System, if it exists, is that strong? One hundred per cent reliable?'

'Well, it would appear so, wouldn't it? They've got a 100% success rate so far, if you discount the horse from Lambourn Collier's stable. And they're making a lot of money. It's not every day people pick 18/1 outsiders that win. They appear confident. They have purchased a brand-new car. They are obviously willing to travel. Goodwood was a five-hour journey... At this rate, we could see them heading up towards Scotland next.' Griffiths paused whilst Price took a phone call. 'All I'm saying is – it would be a good idea to get our hands on the information they're using, to see for ourselves.'

'What do you have in mind? Stealing it?' Price's tone was a little uneasy. He'd had brushes with the law in the past, and he was not the firm's most trusted employee. Security services had investigated him on a few occasions, the most recent resulting in a written warning for conduct likely to bring the company into disrepute. He had to stay clear of trouble and squeaky clean for two years before his recent indiscretion would be removed from his employment record. The alternative to two years of unblemished behaviour was instant dismissal and the loss of numerous loyalty bonuses.

In a rare moment of frank openness, Price explained his current low standing in the organisation and said he couldn't condone any activity outside the law – his employers would crucify him. 'Meet me in the Red Lion at eight tonight!'

Andy Wheildon

*

Price was sitting in the corner of the saloon bar as far away as possible from the throng of people buying drinks. In front of him was a large Scotch, the *Sporting Life* and a packet of pork scratchings. He'd had to discard some of the pieces of scratchings because they were too damn hairy. The rest were being gradually consumed, whilst he cognitively digested the contents of his paper.

He sat back for a moment and contemplated the final piece of pig before popping it into his mouth. Years ago, a packet would have lasted no time at all, but now, with his teeth letting him down, it was necessary to suck on the pieces for a few minutes to soften them up before chewing commenced. He smiled inwardly as he dwelled on the word mastication. He had done too much masticating in his early years, and his teeth had suffered as a result.

Griffiths walked into the bar area and looked around for a while before deciding to take off his glasses and wipe away the condensation. He put them on again. 'Ah, there you are.' He walked over to Price who pushed his empty beer glass across the table. Griffiths picked it up and waited. Price sighed and reached for his wallet.

'And get one yourself,' Price said, as Griffiths walked off to buy the drinks.

A couple of minutes later, Griffiths returned with two large Scotches and two pints of bitter. He smiled as he pushed what little remained of Price's ten-pound note towards Price.

Price let Griffiths sit down and take a sip from his pint. He leaned across the table and drew Griffiths close. 'I want the System.' He spoke slowly and deliberately, with a touch of menace. 'I want to take it from those two bastards who've got it. I want it for myself, and you're going to help me. Is that clear?'

'I was actually offering to do just that in your office this afternoon; but what if I say no now?'

'If you say no, the Old Bill find out about you turning a blind eye when my shop was turned over. If you say no, Grattan finds out it was you who kept his wife company when he was inside. If you say no, a few debt collection agencies will come across your new address *quite by chance*.'

'Sometimes, I think I'd prefer to do a stretch rather than deal with you, you know.' Griffiths knew he was always going to be at Price's beck and call. 'Anyway, I'm in. I know a good thing when I see it, and like I said at your office, they've got something. Unfortunately, the something they've got is a computer. I reckon any system which can predict the outcome of a handicap with thirteen or more runners must be on a computer. The trouble is I know nothing about computers. But my daughter is a bit of an expert, so we could ask her to look at the kit if we get it?'

'Yeah, that would be good. But all in good time. We don't move in just yet. Watch them, learn their habits, and we'll take them on when I'm good and ready.' Price drained the last of his pint and left his whisky untouched as he stood up to leave. 'Keep in touch. I'll hear from you two weeks from today. 'Phone me at the office, don't bother paying a visit. I don't want anybody putting us two together, just in case anything goes wrong.'

'I see. You want me to take the fall if something happens, is that it?'

Price gave a wry smile. 'It'll keep you on your toes. I'll expect to hear from you in two weeks.' He walked out of the pub and went home.

Griffiths stayed and got drunk. Alcohol was the only companion he had apart from his daughter.

*

The following evening, Ian struggled through the back door and into the kitchen. Making a bit of a din as he dropped the weight from his shoulders, he closed the door, took a deep breath and sighed.

'What on earth have you got there?' Nigel could hardly believe his eyes.

'It's a train set,' Ian replied sarcastically, having given the question a little thought.

'It looks more like a set of golf clubs. But you don't play golf. Come to think of it, you don't play anything… except Elton bloody John and ELO!'

'*Didn't* play golf. I didn't play golf. Past tense, previous life. This is the new me. Well, it's a bit of the new me. I'm still working on the rest. I'm taking up golf, and I'm going to have lessons.' Ian picked up his bag of Wilsons and lugged them to the far side of the kitchen where he propped them up against the fridge.

Studying Form

He extracted a shiny putter from the bag and demonstrated the art of putting to his friend with an imaginary ball. 'If we are going to win lots of money—'

'*Earn* lots of money. It's our profession, remember?' Nigel corrected his friend.

'Either way. If I'm going to have lots of money, I want to enjoy it. This is the first step.'

'What, getting a hernia?'

'No, getting a set of golf clubs.'

'Same thing if you ask me. You're going to break your back carrying all those around.'

'OK, so maybe the second step towards enjoyment is buying a golf trolley, who knows?'

'So what's Zoë got to say about all this?'

Ian smiled and got himself a Coke from the fridge, Nigel declining the offer. 'The lessons I referred to will come from Zoë. Well, hopefully, from Zoë's old man. He loves the game. Apparently, he plays off a four handicap. Zoë plays off sixteen. I'm meeting them at the driving range later on. Fancy coming?'

'Actually, no. But thanks for the offer all the same. Will you be ready for the Open in a few weeks' time? Royal Birkdale, if my memory serves me right, or is it Troon? Anyway, I look forward to seeing you striding down the eighteenth fairway on telly one day. Thinking about it, it can't be Troon because it was St Andrews last year. I take it you've heard of Nick Faldo, because he won last year at St Andrews?'

'Vaguely. How come you're an expert on golf all of a sudden? Faldo, Troon, St Trinian's, etcetera. I thought horse racing was your only area of expertise.'

'Horse racing is, and will be for ever more, my *area of expertise*, but golf gets a lot of coverage too if you read the right newspapers, especially in the run-up to the Open. Ian Wooldridge did an excellent piece not so long ago in the *Daily Mail*. Now, there's an excellent sports journalist, Mr Wooldridge.'

*

The following morning, Ian walked into the living room, rubbing his ribcage, his face expressing a level of discomfort. The previous evening had been most enjoyable. However, the morning after the night before found him very stiff round his lower back and extremely sore down the right-hand side of his rib cage.

'I could hardly breathe when I first got up,' Ian informed his friend as he gingerly lowered himself into one of the easy chairs. 'I didn't realise golf could be so painful. I think I've pulled every muscle in my back and bruised a couple of ribs.'

'Rubbish, you're just a bit stiff, you big girl's blouse. A hot bath will sort you out, but first, I want to talk about our system – something we've neglected for a few days.'

'Fine. Hopefully, we can get cracking with updating the database. There's two weeks of data I've got to catch up on, and we've got to pay RLDS. We got another statement from them on Saturday for £250, I think. I'll go and get it.'

Studying Form

Ian gingerly rose to his feet and winced, clutching his side again. He went through to the kitchen and retrieved the statement from the worktop. 'Fancy a coffee?' he called back to Nigel. He put the kettle on, despite not hearing a reply, then returned to the living room.

'I've put the kettle on if you want a coffee,' Ian said, walking across the room to the sideboard. He pulled open the top drawer and extracted a chequebook and pen. He filled out a cheque to the value of £257.83, signing and dating it. He passed the chequebook to Nigel, who further endorsed the cheque, then put it into a prepaid envelope with the payment slip. 'That should keep them happy.' He licked the envelope and grimaced at the taste of the gum. 'I definitely need a coffee now!'

'Yeah, I'll have one too,' Nigel said. The two of them went into the kitchen. 'I was a bit busy last night, locked away in my bedroom. Sorry I didn't join you when you got in from the driving range – I wasn't in the mood for socialising. I got myself too engrossed with our next step and didn't want to put it down.'

'Zoë was a little disappointed; she brought round a lasagne to share. Actually, we've left some for you in the fridge. Zoë said she hopes you enjoy it – twenty minutes at 180°C.'

Nigel smiled. He had really warmed to Zoë and felt a pang of envy that Ian should have stumbled on such a great girl. Nigel's recent loss in love had left him feeling lonely. In the past, if he didn't have a girl in his life, Nigel could always count on Ian being around for a pint and a chat. Recently though, Ian hadn't been around.

'Make sure you thank her for me,' Nigel said as he looked in the fridge at the lasagne and got the milk out for the coffees. 'Now, let's discuss the next step with this system. It's going to be a big one.'

Ian listened intently as Nigel explained he'd been able to sort out a series of races over the next three weeks which would require extensive travel and overnight stays away from home. If all went well, Nigel hoped they'd be able to update the database and modify the System whilst they were travelling. Ian had explained earlier that all they needed was a portable PC and the means to connect it to their main computer once a day or a little less frequently.

He had costed the necessary equipment at around £3,000, since PCs which were more portable were more expensive than those that sat permanently on, or under, the desk. 'New micro-technology,' he explained to Nigel. 'The bits and pieces in the portable PCs are harder to manufacture, and they are the current leading edge in technology. Just like video recorders were expensive when they first came out.'

Nigel left the purchasing to Ian, trusting his expertise and hoping their recent easy money wouldn't cloud his judgement. 'Can you get everything right away? I want to visit Ripon on the twentieth.'

'Three days!' Ian exclaimed. 'You are joking, right? … You're not joking, are you?'

'No, I'm not. Let's do this. I'd hate to miss Ripon.' Nigel smiled, raised his eyebrows by way of a question and waited for a response from Ian.

'OK,' said Ian with a sigh.

He thought for a moment then moaned to Nigel that he'd need to write and test programs to allow him to collect RLDS data on the computer at home without having to be there in person. There was also the daunting prospect of his further neglected college work. He put that issue to the back of his mind.

Nigel wasn't impressed. 'Yes, yes, yes. But can it be done?'

'Yes, yes, yes… It will be done on the road to… Where, by the way? Apart from Ripon.'

Nigel passed his friend a piece of paper with a list of towns on it, with dates by the side of each town.

> *Ripon 20th June*
> *Nottingham 24th June*
> *Brighton 25th June*
> *Doncaster 28th June*
> *Haydock 4th July*
> *Beverley 6th July*

'I don't believe it,' Ian said in his best Victor Meldrew voice. 'Six meetings in the space of, what, two weeks?'

'That's right, give or take a day or two,' Nigel confirmed. 'There are races at each of those meetings which will fit nicely into the System. The Ripon meeting is on the same day as Royal Ascot.'

'So?'

Andy Wheildon

'So, we might go to Royal Ascot. I'm not sure yet. We've got a couple of days to decide before we set off.'

Ian poured the boiling water into a couple of mugs and passed one of the mugs to Nigel. 'How many nights are we going to be on the road, so to speak?'

Nigel wasn't quite sure. They got the maps out to see where they'd be geographically from one day to the next. Clearly, they would have to come home each night if they were unable to access their database from a hotel or guest house. In the end, they decided to postpone the decision over their nocturnal locations until they had established whether Ian could get the necessary equipment and come up with a remote access solution.

Dunking a shortbread biscuit into his coffee, Ian said, 'There's no time like the present. After this coffee, I'll nip into town and visit a friend from the university who'll be able to give me some advice. I just hope I don't meet anybody important. I've had a strong letter from the chancellor asking if I intend to complete the course this year and, if not, if I intend to reimburse the local authority what remains of my grant. God only knows what'll happen when my parents find out I'm not studying... That reminds me, I should pay back the money my mum lent me when I first started this little caper. I suppose it's only fair.'

'Well, they're all your problems. I've got a bit of scouting round to do. Unfortunately, one of the horses we're interested in is trained by Lambourn Collier.'

Studying Form

'Who? The name rings a bell, but—'

'Lambourn Collier is the trainer of the horse that almost had me throw this entire system in the bin. Remember, I told you about my unsuccessful bet on a horse called Tapestry? To this day, I'm certain the horse *should* have won. But it didn't. And the more I think about it, the more I'm convinced something was wrong about that horse on the day, so I'm going to ask a few questions about Lambourn Collier.'

*

By nightfall, the two were back together again in the kitchen going over the day's events. Both were extremely excited but for very different reasons. Luckily, Zoë was there to provide a calming influence.

'If either of you wake the baby, I'll crucify you.' She had been given a lift round by her father, since he and his wife were going away for a couple of nights. It had been agreed Zoë would stay with *the boys*, as her mother referred to them, whilst they were away. 'It's taken me ages to settle him down; he doesn't like it when he's not in his own room. So please keep the noise down.'

Nigel apologised and sat at the table, waiting for his lasagne to warm up, and let Ian say his piece.

'Well, the good news is I've got all the necessary equipment for us to tap into our database from anywhere in the world. Anywhere that has a phone, to be precise,' he said. 'The other good news is it hasn't cost me a penny, because I've got it on loan.'

'Brilliant! If the next couple of weeks pay off, and I'm sure they will, then we'll be seriously richer and well able to afford to buy our own equipment should we choose to make another concentrated attack on the bookies.

'I've got some good news as well. Pity though, because it means one of my chosen horses will have to be overlooked, along with all of the races she's due to run in the future. The trainer I mentioned this morning? Well, it appears he is known to bend the rules occasionally. He's got a string of fifteen horses that have an assortment of owners, one of whom likes to gamble but hates to lose. Tapestry was owned by this guy and so is Ginmist.'

Zoë frowned. 'Tapestry *was* owned?' she asked.

'Apparently the horse broke a leg and had to be destroyed,' Nigel explained. 'Anyway, Collier will train a horse to win, as will every other trainer in the business. But *this* trainer has a habit of ordering his jockeys to hold the horse up in certain races, so the handicapper doesn't put too much weight on its back. Eventually, the horse gets into a race at very generous odds, with hardly any weight to carry, and flies. It wins the race, making both trainer and owner a lot of money.'

'So Ginmist is one of his horses, and now you know you can't trust his horses to get honest results.' Ian tried to summarise.

'Not quite. It's only the horses belonging to this same owner – Mr Derek Trist, a stockbroker with offices in London, Frankfurt and New York. The guy is loaded, greedy and, apparently, ruthless.'

'How on earth did you find all that out?' Zoë asked.

'The bit about the stockbroker came out of a tabloid newspaper – I read a long article on him some months ago. Quite a detailed article with loads of photographs of him from around the world. It was more like an advert than an article. The bit about Collier being bent came straight from the horse's mouth. An ex-jockey to be exact, who knows a friend of mine who goes to the same betting shop as the jockey's brother-in-law.'

'Oh, a reliable source then, twice removed,' Ian quipped, trying to work out whether the brother-in-law was related to the ex-jockey or the friend.

'It all fits, and I'd lay money on Ginmist losing her next race. Unfortunately, this added factor of Collier being occasionally dishonest means we're going to have to disregard all his races when Trist is involved as an owner.'

The prospect of having to ignore races because of Collier and Trist annoyed Nigel. What if Trist became a successful owner with a string of horses at Collier's stable? That would mean a lot of races out of bounds to the System. 'I wonder if we can put a stop to all this? We'll have all the necessary information to expose Collier's shady practices at our fingertips. We'll know when his horses should win… I *am* going to put a stop to this. I'm going to scare Collier with the evidence and threaten to expose him if he keeps Trist's horses. It'll be simple.' He tucked into his lasagne.

Zoë and Ian looked at each other with matching expressions of concern.

'Don't you think you're jumping the gun a bit? You can't confront him with any facts because you can't prove anything. And if what you've said is right, then Trist the Ruthless – your word – might not be too impressed.' Ian looked at Zoë for some moral support. 'You're talking about marching in there and questioning Collier's integrity, threatening to destroy his livelihood. And Trist sounds like a pretty nasty piece of work. Don't get involved. It's not worth it.'

Nigel heard, but he didn't listen. 'All I'm going to do is give him a call, pretend to be a reporter, furnish him with the facts and leave the obvious response – dumping Trist as one of his owners – to him. Then I'll hang up. It'll be fun.'

*

That night was very uncomfortable for Ian. He was worried Nigel might do something stupid with Collier. He was also sharing a single bed with Zoë. She had told him to stop 'messing about' when they first got into bed. The fact they were in single bed and the baby was in the same room had served as adequate contraceptive. It was only for one night, she'd told him. They'd stay at her parents' house the next evening.

Nigel, on the other hand, felt no discomfort. Having already spoken to Collier and made it known he wanted to see Collier and Trist part company, he lay awake staring at a patch on the ceiling where a spider had once dared to walk. The large spider and the sole of a dirty shoe had both left their mark. Nigel hated spiders.

He had phoned Collier at about 10.30 p.m. The theme tune that signalled the end of the *News at Ten* had drifted down the phone line, which suggested to him Collier was relaxing in front of the telly.

'Sorry to bother you at such a late hour, Mr Collier. My name is Bishop. I'm a freelance journalist. I would like to ask a few questions about your association with one of your owners. Trist.'

There had been a slight pause, but Nigel could detect no audible concern.

'Well, Mr… er… Bishop, did you say? Mr Bishop, you are right – it *is* late, and I am trainer to Mr Trist's horses. What would you like to know?' Collier maintained a friendly tone whilst he reached for a pen and paper from the top drawer of his desk. He lived with his family in the country, miles from anywhere – an occupational necessity for trainers, since they needed a great deal of space to go about their business. A great deal of his business was spent on the telephone: talking to trainers, vets, Wetherby's, suppliers, jockeys, lads, his mother, etc. The telephone was his lifeblood, so he always invested in the best telecoms systems available. Tonight, the best came into its own. Collier quickly jotted down Nigel's phone number, which was displayed on a small screen alongside the duration of the call.

Andy Wheildon

Nigel decided to come to the point. 'I have reason to believe, under the express orders of your owner, Mr Trist, you prevent your horses from winning races when they have every chance to do so. I also have reason to believe you have fraudulently extracted monies from insurance companies over accidents that have befallen some of your horses.'

Collier kept his composure. 'I haven't the slightest notion what you are talking about, young man. I have a string of seventeen horses for an assortment of owners, one of whom is Mr Trist. All my owners like to *win* races, none more so than Trist. However, all my owners are in racing for reasons of sport, entertainment and fun. They are aware good horses cost a lot of money, and they are aware they will only rarely make money from winning races. They are in it, I say once more, for the fun of it. My owners are rich enough to enjoy an expensive hobby. As for your remark about insurance, you will need to expand on that. What fraudulent accidents are supposed to have befallen any of the horses in my care?'

'Tapestry.'

'Tapestry.' Collier sighed.

There was a pause in the conversation. Collier recalled the morning he wept at the sight of the horse in pain. He was only now beginning to get over her being destroyed. Trainers don't get sentimental about horses. To them, horses are just a means to an end, just part of the business. Tapestry had been different. Collier felt anger boil over into his voice. 'How dare you make accusations about my integrity. I have been in this business for over twenty years, and I have loved every minute of it. I have earned the trust and support of my owners and of other trainers alike. I have done nothing, nor would I do anything to tarnish the sport I love. I suggest, Mr Bishop, you take your questionable freelance talents elsewhere.' Collier replaced the receiver on its cradle and poured himself a large Scotch. He hated Trist for forcing him to compromise his integrity. It didn't stop him calling the man immediately though.

Trist listened to what Collier had to say, making a note of the telephone number and the name which he assumed would turn out to be fictitious. Trist reassured Collier all would be well and asked him what chances Ginmist had at Beverley.

'All things considered, I think we ought to give the horse every chance. The odds for the race probably won't be to your liking, but I think she can win. With this "Bishop" cloud over our heads, we had better do things by the book.' Collier didn't usually get the opportunity to express his opinions about the tactics for one of Trist's horses. The man was normally too dictatorial in such circumstances.

'I hear what you're saying, and you're probably right. I look forward to her winning then, but don't worry, I'll keep my money in my pocket this time. You concentrate on the next few races, and I'll concentrate on this Mr Bishop. Goodnight.' Trist didn't wait for a response from Collier. He put the phone down and reached for his desk diary, thumbing his way through the address section.

He smiled when he found what he was looking for. Picking up the receiver, he dialled. Danny answered almost immediately with an aggressive, 'Yes?'

'And a pleasant evening to you, Danny. How's it hanging?'

'To the left, as usual.' Danny Parrot, a highly dangerous private investigator chuckled down the phone. 'How are you, Derek? I've not heard from you in ages. Business keeping you filthy rich, is it?'

'You might say that. I'd like to throw some of my filthy money your way, if you're not too busy.' Trist was not keen on pointless banter and liked to keep things business-like. 'I want details on an individual who could be trouble for me. I've only got a name and a telephone number. The name, Bishop, is probably fictitious, but the number is genuine – I just hope it's not a public phone.' Trist relayed the details, and Parrot made a mental note. He had no need for pieces of paper. His memory was astounding, and anyway, bits of paper went astray or ended up in the wrong hands.

'OK,' Parrot said. 'I'll get on it straight away. I should have something for you in a couple of days. Do you want me to call you, or are you going to call me back?'

Trist told Parrot he should wait for a phone call from him as he'd be out of the country for the next forty-eight hours.

Having replaced the receiver and sat back for a moment to think, Parrot reached for the phone once more and dialled one of his numerous contacts. 'Hi there. I have a phone number; I want to find who it belongs to and where they live. I need it within forty-eight hours. I'll post the cheque to you tomorrow morning.'

His contact accepted the commission and took a note of the phone number. Parrot thanked him and terminated the call. He walked over to his bureau and opened two drawers. The first contained envelopes and postage stamps and the second contained an assortment of cheque books. Shuffling through the cheque books he found the account he wanted to use, wrote a cheque to the value of £500 and placed it in an envelope which he addressed and prepared for posting the following day. Then, on second thoughts, he put on a hat and coat and went for a late-night walk to the post box.

Two days later, both Parrot and Trist knew exactly where a certain Nigel Green lived: central Nottingham.

Thursday, 20 June 1991

The previous day, Nigel and Ian had tested the software Ian had written and loaded it on to their brand-new, slightly smaller form factor personal computer and VDU. They had both agreed it all worked as it should and the best time to link the portable with Ian's PC in his bedroom would be any time before 9 a.m. Ian had therefore adjusted his batch files so the computer automatically connected with RLDS to download up-to-date information at 7.30 a.m., with the option of three redial attempts should the RLDS phone lines be busy.

'Good skills, that man,' declared Nigel when he saw everything working like clockwork for a fourth time. 'It looks like we've cracked it. Now, let's get ourselves to Ripon and take another couple of thousand pounds from the bookies.'

The following morning, they loaded the car with suitcases, new computer and sandwiches, made by Zoë and Ian the previous night.

'I'm going to miss her, you know. I'm in love. It's amazing.'

'Don't worry, I'll keep you warm!' Nigel quipped

'Bugger off,' Ian replied, without thinking.

'Very apt. Only joking.'

Studying Form

Ian started the engine, whilst Nigel flicked through the pages of the *Reader's Digest Road Atlas of Great Britain*.

'So, you know where we're going, do you?' Ian enquired.

'No problemo, Mr Turner. Straight on, my good man, left at the lights and then head for the motorway.'

As the Calibra pulled off, Griffiths started his engine and nipped out behind them. Danny Parrot saw everything and unexpectedly found himself at the back of a three-car convoy. He reached over to the glove compartment and retrieved a small pair of binoculars, using them to read the number plate of the car in front. Committing it to memory, he would call in a favour later to find out who the driver was and, hopefully, why he was interested in the same quarry.

Conversation in the front car was light-hearted and had little to do with the job in hand.

'So, what's she like in bed?' Nigel asked. 'The journey's about two and a half hours, so we've got to talk about something!'

'I'd prefer it if the subject of conversation was something other than my sex life, if you don't mind.'

'OK. Let's talk about my sex life then.'

There was a moment's silence.

'That didn't take long now, did it?' Nigel said in mockery of himself. He had been single for about three months and was beginning to worry.

'There's more to life than sex, you know,' ventured Ian. 'How old were you when you did it for the first time?'

'Er, you won't laugh, will you?'

The two turned to look at each other, and Ian raised his eyebrows as if to repeat the question. Then they both looked back to the road: Ian to ensure they didn't crash, Nigel to ponder on his reply.

'Dix-huit ans, achtzehn Jahre, eighteen years old. I thought it'd never happen. I used to walk round town and see kids half my age walking hand in hand.'

'Yes, but it doesn't mean they were bonking.'

'I know. But there I was, a virgin at eighteen with no-one to hold hands with, let alone *bonk*.'

'You're joking. No girlfriends?' Ian couldn't believe his ears. For two years, Ian had thought Nigel was both confident and competent when it came to chatting up women. It had seemed to Ian that Nigel had always had a girl in tow. In fact, he remembered Nigel joking about how he'd pulled in the maternity ward three days after he'd been born. 'I thought *I* was the timid one, when it came to the opposite sex.'

'Don't worry, you are! I started late, that's all. I've made up for lost time, though. The last three years have been quite enjoyable. The only thing that's ever got in the way of my sex life is horse racing. These past three months it's been all horses and nothing else. I can't say I'm that bothered though.'

'Liar.'

'Correct,' Nigel confirmed. 'I am bothered. I need a woman. I miss the company more than anything. Does that make me sound old?' Nigel didn't wait for an answer. 'You know, in the past, if I was on my own, you'd be around to have a pint or a chat. Not anymore though. Oh no, now it's all "Zoë this, Zoë that". You're never around these days. Call yourself a friend?' Nigel was smiling.

'You're just jealous,' Ian observed.

'Correct again. She's lovely, young Zoë. She's got a nice figure on her as well.'

Ian turned to look at Nigel with an uneasy frown.

'Don't worry, I wouldn't dream of it. She's lovely, she's got a great figure and she's got you. She's not my type, honest!' Nigel did his best to reassure his friend, genuine in what he said. 'You could do with oiling the springs on your bed though – squeaking to all hours of the night… it's very disturbing!'

'Yes, I know – especially when she's on top! Point to note: it's not my bed.'

After a while, they pulled into a service station, closely followed by their two pursuers. Parrot grabbed the chance to refuel and make a couple of brief phone calls. Like most successful people, he had useful friends. The type of friends you would deny knowing if anyone were to ask, the type of friends who would disown you at the drop of a hat, friends who became enemies if you didn't tread carefully. Parrot had lots of those type of friends. After making the calls, he had all the information he needed. He could relax behind the wheel of his car now that he knew Griffiths would be easy to handle.

'We've got two choices: either the A1 all the way or go via Harrogate on the A59 and A61. We have enough time on our hands to stop for a bite to eat in Harrogate if you're interested?'

Ian decided it would be nice to stretch their legs in Harrogate, so they dropped off the A1 and headed west on the A61 towards Knaresborough and Mother Shipton's Caves. Reaching Harrogate, they stopped off at a café to the north of the town. Parrot decided to join them in the café, confident the two lads wouldn't clock him. Griffiths, on the other hand, stayed in his car. He was hungry and tired but didn't want to risk getting too close to his quarry.

'So how was Zoë?' Nigel cnquired as they walked back to the car.

'How should I know? I was on the phone to my aunty. It's her birthday today, and I forgot to send her a card. I'm sure Zoë is fine – thanks for asking!'

They soon joined the local traffic heading towards a well signposted Ripon racecourse. Idle conversation ensued until the outskirts of Ripon when keen navigation and explicit clear instruction became the order of the day once again.

The Nigel, Ian, Griffiths and Parrot entourage arrived at Ripon racecourse with ample time to spare, all three cars parking close to each other in the car park. Nigel looked Griffiths straight in the eyes as he and Ian walked towards the racecourse entrance. He frowned. *Where had he seen that man before?*

The two friends had decided to place bets to the value of £1,200 this time. The odds for the horse would be quite generous since it was moving up a class, but the System still showed this horse was a class above the rest, so it was worth the risk. Walking around with £200 in his trouser pockets and £200 in each of his coat pockets made Ian feel uneasy, but Nigel reassured him it was impossible to tell he was carrying such a large wad in his trousers!

Parrot kept his distance behind Griffiths and spoke briefly to Trist on his cellular phone, getting a few funny looks from passers-by intrigued by this new technology. Trist made it plain he didn't want a couple of kids interfering with his plans and that Parrot was authorised to do whatever he thought necessary to remove them from the picture. Trist also reminded Parrot that nothing should be traceable back to either of them. Parrot had never let the wealthy stockbroker down before and was far too appreciative of their working relationship to put either of them at risk – Trist was very generous when it came to rewarding a job well done.

At 2.15 p.m., the racecourse was a hive of activity. The first race had been won by a well-backed horse which had started second favourite, so it was taking a while for the bookies to pay out on winning bets. Eventually, the bookies and punters turned their attention to the 2.45 whilst Griffiths and Parrot concentrated on Ian and Nigel.

Parrot decided to follow Nigel and was amazed to see him put £600 on a horse called Broughton Blues, placed midway down the betting in a field of twenty runners. The horse looked like it was going to start at about 12/1. Nigel was going to win nearly eight grand, and presumably, so too was Ian. Parrot absentmindedly wondered where Nigel would put £8,000; it was quite a large herd of ponies.

The horse won with ease, and both Nigel and Ian went about collecting their winnings along with a few other people. The horse had started at 10/1, and the bookmakers on the course were relieved that the favourite had been beaten into fifth place with the second favourite Kalabridge finishing last.

It didn't take long for the two lads to finish collecting their winnings, and with pockets nearly bursting at the seams, they made their way back to the car. Now they needed to find a bank where they could pay in the cash, and they needed to find suitable accommodation for the night.

Midland Bank was kind enough to accept £13,200 in a variety of denominations, though there was a degree of suspicion initially. Ian and Nigel were ushered into a room when it became obvious pushing that volume of cash under a bandit screen was a bad idea. The bank manager verified the two individuals were account holders and asked them where the money had come from – it wasn't every day two young men deposited such a large amount of cash in a provincial branch. Nigel got annoyed at the treatment they were receiving, but he eventually convinced the manager that all was in order.

They left the bank and found a guest house, booking in for one night.

'Is there a telephone in the room?' Ian enquired.

'Yes, along with a television, coffee-making facilities and a trouser press. Breakfast is served between seven thirty and nine. Will you need a wake-up call?'

Nigel thought it a good idea, so they booked an early call for 7.15 a.m. He also ordered a copy of the *Daily Mail.*

The two friends went to their room, and each had a shower in preparation for exploring Ripon later in the evening.

'It worked really well,' Ian called out to his friend who was spending longer than usual in the shower.

Nigel poked his head round the door, his hair dripping wet. 'You called?'

'No, I advised. I was just saying the download from home worked a treat. I've got all the race results from last week and today. Apparently, a horse called Broughton Blues won the 2.45 at Ripon this afternoon!'

'And we won a fortune!' Nigel returned to the task of drying his hair and readying himself for the world at large, whilst Ian lay back on his bed and dozed.

Twenty-five minutes later, the two of them were heading into town in search of a pizza and a pub. A brief discussion had them agreeing on a swift pint before they ventured too far. So the first pub they found became their first watering hole. It then turned out to be their only watering hole for the evening since it was cosy, warm and had a comprehensive evening menu. It also had a comprehensive choice of skirt, according to Nigel. Ian maintained he hadn't noticed.

Andy Wheildon

'But now you mention it, there *are* some pretty women here. That reminds me, I promised to call Zoë. Have you got any change I can scrounge for the phone? I might not have enough, and Zoë has been known to go on a bit – not that I'm complaining.'

Nigel fished a couple of twenty pence coins out of his pocket and handed them to Ian. 'I'll get the next round in. Have you decided what you want to eat? I might as well order whilst I'm at the bar.'

Ian had a quick glance at the menu to confirm his earlier choice then decided to change his mind. 'Oh, I'll have some skinny dips for starters, with chilli, and then cod and chips. And don't forget the tartar sauce.'

He left Nigel to deal with the food and drinks and went in search of a phone. Fifteen minutes later and £2 poorer, he returned to the table to find it empty. Empty of glasses, empty of discarded crisp packets and definitely empty of Nigel. A quick glance to the bar saw Nigel deep in conversation with a very attractive girl who had an equally attractive friend.

'Oh no.' Ian sighed as he walked up to Nigel in search of his pint. There was no way he wanted to chat to two complete strangers, especially knowing what Nigel probably had in mind for the evening. All Ian could think of was Zoë and how much he wished he could be with her.

'*There* you are,' Nigel said. 'Was she in? I suppose she must have been, the time it took you. That conversation lasted longer than forty pence!' The girls smiled and looked at Ian who blushed.

Studying Form

He returned Nigel's two coins and informed his audience that, yes, Zoë had been in, and yes, the call had cost more than forty pence. 'Two pounds to be exact. Is that mine?' Ian pointed to a full glass of beer on the bar. One of the girls passed it to him and smiled. Again, Ian blushed. 'Thanks.'

'Number forty-seven!'

Nigel jumped from his barstool and picked up his glass from the bar. 'That's us.' He turned to the girls and said he hoped to see them later before walking across to the servery.

Ian followed, smiling a farewell to the girls then turning to Nigel with a frown. 'You are joking? Surely, you're not on the pull tonight?'

'Oh, behave. You're not me bloody mother. They're pretty, and they're not with anyone. I just got chatting to them, that's all.'

They took their food over to their table and tucked in to a well-earned meal.

Whilst they enjoyed their food, Parrot was on the public phone just outside the bar area, speaking to Trist.

'Deal with these boys the way you dealt with Jenkins, if you like. Scare the living daylights out of them but keep me out of it. Whatever you decide to do, I don't want to know. If they've got a system, good luck to them. I've got my own system, and it's working fine for me.'

'But whatever I decide to do, Griffiths will be there to witness it. He's sticking to them like glue. He actually bumped into them at the last meeting, he was so close.'

'That's your problem. Again, I don't want to be implicated, just do something decisive. Get this problem resolved. I take it you still have the same bank account? I'll put some money your way in the morning. Goodbye.' Trist hung up abruptly, not waiting for a response.

Parrot replaced the receiver and looked out to the car park, to where Griffiths had parked his car. 'It's about time we had a little chat.' He left the pub and dug his hands into his coat pockets, taking hold of a small handgun with his right hand.

Looking up and down the street to ensure there was no-one around, he walked up to Griffiths' car and saw the door lock was pressed down. He tapped on the window, hoping Griffiths would wind it down. It actually made Griffiths nearly jump out of his skin. Ultimately, it had the desired effect though.

'Bloody hell, mate! You scared me half to death,' Griffiths said as he lowered the window. Parrot moved like lightning, pushing the gun into Griffiths' neck, forcing his head back, then reaching into the car, Parrot removed the keys from the ignition.

'Now sit still and keep quiet, Mr Griffiths.' Keeping the gun trained on the ex-police officer, Parrot moved round the front of the car and let himself into the passenger's seat. 'Put both hands on the steering wheel, where I can see them. My gun is pointing at your abdomen. If you cause a fuss, you will hear a cough, as I shoot you. You will feel intense pain. But don't worry, that won't kill you. Loss of blood, then shock, then blood poisoning as your own gut leaks its contents into the rest of your body – *that* will kill you.

'Alternatively, we could have a friendly chat, after which I'll be gone, leaving you to go about your business.'

Griffiths turned to look at Parrot and opened his mouth to speak.

'Keep quiet, Mr Griffiths.'

Parrot spent five minutes giving Griffiths an insight into everything his carjacker knew about the last fifteen years of the ex-police officer's life. Parrot knew things about Griffiths that Griffiths had forgotten. Parrot knew everything about him. He also knew Price. 'But what I don't know is why you're so interested in those two young gentlemen you've been following all day. What is it you want from them?'

Reluctantly, Griffiths told Parrot about their potential computer system and how he'd been engaged, as a PI, to follow them whilst his employer decided what to do for the best. 'If the System is out there and works, and it seems as though it does, then it could undermine the whole betting industry. My boss thinks the System needs to be destroyed.'

'Thank you, Mr Griffiths. I don't care what your boss thinks, but I'm going to tell you what I think you should do. Go home. Report back to your employer about this conversation and tell him the two young gentlemen will no longer be a thorn in his side. I suggest you visit their house and take whatever you require; they won't be in need of it anymore. Go home.

Leave those two to me.' Parrot handed back the car keys to Griffiths and got out.

Griffiths started the engine and pulled off.

Parrot smiled and watched him leave the pub car park, turn left at the traffic lights and drive away. With shoulders hunched against a bracing wind, Parrot turned up the collar of his coat and walked away from the pub in search of somewhere else to have a meal, just in case Griffiths decided to double back and see where Parrot may have gone.

In fact, that was precisely what Griffiths had considered doing, right before considering the gun he'd had pressed into his side. Retreat, rather than confrontation, would be the prudent course of action, he decided. At the first opportunity, he stopped at a payphone and called Price who was intrigued at what Griffiths had to tell him.

'You'd better come home then,' Price said. 'This situation doesn't warrant guns or any sort of violence, not as far as I'm concerned. The powers that be, my direct bosses, have decided to ignore my letter of warning. The case is therefore closed.'

'But what about the System? It works. You've seen it in action in your betting shops, and more recently, I've seen it succeed a few times now. We can't just let it go.'

'No, I realise that. Those two lucky bastards have developed a system so good it's now got them in trouble with a gunman. But they don't know it yet. We back off. He takes over. Good luck to him. As he told you, he's not interested in the System itself. It's ours for the taking now. I reckon the two boys have trodden on someone else's toes. And now it seems they're going to pay, quite dearly. We, on the other hand, or rather you, are going to return to their house, take everything that appears relevant and scram.'

'Yes, if it's going to be done, it's something that needs done sooner rather than later.' Griffiths didn't like it one bit. He would have preferred it if Price had decided to walk away from this whole business, but it was clear he wouldn't.

'I agree, so... while the cat's away! Do it tonight and call me in the morning. Goodnight.'

Griffiths could hardly believe his ears. Three nights with hardly any sleep, thanks to sleeping in the car, and now he was expected to commit burglary. If he got caught, he was going to make sure he took Price down with him.

Parrot walked for five minutes but could not find a restaurant he liked the look of, so he returned to the same pub as Ian and Nigel, sitting on the same bar stool Nigel had used when chatting to the two girls. He ordered a large Scotch, without ice or water, and then had a general browse around the bar. For a moment, he looked quizzically at a lampshade in the shape of what seemed to be deer antlers. His mind returned to more serious matters. He had seen the two boys the moment he entered the pub and smiled to himself at the irony of having thought Griffiths a fool when he had nearly walked straight into Nigel at Ripon. Parrot was confident he had not been seen by either of the two before now and their contentment with the day's events would have left them relaxed and unobservant. He swivelled back to the bar and leaned forwards to get the attention of the barman.

'The guy at the bar, I'm sure I saw him earlier today.' Ian was the observant one of the two, and he gestured to Nigel to take a discreet glance.

'So?'

'I just thought I'd mention it, that's all. Anyway, I'm knackered. I'll see you back at the room. Don't bring anyone back!'

'Don't worry. And don't wait up.'

Friday, 21 June 1991

The following morning Ian woke up to find the other single bed empty and untouched. Where the hell was Nigel? He picked up the phone and dialled the guest house reception. 'Any messages for room 214?'

'One moment, sir, I'll have a look... Sorry, sir, no messages. Will that be all?'

'No. How long do you serve breakfast till?'

'We require guests to have ordered their breakfast by nine.'

Ian gave his thanks and hung up. Fifteen minutes later, after a quick shower, he was downstairs and walking into the breakfast room. Nigel was sitting at a table, tucking into a full English breakfast. 'Mind if I join you?' Ian asked.

Nigel looked up from the *Racing Post* he had open next to his plate, and smiled. 'By all means, help yourself. Care for some toast? And there's the *Daily Mail* if you're interested?'

'Where the bloody hell have you been?'

'I'll tell you later. You missed out last night, you know. You definitely missed out. Anyway, our next meeting is Nottingham, next Monday, so we could go home now except there's a horse running at Redcar today I'm interested in. If it's OK with you, can we nip across to the meeting?'

'You got lucky, did you?' Ian was more interested in the happenings of last night than the day ahead.

'It's not luck, Tod,' Nigel quoted from *Trading Places*. He then changed tack. 'We can get to Redcar from here, easy-peasy lemon-squeezy as long as the A19 stays clear. Order some food. I'm off to freshen up and get a change of clothes. Hopefully, we can be on the road in about forty-five minutes.'

Ian ordered a full English breakfast and ate it on his own, whilst Nigel went back to the room. Once he had finished his breakfast, he went to reception and asked for the bill. To his surprise, the bill had been paid in full already.

'Your colleague paid earlier. He's a bit of an early bird, isn't he?'

Ian smiled. If only the receptionist knew the half of it.

Forty-five minutes later, they'd packed, vacated their room and were on the road to Redcar – a mere fifty-minute drive and a good opportunity to catch up on the events of the previous night.

'So, where did you end up then?'

'I thought you'd never ask!' Nigel could hardly contain himself. 'Left at the lights and take the third exit at the next roundabout. And listen very carefully, coz you ain't gonna believe it.'

'I'm not sure I really want to hear it, but go on. You obviously pulled. So, which one?'

Studying Form

'Well, it seems you are assuming I pulled one of the girls you briefly met at the bar, Ruth or Sharon. You're assuming it was either Ruth or Sharon?'

'I'm assuming it was either Ruth or Sharon, yes.'

'Well,' Nigel's face was a picture, this cat had definitely got the cream. 'Both of them.'

'You're joking!' Ian nearly hit the curb as he turned to look at his friend. 'You slept with two women. You got off with both of them. Practise safe sex, did we?'

'Do watch where you're going. You could get us both killed! And don't worry, it was all very safe.'

There was silence for a few moments whilst Ian negotiated some roadworks, and Nigel consulted the map. Eventually curiosity got the better of Ian once more. 'So, how did you get on then? Satisfy them both, did you?'

'Probably not. I was satisfied though, completely. They were amazing. When they had finished with me, they turned to each other. It was great. What a show.'

'You're kidding.'

Nigel laughed. 'No, I'm not. We had a great chat after you went back to the guest house, and they invited me back to their place after last orders. They suggested £200, and it didn't take me long to agree.'

'Blimey. You paid them? Have you ever paid for sex before?'

Andy Wheildon

'No.' Nigel stared out of the car window and reflected for a while. 'It was amazing, but no, I never have, and I don't think I ever will again.'

*

Parrot was on their tail, about five cars behind. Thankfully, the A19 was relatively clear of traffic, making his job a doddle. He hummed to the strains of Annie Lennox and Dave Stewart singing 'I Love You like a Ball and Chain' on the local radio station.

He had opted for an uncomfortable night in the car and, as a result, had had little sleep. When he had finally nodded off, a milkman, the dawn chorus and the early morning sun had all conspired to revive him. A brisk walk to a newsagent was all that was required to shake off the strains of fatigue. He had purchased the *Sun* and a pint of milk. The *Sun* had revealed an ample chest on page three and the probable venue for the next race meeting on page twenty-six. The pint of milk had quenched his thirst and overcome his desire for food. He had presumed his next meal would probably be at Redcar on the east coast, since Redcar was the nearest race meeting of the day. The journey north-east was proving him right.

Parrot had also decided this would be the day on which to finish this business and return home to a comfy bed and a healthy bank balance. The end for the two boys would be either eternal or everlasting, depending on the outcome of an accident Parrot was going to prepare for them. If they died: eternal. If one or both of them survived: the fright should be enough to ensure their everlasting retreat from racing. He sighed as they continued to drive east. The thought of these two men dying at his hands made him feel uneasy. He had killed before. Six people. Those killings had been business: justified, necessary. They hadn't even pricked his conscience. This was different. These two youngsters had trodden on the toes of a greedy, ruthless man who would not stand for anyone getting in the way of his business or, it would seem, his hobby. Parrot felt sorry for them, but at the same time, he had a job to do to his client's satisfaction… or he wouldn't get paid.

*

Redcar is a pretty, provincial course. It was the first time Nigel had been there. He'd often seen it on TV, and as always, the atmosphere on the course made all the difference. It had been a cloudy morning with the threat of rain, but now the sun was shining, and everyone walked about with an air of expectation and a smile on their faces.

Coachloads of people spilled from the parking area. They were all looking forward to something special – maybe an excellent meal, maybe a few beers with friends and, hopefully, a flutter on a winning horse. They all expected to see some fine racing, and with the sun shining, they were all relieved to see some fine weather.

For a moment, Nigel stood and watched the hive of activity, the hustle and bustle of racing that occurred almost daily throughout Britain. Horse racing was a friendly sport; it appealed to all age groups from all walks of life. Racing could offer something for nearly everyone. Children could play unattended on the grassy banks overlooking the course. Kite flying, frisbee throwing, and an assortment of ball games were the order of the day. Parents could mingle and become punters, choosing either to have a flutter or to abstain from the monetary activities. Everyone could marvel at the grace and commitment shown by the jockeys as they went about their business. Everyone could be enthralled at the sight of numerous horses in full gallop attempting to outrun the rest of the field.

Whilst everyone went about the business of preparing for the first race, Nigel thought about his next winner and smiled.

Ian noticed Nigel's look of contentment. 'Stop thinking about last night, you dirty bugger. Nice course though, isn't it?'

'Actually, it was the course I was thinking about. Don't you just love racing? Everyone seems so happy.'

'Probably because they haven't lost their money yet. Give it a couple of hours and a rain shower, and I'll bet there will be a few disgruntled characters walking away towards the car park.'

'Yes, you're right,' Nigel agreed. 'Well, somebody has to lose, to keep us in business!'

Parrot had decided not to follow the two lads into the meeting. He relaxed in his car, listening to the radio and reading the paper. Unfortunately, the paper he was reading didn't take too long to finish. The most popular paper in the country, and it was nearly all adverts and photographs. Once he'd finished, he ambled across to a vendor and purchased a copy of the *Sporting Life*. Back in the car, he was quite surprised to find himself enjoying this specialist publication covering a subject he'd never had the slightest bit of interest in before.

The third race of the afternoon brought the punters out in their droves. The second race had gone to a horse called Sizzling Saga, and the on-course bookies were extremely busy paying out on this odds-on favourite. With so much time spent settling the winning bets for the second race, there wasn't much time to scour the lines of prices on offer for the third. Nigel and Ian stayed together as they mingled with the crowd. This time they were merely spectators. Nigel had mentioned a horse called Polistatic when they had entered the course, and it was favourite across the board.

The two retreated to a high vantage point in the stands, in line with the finishing post, and waited patiently for the off. Nigel's binoculars were trained on the horses mingling around the starting stalls at the one-mile-three-furlong marker to the left of the main stand. There was a slight commotion in one of the stalls when a horse became nervous whilst other horses were being loaded.

'Oh dear, one of the horses is making a bit off a fuss.' Nigel consulted his race card to determine the culprit and laughed. 'Fancy that. A horse called Heir of Excitement is playing up!'

'So?' Ian couldn't see the significance of an outsider getting excited before the race.

'So, it might unnerve our horse. It's in the next stall.' Nigel lifted his binoculars once more and was relieved to see the handlers were in no hurry to put their horse in the stalls. In fact, they chose to insert Polistatic last of all.

As soon as the horse was in the stall, the white flag was raised to put them under starter's orders, and all at once, there was a cavalry charge of ten horses tearing up the first three furlongs. The course commentator kept the crowds informed of the general progress of all the horses, whilst Nigel concentrated on Polistatic.

'Fourth, tucked behind a couple on the rails. One horse has gone off far too fast – he'll soon burn out.' Nigel was proved right, as the field began to pass the leading horse after five furlongs. Most of the horses were still in with a shout as they approached seven furlongs. Polistatic had to stutter when another horse moved away from the railings.

'Damn, he's lost a bit of ground. He's about four lengths off the pace.'

'I can see that.' Ian could also see the two horses in front of Polistatic were moving very smoothly, neither jockey having to do much work. Nigel put his binoculars to his side as the race reached a climax. The crowd began to shout encouragement at their respective horses, and in an instant, due to the noise, the course commentator became somewhat redundant. Jester's Farewell pulled clear of Top Scale and took a two-length lead, whilst Polistatic moved up a gear and raced from third to second. In the last fifty yards, the jockeys on both Polistatic and Jester's Farewell began to use their whip and frantically work on their horses to extract the last ounce of effort, a longer stride and a bit more pace. Polistatic was now flying and, had the finishing post been ten yards further away, he would have won with something to spare.

The finishing line was, however, much closer than that, and the two horses passed the post together. It was close, very close indeed. Nigel recalled the afternoon when he'd been watching a race with Ian and Zoë. That race had been close. He turned, open-mouthed, to Ian who was staring at the finishing post. 'Well?'

Ian closed his eyes and tried to re-run the last few strides in his mind. 'It was close.'

'I know it was bloody close. I don't need you to tell me it was close. It was too bloody close.'

The course commentator announced the result would need to be determined from a photograph. 'Concerning, in race card order, number six and number ten.'

'Well?' Nigel knew Ian to be good at predicting the result of a photograph.

Again, Ian closed his eyes and thought for a while. Then, before opening his eyes, he began to smile.

'Yes!' Nigel punched the air. 'You'd better be right. Just to prove a point to myself I can still pick winners on a day off. '

Andy Wheildon

The result of the photograph was duly announced, and Polistatic was deemed to have won by a short head.

'Weighed in.' It was official: no objections, no stewards' enquiry.

Nigel and Ian laughed. 'Phew, exciting, wasn't it?' ventured Ian.

'Yeah, let's go home.'

In the car park, a light drizzle turned into heavy rain, and Nigel suggested Ian get the car unlocked without delay.

'Alright, alright. Keep your hair on.' Ian searched his pockets for the car keys and, as usual, found them in the most unlikely pocket 'God knows why I put them in there,' he said, fishing them out and unlocking the car doors.

There was a slight sigh, followed by a metallic click, as both doors unlocked in unison. Nigel jumped in first and immediately reached for the map. Ian was laughing as he started the engine. 'Left at the exit. We need to take a trip round the other side of the racetrack and then back towards the A19.' Nigel began to plan their journey home.

As they approached the exit, Ian noticed, in his rear-view mirror, another car leaving the course. The meeting was only half-finished, but someone else had decided to leave at exactly the same time. The main road was busy, so it was impossible for Ian pull out and join the flow of traffic. Whilst he waited, the other car pulled up behind him. He could hardly believe his eyes. The occupant of the car behind them had been at the race meeting in Ripon the previous day and had been in the same pub as them last night. 'Will you look at that?' he said to Nigel. 'Behind us.'

Nigel glanced over his shoulder at the car as Ian pulled out onto the main road. 'Hmm, very nice.'

'No, not the car – the driver. He was in the bar last night, remember. I pointed him out to you. He was sitting at the bar, and I mentioned he looked familiar from earlier in the day. And now here he is again.'

Nigel turned around again, and this time looked directly at the driver.

'Shit.' Parrot knew he'd been recognised. The traffic on the main road had been his downfall. He had got too close too soon. He would have preferred the element of surprise for creating the accident. All was not lost, however. He would just have to be more careful about choosing his moment.

Nigel looked anxiously at his friend, not quite sure what to say. Eventually, whilst looking back at their pursuer, he decided there was nothing they could do except drive. And keep on driving. 'You never know, it could be a coincidence,' he suggested, somewhat feebly.

'You are joking?' Ian replied. 'Three times in two days, I've clocked that guy – that's twice too many. Coincidence only comes in twos as far as I'm concerned. We've got somebody following us. We've got a problem.'

'We're going to have to lose him then. Put your foot down.'

Ian tutted, looked to the heavens for a second and motioned Nigel to look to the front of the car. They were stuck behind a cement mixer busily mixing cement and annoyingly moving at a snail's pace. Cars flew by in the opposite direction, making it impossible to overtake.

'Cancel that.' Accelerating into the back of a slow-moving vehicle would probably not be a prudent means of escape. Nigel consulted his map and decided the best option was to find heavy traffic in an area with a myriad of exits any of which they could choose to take at the last moment. 'We'll head back towards the course and try to lose him in the heavy traffic. So, all the way round the roundabout that's coming up and back the way we came.'

'Good idea,' Ian agreed. 'That way we'll definitely know if he's following us.'

As the roundabout approached, the cement mixer indicated left and took the first exit. 'Thank Christ for that.' Nigel sighed. Ian agreed and focused on his rear-view mirror.

The next fifty minutes saw Ian spending too much time watching the rear-view mirror instead of looking where he was going, whilst Nigel continued to review the map trying to find a way to lose their pursuer.

The A19 and the A168 took the two cars to the A1 which Ian knew he had to take. So they would then be on a dual carriageway with Parrot still right behind them.

Studying Form

As they joined the A1 traffic, Nigel repeated his earlier suggestion, his tone calm. 'Put your foot down.' Ian duly obliged, entering a stream of traffic heading south towards Grantham.

Their pursuer was behind them, keeping a reasonable distance.

'I don't think it's going to be very easy losing him on a dual carriageway. How can we lose him on a straight road?' Nigel looked back over his right shoulder, watching their pursuer following them.

Ian swerved violently into the stream of traffic currently using the outside lane to overtake some fifty-mile-an-hour cruisers. *At least they're not hogging the outside lane,* he thought. Whereupon he caught up with a Metro driver obstinately sticking to the national speed limit when the inside lane was free.

'Get out of the bloody way,' Ian shouted as he flashed his lights impatiently.

The Metro driver looked over his left shoulder to check the inside lane was clear, which it had been for at least half a mile, and indicated left. A hundred yards later, he eventually decided to complete the mirror, signal, manoeuvre procedure and tucked himself neatly into the slow lane, slightly overdoing it and running over the paintwork that separated the carriageway from the drainage gutter.

'About time too,' Ian exclaimed. He put his right foot to the floor and waited for the car to respond, which it did. Unfortunately, Parrot was now directly behind them and was not about to let them out of his sight. For the next fifteen miles or so, Parrot kept close enough to ensure no other car nipped in between them.

'He's smiling at us,' Nigel observed.

'I know. Planning his next move, I reckon. I wonder why he's got a left-hand-drive car. And more to the point, I wonder what he wants.'

'Well, that's easy enough. He wants our money from yesterday, obviously. Hold on, he's overtaking.'

Ian watched the car gradually pull out and move alongside their car. The road behind them was clear of traffic, probably for the first time since they'd joined it, very unusual for this neck of the woods.

Nigel also watched and noticed the left-hand front window begin to lower. 'Bloody hell, he wants a chat by the looks of things – he's opening his window.'

Parrot lifted his left hand and pointed a gun towards the front offside wheel of Ian's car.

'Shiiiittt, he's got a gun. Do something!' Nigel's demand came with no instructions on what the 'something' should be.

Ian hit the brakes, putting the car into a skid and burning a great deal of rubber.

Parrot shot past, cursing at having missed his opportunity to finish the two with one easy accident. He slowed down and moved over to the side of the road, turning on his hazard lights. To anyone else, it would appear he had broken down and was just coasting to an emergency telephone. To Nigel and Ian, however, it was a ploy to allow them to move past him so he could begin the pursuit once more.

Studying Form

'What are we going to do?' Nigel turned to his friend. They were both scared out of their wits.

'Whatever we do, we can't let him get on the outside of us again. That's probably why he's got a left-hand-drive car – so he can shoot people easier!' Ian took a deep breath and accelerated into the right-hand lane and past Parrot who turned off his hazard lights and took up the chase again.

'This is impossible. Slow down and let some traffic catch us up, then we can mingle with it,' Nigel suggested.

'Mingle, mingle! This isn't a bloody party, you know. I'm not hanging around.' Ian looked in his rear-view mirror and swore under his breath. Ahead of them was an open road. The carriageways were empty. And the scenery was quite pleasant. Fields of green and yellow on either side of the road. The only thing that was clear in Ian's mind was someone wanted to kill him. And Ian didn't want to die. After all, he still owed his mother £100, he hadn't finished paying for his old Fiat Panda and he wasn't wearing clean underwear. 'You can't have an accident in dirty underwear,' his mother used to say. And he didn't want to die because he had Zoë now.

'Well, have you got any better ideas?' Nigel asked. 'He's gaining on us.'

Ian didn't have any better ideas. But then, all of a sudden, the answer was staring him in the face. He looked in the rear-view mirror once more and saw a few cars some way off behind them. 'Hold tight,' he said to Nigel. 'And if you've got a guardian angel, say a little prayer.'

Nigel looked at Ian then looked out of the front of the car to where Ian was looking. 'You can't be serious.' He turned back to Ian. 'You'll kill us both.'

'Just hold on and pray.' At the last moment, and at 115 miles per hour, Ian flung the car left from the outside lane towards a raised Police Observation point. The car hit the bottom of the ramp and, momentarily, ducked down on its front suspension. The front bumper disintegrated on impact, throwing sparks and debris in all directions. The sudden impact caused both airbags to inflate.

'Aaagggghhh,' was all Nigel could muster. Ian, on the other hand, held on to the steering wheel so tightly his knuckles turned white. He closed his eyes, left his face to be engulfed by the airbag and left his destiny to the gods who proceeded to catapult him, Nigel and half a tonne of metal skywards towards a field of rape.

Parrot couldn't believe what he was seeing. There was no way he was going to follow them off the road in that, somewhat unorthodox, fashion. He smiled as he watched the car leave the road and take off, wheels spinning out of control. 'Safe landing!' He laughed to himself and pulled on to the side of the road once more. He got out of the car and looked towards the field. He could see nothing. The rape plants were six feet tall. For all he knew, the car could have somersaulted, the occupants could be dead.

Studying Form

The car had actually landed on its back axle, causing the rear bumper to disintegrate. Two bounces and the car had come to rest quite safely. The engine was racing because Ian had his feet hard down on both the clutch and the accelerator. Eventually, he regained his senses and began to splutter. 'Jesus Christ, these airbags are dangerous. You can't see where you're going! Where are we anyway?'

'Turn off the engine.' It was more of a plea than a request. Nigel had had enough.

'Do you think we've lost him?' Ian enquired.

Nigel stared at his friend then looked out of the back window. There was nothing but rape plants. 'I don't think he's following us, somehow.'

'No, no. You're right.' And then on reflection, Ian said, 'Pretty good move then. I knew we'd lose him. But now we've got to get out of here. Which way do we go? You're the one with the map.'

Nigel stared out of the car, straight on and straight into a field of rape. 'You know what? I have absolutely no idea. Let me consult the map for a moment. Hmm, I'm not sure which field we are in. I have the A1 it's this red line here, and I know we are heading down the page but that, unfortunately, is all I can offer. Straight on, if the car still works, is all I can suggest.' Nigel sighed and looked towards Ian for inspiration.

'OK, OK, let's think. We've just given a bad guy with a gun the slip. Now all we've got to do is find a gate and then a road. Simple.' Ian opened the sunroof and gestured for Nigel to stand on his seat and poke his head out of the roof and above the crop. Reluctantly, Nigel complied with his friend's request and raised himself above the tall vegetation.

After a couple of moments, Nigel got his bearings and suggested Ian drive slowly straight on. There was, Nigel thought, a hedge which would, in turn, lead to a gate.

Parrot watched with some amusement. Nigel's head seemed to float through the field, the car completely obscured by the rape crop. 'Well, I'll be...' He got back into his car and pulled out to re-join the traffic.

Eventually, Nigel found a gate and thus an exit from their rape-field maze. He jumped out of the car and opened the gate to let Ian drive through.

'I don't know where we are, so you'd better just drive for a bit,' Nigel suggested quietly.

Ian was strangely silent. The reality of the last fifteen minutes was beginning to sink in; the adrenaline had left his bloodstream, and he was consumed by a sudden fear. He stopped the car and turned off the engine. Nigel looked towards him, saying nothing. A tear rolled down Ian's cheek. 'We should be dead right now.' He sighed and opened his door. 'We'd better look at the damage. I think we might have dropped something on take-off and landing.'

Nigel made his way to the back of the car whilst Ian went to the front. 'No bumper!' They said in unison and both laughed nervously.

Studying Form

'What's done is done,' Ian said, somewhat philosophically. 'We'll have to find a garage because we're illegal without lights and number plates.'

'And bumpers!' Nigel added.

'And bumpers,' Ian agreed, absentmindedly. 'Why does someone want us dead? Were they trying to kill us or just scare us? Were we their intended target, or could it have been a case of mistaken identity? Are we safe now, or still on some person's hit list? What the fuck is going on?'

'Let's find a garage, a pub and a hotel – in that order. Then we'll run through all those questions again.'

A signpost greeted them at a T-junction, and Ian decided on a left turn towards Marton and Grafton.

'Why left?' Nigel asked.

'It's north, and there are a couple of villages which are close to a junction where we can easily get back on the A1.'

After a few miles, they pulled into a garage which had a large sign reading 'MOTs while u wait', so it was reasonable to assume they would have an onsite workshop. Ian went in search of the proprietor to see if they could have the car looked at, whilst Nigel went into the garage kiosk to ask about accommodation in the area.

They met back at the car, where Ian pointed out the absence of bumpers, number plates and light clusters to a bemused mechanic.

'How do you lose two bumpers?'

'We hit some bumpy terrain earlier in the day. Mucking about along some dirt tracks in a forest.'

Dirt and plant life were evident under the wheel arches, so the mechanic didn't see fit to ask any more questions. 'I can do it, but not until tomorrow. I'll have to go into town to pick up spare parts. There's a bit of panel beating needs to be done, and you've completely lost a bracket at the front, so I'll have to weld a new one on. You've also picked up some deep scratches along the left-hand side of the car. You must have scraped past some bushes or something. I can't do the paintwork. But I've got this mate—'

'No, you're alright there – the re-spray will have to wait. Just the front and back, that's all. Oh, and I'd appreciate it if you'd look at the suspension as well. We, er, hit some big potholes.'

The mechanic shook his head in disbelief. 'I don't know… you youngsters. Well, at least it keeps me busy. Leave it with me, and I'll have it ready for you by six or seven tomorrow night. I'll need proof of car ownership for the number plates though.'

'No problem, it's all in the glove compartment.'

'I've found somewhere to stay, but it's about five miles down the road. The Swan?' Nigel looked at the mechanic, to see if he knew the place.

'Yeah, you'll like it there. Especially if you drink bitter. Try the Bass.'

'Any idea how we get there? We've got quite a bit of luggage.'

'Bloody hell, so now I'm a taxi service, am I? I'll get the truck.'

Friday, 21 June
– Evening

'They did what?' Trist was furious as he listened to Parrot recount the events of the afternoon. 'Cars don't fly off the side of roads. Cars don't hide in fields of corn!'

'It wasn't corn, and yes, they do.' Parrot knew he was in for some stick from Trist, but he also knew how to handle it. 'You told me to scare them and to choose my own methods. Well, I reckon they are as scared as hell right now. I saw their faces. They saw my gun. They ran for their lives. I don't think you'll have any trouble with them going forwards.

'By the way, that computer system of theirs works, you know. I saw them pick up a considerable amount of money at Ripon.'

'I thought you said Redcar?'

'Today they went to Redcar, but it seems they were just spectators this time. Yesterday, it was Ripon, and they won a lot of money.'

'OK, so they might have a system, but I'm not interested in their system. I just don't want them troubling Collier again. He's getting nervous, says he doesn't want to train horses for me anymore. He thinks he can do without me, now he's had a few winners for other owners. I've decided to let him get on with it for a few months, until this whole thing blows over.' Trist went across to a drinks cabinet and picked up a bottle of Talisker. He poured himself a generous measure then lifted the bottle, offering Parrot a drink.

'No thanks, it's a bit too hot for me I'm afraid, a bit too peppery.'

'Suit yourself.' There were a multitude of bottles on display – whiskies, ports and gins, but it seemed Parrot had missed his chance – Talisker or nothing. 'So what now?'

'It's up to you.'

'It was rhetorical,' Trist said, a bit too forcefully.

'I know, but I think they'll stop their betting activities for a while because that Griffiths guy will have probably stolen their computer by now.'

'What? What makes you say that?' Trist asked as he turned abruptly towards Parrot.

'Well, I had a word with the bloke a couple of days ago. He was very accommodating when I suggested he leave the two lads to me. I suggested he make himself scarce, and he left immediately.' Parrot smiled as he recalled the look of terror in Griffiths' eyes when he was confronted with the dangerous end of a gun. 'I suggested he went looking for their system elsewhere. I'm assuming that is exactly what he will have done.'

'OK. I think I'll call the matter closed, for now. Just make sure the two kids keep away from Collier for the next couple of weeks. Let me know what they do next.'

Studying Form

Parrot wasn't happy with the ambiguity of the final request. Nonetheless, as he picked up his coat, he agreed to keep Trist informed, then he let himself out.

Trist walked over to his phone and picked up the receiver. Pushing a button on the inside of the receiver, the phone dialled a pre-programmed number, and he heard the ringing tone almost immediately. Eventually, Collier answered.

'James, Derek here.'

'Oh, hello.' There was an audible sigh. 'It's late, what do you want?'

Trist paused to take another sip of whisky. 'I fully accept you have not enjoyed our relationship in the past, and I appreciate your honesty and integrity. I understand the contact you have had with that so-called journalist has been both unnerving and worrying to you. For that, I apologise. I would, however, like to maintain our relationship. I want to buy another horse. Would you be prepared to find one for me and, obviously, train it?' Trist knew Collier's stable was not full and trainers never liked to turn away a new, lucrative challenge.

Collier sighed, and his shoulders sank. This game was making him old before his time. 'I'd be delighted. But please. I do not like it when my integrity is questioned. I accept I have helped you see a few more winners than is strictly legit., but I cannot accept being challenged in that way. Integrity is everything in this industry. If I lose my integrity, my career is over.'

Trist reassured Collier he was free to train as he saw fit, and he, Trist, would ask no non-legit favours for the foreseeable future.

*

Ian and Nigel made themselves comfortable in the amply appointed family room which was the only room available at the hotel. Ian flicked through the channels on the TV, hoping to find some satellite entertainment.

'What are you looking for?' Nigel shouted from the bathroom. He could hear Ian channel-hopping. Poking his head around the door, his face covered in shaving foam, he asked, 'You're not looking for *adult* entertainment, are you?'

'It would be better than all this reality TV and DIY garbage!' Ian replied.

'Any luck?' Nigel enjoyed the occasional skin flick when the mood took him.

'Nah, we've just got the four terrestrial channels, by the look of things. I'm going to nip downstairs to make a phone call and see how Zoë is.'

'What's wrong with the phone up here? I promise I won't listen!' Nigel felt somewhat aggrieved.

'It's not that. But yes, you would listen, and you know it. It's the cost of the call that gets my goat. There's a payphone outside, and it'll be cheaper than whatever this place charges.'

Neither Nigel nor Ian had noticed the telephone box was actually within the boundary of the hotel, and that it was one of the old traditional red boxes rather than the type British Telecom had replaced them with for the updated public phone network throughout the eighties. The hotel owned it. So, Ian actually made his call from a payphone outside which charged the same rate as the telephone in their room.

The hotel manager could see the phone box from where he was standing behind the bar, and he smiled to himself as he poured a pint of bitter for one of his regulars. The customer took his beer from the manager and glanced in the direction the manager had been looking. 'You're a cheeky sod.'

'Business is business,' the manager replied.

Ian spent longer than he intended on the phone to Zoë and was surprised at how little time he got for his twenty pence coins. He made his way into the bar and ordered himself a bottle of Newcastle Brown. Taking the bottle and leaving the half-pint glass on the counter, he made his way to a chair by the window and settled himself down, deep in thought.

The manager walked over and put the glass on the table next to Ian's bottle of Brown. 'I'd prefer it if you used this,' he said politely.

Ian raised his eyebrows but decided against a sarcastic remark. Things were not going very well at the moment. This was proving to be a very bad day. 'Why?'

'I'm not too keen on the impression it gives to other customers. I accept it's a bit old-fashioned, but I'm sure you understand.'

'Completely, don't give it another thought. I'm alright sitting here though, am I?'

The manager smiled and went back to the bar. Ian poured some beer into the glass and then continued to drink from the bottle. He didn't usually drink from the bottle and, if truth be told, he agreed with the sentiments of the hotel manager. But right now, Ian was totally fed up and in no mind to comply with any social rules of etiquette.

Nigel made his way over to Ian half an hour later, having nicked himself shaving and smelling a bit too much of shower gel. Why on earth someone had invented menthol-scented shower gel was beyond Ian's comprehension. The stuff stank. Nigel knew Ian didn't like it. 'My two friends liked it, last night.'

'For £200, I'm not surprised. We are in trouble, mate, serious trouble. Get yourself a drink and bring over the menu. I need some food, some serious food.' Ian drained the last of the brown ale from his bottle and passed it to Nigel. 'And I'll have another one of those, please.'

Nigel spent the next few minutes talking amiably with the hotel manager, seeking advice on the best bitter behind the bar and the best meal on the menu. Eventually, he returned to the table with a pint of Sam Smiths and a second bottle of Brown for Ian.

'The manager apologises for the bottle being warm, but he said there were no more on the cold shelf. He also said the glass would cool it down. Gave the impression you'd know what he was talking about?' Nigel enquired.

'Oh, it's nothing. He just prefers the customers to use a glass rather than drinking out of the bottle, that's all. I tried to be clever and refused to use a glass, so warm beer is my reward. Serves me right, I suppose,' Ian said, philosophically. 'Anyway, you're not going to believe what's happened. Where's the menu, by the way?'

'Damn, hang on a minute.' Nigel returned to the bar and picked up the menu he'd left behind. He also picked up his change. Returning to the table, he tossed the menu to his friend, suggesting the beef wellington. 'The manager recommends it.'

'We've been robbed.'

Nigel laughed into his pint. 'You're not kidding, we've been robbed. We've been temporarily robbed of our car. We've been nearly robbed of our lives. And I feel like I've aged ten years today, robbed of my youth. You're damn right we've been robbed. That's probably the understatement of the year.'

Ian just stared at Nigel, expressionless and very tired.

Nigel saw his friend was not happy. He put down his pint, centring it on the beer mat and turning the mat carefully through ninety degrees. 'What do you mean, robbed?' he asked quietly.

'Burgled, we've been burgled. Zoë went round to the house last night. The back door was open, and lights were on. She went in. I can't believe she went in, but she did. A bloke ran past her carrying our monitor and knocked her flying. He ran out of the house and shouted, 'Tell them to back off.'

'Is Zoë OK? Has she called the police? Are you OK?'

Andy Wheildon

'No, I'm not OK, and Zoë is bruised along one of her arms. In Zoë's words, things are missing.' Ian paused. 'Like I said, I can't believe she went into the house.'

Nigel was ashen-faced and, for a moment, quiet. 'What things are actually missing? You're very calm.'

'I'm very numb. I'm tired. And to tell the truth, I'm scared. We've had a gun pointed at us today. We've been burgled today... well, last night. What else can happen? What's going on?' Ian took a mouthful of beer, having poured some into his glass.

'I'll put some bottles in the freezer, to chill them quicker, if you like,' the manager called over from behind the bar, looking pointedly at Ian drinking from the glass.

Ian smiled at the manager and acknowledged it was a good idea. 'The computer has gone – the computer, the monitor, the keyboard and all the cables. The modem has been left, if that is the little box Zoë referred to. Apparently, there's nothing missing downstairs. The telly, stereo and video are still there. So are all the tapes.'

'What about my room?' Nigel enquired. 'What's missing from there?'

'Zoë has never been in your room. At least I hope she hasn't! So she wouldn't know one way or the other.'

'Of course not, silly me. What a nightmare. Is the house secure now, do you know?'

'Zoë called the police last night, and they advised a locksmith. She was up until two this morning, and her parents are not happy at all. The house is, however, secure.'

'Jesus Christ, what a mess.' Nigel thought for a while then stated the obvious. 'When we get the car back, we'll have to go straight home.'

'Thank God we password protected the computer and the files. No-one will be able to use them, I hope.'

'Thank God I changed the insurance to cover the computer equipment. And I exaggerated the value!'

'All things considered, the damage isn't too bad, is it?' Ian was beginning to relax. Newcastle Brown was powerful stuff on an empty stomach. He took another mouthful and burped as he swallowed. 'It always makes me do that when it's warm,' he said, looking into his raised glass. 'The damage is purely material and psychological, I suppose. The material damage is superficial and can be repaired or replaced. The psychological scars may be more difficult to overcome. You said you were scared. Well, so was I this afternoon. I had no idea backing a few winners could be so dangerous.'

'Zoë can't be too happy either. When you call her, tell her I said hello. And tell her I'm sorry, for what it's worth.' Nigel picked up one of the menus.

'There's no need to apologise to her, but a word of thanks when you see her next won't go amiss.' Ian picked up the other menu and quickly scanned its contents. 'Surf and turf for me, I think. I also think a couple of bottles of wine should be the order of the day. I don't mind if I have a hangover tomorrow. We won't be going anywhere until the end of the day, if the mechanic has got his estimates right, so I think I'll have a drink.'

Nigel sighed. His friend was not the best of drinkers. Tommy-Two-Pints was a nickname which came well-earned.

*

Fortunately, the mechanic was true to his word and the car was ready to be picked up at 7.15 the following evening.

'It cost us £500 for labour and £450 for parts, but it seems as though he did a good job.' Ian rested his head in his hands, elbows on the kitchen table, as he finished recounting the previous day's events to Zoë.

Nigel had taken himself off to visit some friends for the evening. His parting comment had been 'Don't wait up', winking at Ian, knowing Zoë would see.

Zoë turned to face Ian, wiping her hands on a tea towel. 'You'll have to tell the police, you know. They were very suspicious when I told them what had gone missing. It wasn't a normal burglary, as far as they were concerned. TVs and videos get pinched in normal burglaries. This one, according to one of the policemen, was a professional job. The burglar knew what he wanted and didn't waste any time on incidental items.'

'Pity really, we could have done with a new video recorder. Seriously though, I don't think Nigel wants to tell the police anything. I'm not sure why. What we've been doing is legal. At least I think it is.'

Studying Form

Ian sat up and drew back on the chair, away from the table.

Zoë sat on his lap and ran a hand through his hair. 'I've missed you, you know. I don't like the idea of you driving off roads at a hundred miles an hour. I can't believe the two of you are so blasé about the whole incident. Guns? It's ridiculous.' Zoë gently kissed Ian on his forehead.

'Now that's just what I need,' he said, staring into her eyes. In no time at all conversation had ceased in favour of a passionate interlude where they got intimately reacquainted with each other beneath the kitchen table.

Saturday, 22 June 1991

Price and Griffiths sat quietly at a table in Griffiths' front room, whilst Rebecca, Griffiths' daughter, busily connected cables between computer and monitor, and eventually plugged both into a four-gang power supply on the floor beneath the table.

'Right, that's everything connected,' Rebecca informed her audience, brushing her long auburn hair off her face with a quick flick of a hand across her forehead. She noticed Price looking at her and smiled. 'Where has this come from, Dad? Or should I not ask?'

'You can ask,' Griffiths replied, with no intention of elaborating further.

Rebecca Griffiths got the message and chuckled.

'I see, I see, I get the picture,' she joked, quoting from a Monty Python sketch. The quote was lost on her father and Price. 'Here goes then.' Rebecca turned on the computer and then the bulky CRT monitor which came to life with a few crackles of static electricity. The computer clicked merrily through its boot-up sequence.

Griffiths watched closely as the screen began to display information. It all meant nothing to him, the relatively new digital revolution having passed him by completely. Rebecca noticed his look of bewilderment and decided to help him out. 'It's checking the Random Access Memory,' she informed him.

'I knew that!' Griffiths replied defensively. He hadn't got a clue.

'The what?' asked Price, not wishing to be left out.

'The Random Access Mammary,' said Griffiths authoritatively.

'Oh, I see.' Price seemed happy. Griffiths and Rebecca laughed. '`Enter Password`.' Price was now reading from the screen. He looked towards Griffiths then to Rebecca.

'Well?' Rebecca asked, hands poised over the keyboard and ready to type.

Price looked at Griffiths once more, then they both looked at Rebecca and shrugged. 'Your guess is as good as mine,' Griffiths informed his daughter. 'We haven't the foggiest. That's why you're here. You're the expert, aren't you?'

'Well, yes. I know my bits from my bytes and my objects from my procedures. I could build you an application using Fortran or Cobol. Unfortunately, guessing a password is slightly beyond me.'

'Is there nothing you can do, surely there is something?' Price pleaded.

Without saying anything, Rebecca got up and left the room. Within a couple of minutes, she returned with a handful of floppy disks and a screwdriver. 'First, we'll try the software. If the software fails, we'll take the computer to bits, rip the hard disk out and piggy-back it onto my own.'

'Obviously,' Griffiths said. Rebecca could have been speaking French for all he knew.

'Here, hold these.' Rebecca passed the disks to her father, making him feel useful again. 'Pass them back to me in turn, when I ask for them. They should be in order.'

Griffiths read the disk labels, noting they were labelled 'Disk1', 'Disk2', etc.

After ten minutes of to-ing and fro-ing with one disk and then another, Rebecca announced success, 'We're in.' She got to work scanning the root directory for executable files, finding none other than `autoexec.bat` and `config.sys`, which surprised her initially. Then she noticed a batch file, `DATA.BAT`, which she displayed on the screen. Reading the file contents, she mimicked the batch file instructions, typing each instruction on the keyboard.

Eventually, she launched an executable file called `FORTUNE.EXE` tucked away in a subdirectory, feeling a surge of excitement. *A program with a name like that must be good*, she thought. Almost immediately her high hopes were dashed when the computer beeped and asked for a password.

'Oh, not again,' Price sighed. 'Well?' He looked to Griffiths' daughter.

'No chance. The power-on password was easy enough to get around, but file passwords, especially in executable files, are nearly impossible. I'm not wasting my time on it. You've got just as much chance as a monkey typing randomly. I could try a few, but I would only be guessing: birthdays, girlfriends, signs of the zodiac, anything like that. Why don't you just ask the owner?'

Price decided that that was exactly what he'd have to do. He'd threaten to expose Ian and Nigel if they didn't give him a share of the pie.

*

Ian carried a tray of cheese and biscuits into the living room and set it down on a small table in front of the sofa. Zoë opened a bottle of chilled Chianti and poured a generous measure into each of the three wine glasses, passing the first to Nigel then taking one herself.

All three gathered round the table snatching biscuits and fighting for the cheese knife.

'It's French, I'm afraid, the Swiss was too expensive,' Zoë said, referring to the Emmental.

It was a snack fit for a king, and Nigel said as much. 'You can't beat a good cheese and wine extravaganza. It should be made compulsory.' Nigel sat back in his easy chair, took a drink from his glass and gave an appreciative sigh as he balanced the glass on the arm of his chair. 'Tomorrow, we'll have to replace the equipment. Can you get the files back from your parents?'

Before they had set off on their recent expedition, Ian had taken a full back-up of all the files, including the data files from RLDS. Consequently, they would not have to backtrack, buying data they had already bought from RLDS.

'Pretty fortunate,' Zoë commented. 'So you could be back in business in a couple of days?'

'It's Sunday tomorrow, so yes, let's aim for being back in business by Tuesday. That gives us time to buy the computer, restore the files and download any new data. I want to be working on a fully recovered system by Wednesday night, if that seems reasonable?' said Nigel.

Zoë looked at Ian who shrugged. 'It shall be done, Obi-Wan Kenobi. We'll have to be up nice and early though. We can probably get a good deal on a new computer if we pay cash. So, we'll need to go to the bank first.'

'No chance, we'll pay by credit card. That's as good as cash, and it will be interest free for about sixty days.' Nigel looked smug.

'*And* you get some kind of free insurance if your purchase is over £100, I think,' said Zoë, with less smug confidence.

'OK, two-to-one. Whatever makes you both happy. Just remember to pay the statement on time!'

Ian took a bite out of a Hovis biscuit and followed it up with a bit of Blue Stilton.

Tuesday, 25 June 1991

Rebecca Griffiths walked into the living room and found her dad reading the *Evening Post* in front of the fire. She went over and lifted some coal out of the scuttle and added it to the dying embers. An unseasonal cold snap had descended upon Nottingham a few days after midsummer's day, and her dad did not like cold weather.

'Thanks, love.' Griffiths put his paper on his lap and smiled at his daughter.

'I'm in,' Rebecca said in a matter-of-fact tone.

'In what?'

'The computer you brought home a few days ago. I've accessed the program that was password protected.' She looked smug, her smile broad.

'Really? That's excellent news. Show me. How did you do it?' Griffiths let his newspaper fall to the floor as he got up from his chair and followed Rebecca into the front room, which he noted was a bit chilly.

'A friend of mine at work suggested I decompile the program; he gave me some software and it's worked. I decompiled the file called FORTUNE.EXE and then re-compiled it once I found the password. It's an excellent bit of coding.'

The computer monitor now displayed a menu, and one of the menu items said Build a Race.

Rebecca suggested they try it out. Griffiths agreed and watched intently as she typed on the keyboard.

`'Handicap Range?'`

Griffiths told his daughter to hang on as he went in search of that day's *Daily Mail*.

'OK, type this in: 0–90,' he said on his return.

`'Course?'`

'Yarmouth,' Griffiths read from the back pages.

`'Number of Runners?'`

'Six.'

`'Horse/Jockey?'`

'Blimey, they don't want much, do they?' Griffiths rattled off six horse names and six jockeys which took about ten minutes because Rebecca misspelled some of the names and the program complained about incorrect format from time to time.

Once the sixth horse/jockey combination had been typed into the application, the monitor displayed another prompt.

`'Distance?'` followed by, `'Expected Going?'`

Rebecca typed in `7` and then she successfully typed in `7f` followed by `good`.

The monitor then, almost immediately, displayed NEGEEN.

'Well, I never. Negeen won the 3.15 at Yarmouth this afternoon.' Griffiths' heart was racing.

'Wow,' ventured Rebecca. 'Does this thing predict the winner of horse races? That's amazing and, surely, impossible?'

Studying Form

Griffiths told his daughter all he knew about the System, and they both wondered what their next step should be. 'Whatever happens, I won't be telling Price.' Griffiths was adamant.

'We should try it out for real, shouldn't we?' Rebecca asked. 'Tomorrow? Why not right now?'

'Let me go and get the *Post*. Let's see what the computer thinks about a couple of races tomorrow afternoon.' Griffiths nipped back to the sitting room to retrieve his paper from the floor and returned to the front room where Rebecca sat with an eager air of expectation.

Griffiths turned to the racing page near the back of the broadsheet and had a bit of a fight with the pages whilst he folded the paper in half. He studied the page which detailed runners and riders for the following day and said to his daughter, 'It's a bit busy tomorrow. We've got Carlisle, Kempton, Chester and Salisbury to choose from. Let's go for Carlisle. It looks like there are...' Griffiths scanned the page. 'Three handicap races and one of them is for amateur jockeys so let's ignore that one.'

Over the next twenty minutes, Rebecca entered information, fed to her by her dad, into the computer and, at last, saw a result. Apparently, Miss SaraJane was going to win the 3.15 at Carlisle the following day.

And it did, at odds of 11/2.

Over the next few days, Griffiths had five bets, with the first three proving successful. As the money rolled in, he increased the size of the bets, raising eyebrows in the betting shop he was using. The final two bets, placed on Saturday, were unsuccessful however. The betting shop manager relaxed, knowing he'd seen the last of this new punter now his luck had run out. Griffiths was extremely frustrated.

'Something's gone wrong with the System,' he said to Rebecca who knew full well the program was no longer making accurate predictions. She said she would decompile the program again and try to figure out how it worked to see if there was anything obvious that might be going wrong.

Wednesday, 26 June 1991

A new personal computer, a plethora of 3½ inch floppy discs, and a couple of happy chappies were sat watching the computer consume masses of data previously supplied by RLDS. It had cost approximately £1,500 to purchase the new equipment. The computer was the latest available specification – a Compaq with an Intel 386 processor running at 33MHz on the motherboard. It was now processing the information at breakneck speed. A blink of the eye and you missed a screen update that had been noticeably slower on their previous computer.

'The guy in the computer shop wanted me to buy an operating system called Windows,' Ian mentioned, whilst the two worked on restoring the files. 'Apparently, it's going to knock spots off DOS in years to come.'

Nigel clearly wasn't interested, so Ian didn't press the point.

Having restored the necessary applications and sorted out the modem link, they made contact with RLDS and waited patiently. The RLDS link finally finished transmitting up-to-date data with a parting message telling them a statement would be issued the next working day: Cost of transmission – £34.75.

'Jesus, that was cheap,' Ian said.

Andy Wheildon

'Yeah, you're not kidding. It was a good job we backed up most of the data recently. So, just over two and a half grand to get back to square one. A grand for the car, give or take, and one and a half for the computer. Let's see what the insurance company comes up with; I don't know, but we might be able to claim for lost data too. I'll have to look into it. I'll leave the car insurance alone.' Nigel scribbled a note on a yellow post-it and attached it to the cover of one of his form books. 'And now down to business. There are two races tomorrow which are right up our street.' The doorbell rang, giving Nigel an excellent opportunity to kick his friend out of the room.

Ian skipped down the stairs two at a time and, stumbling on the final step, crashed against the front door before opening it.

Brushing himself down and trying to regain his composure, he attended to the milkman who was in need of recompense for three weeks' worth of milk deliveries.

'Oh, and by the way, I ain't bin gettin' me empties back neither. Sort it out, will yer.'

'Yes, sorry about that. There are loads of bottles by the sink. I'll put them by the front door for tomorrow morning.'

'Good, don't forget to rinse 'em out first though.'

Ian closed the door and made his way into the kitchen. He spent the next thirty-five minutes cleaning the empties, drying them and polishing them until they shone. *I'll show him*, he thought.

Studying Form

*

Overnight, the heavens opened, and the gleaming bottles sitting on the front doorstep got splashed with dirt and ended up looking decidedly ordinary.

That'll teach me, Ian thought as he got in the car the next morning. Destination: Carlisle.

'Crikey, we'll probably sink the milk float with all of those,' Nigel quipped as he fastened his seat belt looking at all the milk bottles on the doorstep. He then turned in his seat, somewhat awkwardly, to reach for the road map on the back seat

'Why didn't you do that before you put your belt on?' Ian asked.

'Alright, smart arse, why don't you start the engine?' Nigel replied light-heartedly, as he turned back in his seat and fidgeted with his clothes, trying to make himself comfortable.

Nigel opened his map then realised he knew exactly where they were going, A50 to Stoke on Trent then north on the M6. Fortunately, Ian knew the A50 too, so there was no need for the map. It ended up tossed back on the rear seat.

He reached for another book – *One Hundred Great Handicaps* purchased in Derby at the end of March – and turned to the Carlisle page.

'Listen very carefully, for I will say this only once,' he said, and began to read from the book in a very poor French accent.

'Hang on a minute, a couple of days ago you mentioned going to Brighton,' Ian said. 'Did we miss that meeting because of the burglary?'

'Good question. Yes, we missed *yesterday's* meeting in Brighton, but it was abandoned after the second race when a sea fret blew in. It would have been a wasted journey.'

'Good job we got robbed then,' said Ian, with an air of sarcasm. 'What's the plan when we get to Carlisle?'

'You know something? I haven't a clue to be honest.'

'Really? So what are we doing driving to Carlisle?'

'There are two races at the meeting we could be interested in. One race has two horses running that are very close in our system, so I can't really decide between the two, but the other race has an outright winner as far as the System is concerned, problem is, it will probably start favourite so we won't win much money if we back it.'

'Surely, we go for the horse that has the best chance of winning?' Ian suggested.

'Yeah, you're right. Why am I being greedy? Ask your question again…'

'I have no idea what the question was but answer it anyway.'

So Nigel went on to explain why they were going to ignore the second race on the card and concentrate all their efforts and money on the fourth race.

Studying Form

Having paid their entrance fee and made their way to the Tattersalls bar, Ian and Nigel busied themselves in their own little worlds. Nigel continued to absorb the contents of the *Racing Post*, and Ian whiled away the minutes daydreaming.

'Penny for them?' Nigel offered, as he looked up, wrestling with his broadsheet, trying to turn a page.

'What? Oh, I'm miles away. Sorry. Just thinking about where this is all going to end. Am I going to race up and down the country for the rest of my life, taking money from the bookmakers? Or am I going to get bored with it all soon? And there's always the chance that maniac could raise his ugly head again. We might get shot at. We might get burgled again. We might get found out and barred from having anything to do with racing ever again. Can you get barred from racing? I suppose it must be possible.'

'Yes, of course you can, if you are found to be breaking the rules. You can be *warned off*, banned from meetings. But we're not doing anything wrong. If you're getting cold feet, maybe I should go it alone. The computer is set up and working. *I*'m not getting *bored*.

'I've put a lot of work into this,' he added. 'And so have you recently. The reason I'm doing it is to make money. Yes, horse racing is a hobby for most punters. It was for me, once-upon-a-time. But now it's my job. I'm going to make a living out of it: no nine-to-five job and no routine. Hard work during the Flat season and loads of fun during the winter months.'

'Hmm, that's a good point. Winter. I'd forgotten the Flat season takes a break. I don't suppose your system would work in Australia, would it?' Ian was beginning to relax once more. His bouts of uncertainty and a general lack of confidence often caused subdued periods. He had just spent fifteen minutes being uncertain and, as a consequence, had become subdued.

'You never know. But I was thinking more of a holiday in Florida. By the way: what's the capital of France?' Nigel asked.

'Paris,' Ian replied.

'No, F,' Nigel corrected, laughing at his poor joke as he walked away.

Ian shook his head in disbelief and smiled. All was well in the world once more.

Following Nigel towards the parade ring, Ian stopped abruptly to avoid walking into someone who passed him by. 'Did you see that?' he asked his friend, once he'd caught up. 'That bloke nearly knocked me flying.'

Nigel looked in the direction Ian was pointing. 'Well, I never,' he said. 'Now there's a turn up for the books. I knew he had a runner at the meeting, but I didn't think we'd actually see him.'

'You know him? Who is he?' Ian asked.

'That, my son, is the one-and-only *Lambourn Collier*, Mr James Frederick Collier. He might know something about our burglary and our altercation on the motorway. Let's find out.'

'Hold on a minute. You can't do that. Where do you get the notion he has anything to do with it?' Ian asked, somewhat anxious and reluctant to let Nigel confront the man.

'I've been thinking. We've been told we can't bet locally by the bookies in Nottingham, so we have stopped betting locally. The only other thing, in all of this, that could have caused a stir, is me phoning Collier and asking him about Tapestry. If that phone call put the wind up him, and he has shared his concerns with others, then he may have been the catalyst for our unfortunate adventure. Come on. We're going to talk to him.' Nigel made off in the direction Collier was heading.

'We?' Ian looked towards the heavens, knowing he was going to regret the next few minutes.

'Mr Collier,' Nigel shouted. 'A quick word, if you please.'

Collier stopped in his tracks and turned to Nigel. 'How can I help you? I'm quite busy.'

'I understand, Mr Collier.' Nigel held out his hand. 'Allow me to introduce myself. My name is Bishop, Conrad Bishop. We spoke some weeks ago, regarding your connections with one of your owners, Mr Derrick Trist.'

Collier withdrew his hand from Nigel's grasp. 'Well, Mr Bishop. I have absolutely nothing to say to you. I found your phone call very disturbing, especially because your accusations were without foundation. Good day to you.'

As Collier turned to walk away, Nigel grabbed him by his arm, and Ian's heart missed a beat. 'In the last seventy-two hours, Mr Collier, I have been shot at and burgled. If I find out it is Trist who has decided to get aggressive with me because of something you said to him…' Nigel paused, allowing his words to sink in. 'If I find out you are involved. I'll make such a fuss, such a commotion, you'll have empty stables in no time. I hope I've made myself clear.'

Nigel let go of Collier's arm and walked away.

Ian stood there for a few seconds, rooted to the spot, mouth open, not believing what he'd just heard. He stared at Collier who stared right back.

It was Collier who made the first move. He approached Ian and shook his head in disbelief.

'I assume you are with that man,' Collier said, pointing at Nigel who continued to walk away without looking back. 'I am a capable trainer of horses, and I conduct myself professionally with a high level of competence and complete integrity. I discuss the horses in my charge with the owners on a frequent basis, including any concerns I may have regarding external influences. Following the call from Bishop, I advised Mr Trist immediately and nothing, I repeat, nothing that has happened to your friend there was a result of that phone call as far as I'm concerned. Good day.'

As Collier walked away, Ian felt the blood drain from his face. His heart was pounding. He was not enjoying this one little bit. He chased after Nigel who was mingling in the crowd congregating around the parade ring. Grabbing hold of his friend's arm, Ian turned him round so they were facing each other. 'Collier *has* told Trist about your phone call, but he maintains he has done nothing else. I believe him.'

Studying Form

'Relax. I've told him I know what's going on between him and Trist.'

'Yes, but you don't *know* what's going on, do you? You're only guessing. You could be wrong.'

'Not after that reaction. He was scared. He has something to hide, and now he thinks we know, he'll run to Trist.'

'And Trist will have someone shoot at us again, for Christ's sake.' Ian was aghast at Nigel's lack of concern. 'We're heading home straight after the race, you got that? I'm not staying here any longer than I have to.' Ian looked at Nigel, not sure if he really knew his friend anymore. 'Why antagonise the trainer?'

Nigel reflected for a moment and sighed. 'I don't like the idea of a dishonest owner jeopardising our system. Also, I don't like dishonesty,' he said, shrugging his shoulders. 'Anyway, I'll meet you back at the car. Good luck, and be careful out there!'

Ian found himself in no mood to walk amongst the betting public, placing his £50 notes with a string of bookmakers. Instead, he chose to pass £500 over the counter on the Tote, receiving looks of astonishment from the cashier and a punter to his left. 'Home improvement loan, courtesy of Barclays Bank,' Ian joked, and walked away.

Nigel had busied himself, as usual, with the task in hand, trying to extract the best odds from the line of bookies basking in the afternoon sun. He had been careless on some of his bets, waiting too long and seeing prices rubbed off and lowered before his very eyes. If truth be known, his mind was not on the job.

He was preoccupied with what both Collier and Ian had said. He would have to apologise to Ian. He would also have to decide whether to take the Trist/Collier matter further. He wondered if he could placate Collier by assuring him the matter was closed.

Anyway, the money was with the bookies and the horses were cantering to the start line to the left of the stands. Nigel had an excellent vantage point where he could see most of the racetrack and a TV monitor which would televise the race. It would also provide an instant replay, but Nigel knew he wouldn't be interested in that part of the broadcast.

Their horse, Trojan Lancer, was guided to an easy finish, taking victory from Azubah by a relaxing two and a half lengths. There had been no real contest from the four-furlong marker onwards – that's when it became obvious the only horse who could pose any real danger had run himself into all sorts of trouble on the rails, following a slowly run first mile. Trojan Lancer relished the uphill part of the run-in before the track levelled out near the winning post.

Some five minutes later, the 'Weighed In' announcement was made over the tannoy system, and Nigel began picking up his £1,800, Trojan Lancer having been returned at 9/4 favourite. Unfortunately, Nigel hadn't got 9/4 on all his bets. He was happy with the outcome, nonetheless.

The Tote dividends were announced as Nigel made his way to the car. The win dividend was declared at £3. Unbeknownst to Nigel, at that very moment, Ian was collecting his £1,500 and informing the cashier his *home improvements* were coming along nicely.

Fifteen minutes later, with both in the car and Ian driving towards the exit, Nigel asked how his friend had got on. 'Well?'

Ian turned to Nigel and forced a smile. 'Just the Tote today. I wasn't in the mood, to be honest. One and a half grand exactly'.

'Cool, I picked up about £1,800, I think.' Nigel offered his own return as a prompt to provoke Ian into conversation.

'We're dead anyway,' said Ian. 'What's three thousand three hundred quid between two corpses, arsehole?' Ian hit the brakes abruptly in a fit of anger.

Nigel lurched forwards, choking slightly on his poorly positioned seat belt. 'We're not going to die, you silly billy,' Nigel said, his tone mocking.

'Oh, how reassuring. It's pointless planning a pension with you and your big mouth around. I think life assurance would be a better bet. Leave a bit of money to Zoë and my parents. They'd like that. No, on second thoughts, I know what I'll do: I'll learn to fly... without a plane. Who needs a plane when you've got Doctor Death as your navigator? Left or right, by the way?'

Dr Death pointed left and started apologising for the afternoon's events.

Andy Wheildon

*

When the race meeting was over and the horses had been tucked away for the night, Collier contacted Trist who was just about to leave for the opera.

'Make it quick, I'm in a hurry,' Trist snapped.

'Remember Bishop? I saw him today, at Carlisle, somewhat annoyed at being shot at and burgled,' Collier said, in a matter-of-fact tone. 'Not very happy with me, this Bishop fellow. You wouldn't happen to know anything about guns and burglars, would you?'

Trist removed a white silk scarf from around his neck and sat down.

'You still there?' Collier enquired.

'Yes. I'm thinking.' After a brief pause, Trist said, 'Say nothing, do nothing. If you see him again, listen to what he says, because I'll want to know his exact words. But give him nothing. Understand?'

'You're a bastard, Trist. I've got nothing more to give. You've taken my honesty, robbed me of my integrity. You'll have taken everything dear to me if this gets out. Just get Bishop out of my hair.'

It was Collier who hung up first, which took Trist aback. He stared at the phone receiver as he placed it gently back on its cradle. Reaching for his Filofax, he flicked through the pages of the phone number section and contacted Parrot.

'Danny, Trist.' This kind of conversation had taken place between the two before, and Parrot instantly recognised the tone in Trist's voice. 'There

244

will be £30,000 in your account tomorrow. Mr Bishop and his friend require your immediate attention. Goodbye, Mr Parrot.' Trist hung up and sighed – his ruthless streak was becoming wearisome.

*

Parrot shook his head and walked over to a table, pulling open the left-hand drawer. There were three passports, carrying three different identities. Each had the same photo of Parrot. He chose the passport with the name Blundell – Rodney Blundell, bank manager. The other two he carried to an open fire and destroyed.

Rodney Blundell was his real name. He had been a successful bank manager for thirteen years, having progressed through the ranks with an exemplary record both internally and academically. He'd provided loans and finance to the general public and, of course, to friends, asking few questions when large deposits were made. Unfortunately for him and for the investigator he had had to kill one autumn evening, his career in banking had come to an abrupt end. His friends, whose money he had helped to launder, had looked after him, providing a new identity, with all the necessary papers, and a safe haven whilst police enquiries ensued.

The enquiries into the killing of a senior bank investigator had resulted in the trial and conviction of a petty thief who had been set up to take the fall. Gordon Price was now growing old gracelessly in Parkhurst Prison on the Isle of Wight, serving time for a crime he didn't commit back in 1984. The fact that he had eventually admitted to the killing had more to do with his diminished mental capacity than any evidence presented by the prosecution.

Picking up a holdall, Blundell left his flat, for the last time. He pushed his keys through a letterbox and listened to them land on the floor on the other side of the door. His landlady would be sad about his departure. They had had some good times together whilst her husband worked away from home. Blundell closed the front door to the house and his landlady became a distant memory.

Walking to the car, he hummed one of his favourite classical tunes 'In the Hall of the Mountain King' by Grieg, whilst he thought about the best course of action to earn his £30,000 and make good his escape. He had an open airline ticket and AUD$25,000 in a safe deposit box at his local bank. Unfortunately, the bank was closed at 7.45 p.m. He would have to call in later on his way to Heathrow.

Driving north and occasionally breaking the speed limit as he went, Blundell calculated he'd arrive at his intended destination at about 10.30 p.m. He would enter the premises, having been cordially invited to do so by one of the inhabitants. He would assess the situation and react accordingly. People would die tonight. He had his orders from Trist: the final orders he was prepared to take from anybody.

As he drove through the darkness, his thoughts wandered. He began to realise the enormity of the task he'd agreed to undertake. It was ill-conceived, pointless and totally futile. Seeds of doubt began to cloud his thinking and uncertainty raised its ugly head. He felt compassion once more for the two youngsters he was about to kill. A compassion he'd initially felt when his quarry had eluded him in the golden fields of rape only a few days before.

'Oh, just get on with it,' he told himself as he pulled out into the fast lane to overtake a number of slow-moving vehicles in the middle lane.

Friday, 28 June 1991
– Late evening

James Price pulled up a few houses down from where he knew Ian Turner and Nigel Green lived. The car was facing downhill on quite a steep slope, so he made doubly sure the handbrake was on and put it in third gear. Price got out of the car and straightened his coat. He had no idea how things were going to pan out in the next hour or so, but he had mentally prepared a script he hoped to follow. He took a deep breath and walked up to the front door.

'Good evening, Mr Turner. Ian Turner, isn't it? My name is Price. James Price. May I come in?' Price removed his cap and rolled it up, putting it in his overcoat pocket. He motioned into the house, but Ian stood his ground.

'No, you can't come in. It's late, and I don't know who you are. If you've come to read the meter, I suggest you go away and return at a more sociable hour. Goodnight.' Ian began to close the door, but Price blocked it with his foot.

'My business is horse racing, Mr Turner. And recently, I have made your business my business too. I know you have a betting system. I know the horses you've backed. I know where you've gambled, when you've gambled and how much you've gambled. I know, Mr Turner, you and your colleague have something quite remarkable. And I know, Mr Turner, I want a part of it, or I'll see it destroyed.' Price stared at Ian who fidgeted uneasily. 'I will probably destroy you as well.'

'You'd better come in.' Ian moved back, making room for Price to pass. He motioned for Price to continue straight through to the kitchen where Nigel was preparing a snack for the two of them.

'Something smells good,' Price said. 'Table for three?' His flippancy went unnoticed.

Nigel turned to look at the two of them as they entered the kitchen. He noticed Ian looking anxious. 'What's going on?' Nigel asked Ian. 'Who the hell is this?'

Price made himself at home, sitting at the table and picking up a slice of bread and butter. He looked at Ian, his expression inviting a formal introduction.

Ian shrugged his shoulders. 'His name is Price, and he reckons he knows about our racing activities.'

'Yes, I do know, gentlemen.' Price spent the next two minutes summarising what he knew of Nigel and Ian's betting activities over the past three months, detailing bank accounts, hotels, bars and racecourses. He read from a notebook, listing the horses backed, both in the betting shops and on the racecourses.

Ian and Nigel stood, silently, absorbing what was being said, gradually realising this person knew everything. Finally, when Price had finished, it was Nigel who asked the obvious question.

'So, what do you want?'

'A percentage, that's all. You two are the experts. You've got a computer system. Fortune dot exe is password protected. We work together, or I destroy your system. But I'm a reasonable man who wants to put money on racing certainties, just like you do.'

'Are you saying you've got my computer, you bastard?' Ian was beside himself with anger. 'I'm going to call the police.'

'Wait.' Nigel motioned for his friend to stop. 'What if we call the police, Mr Price?'

'Well, let's see now. No, I haven't got your computer. I'm not stupid. But maybe I know a man who has. If you call the police, I'll deny this conversation took place. I'll deny being here. I have done nothing wrong. The police, if you choose to involve them, will probably charge you with wasting their time. I wouldn't call them, if I were you.' Price shook his head and smiled.

'And don't bother calling Zoë, Mr Turner. I know where she lives. I know where she works. And I know who, on occasion, babysits her young child.'

As Price continued with his lecture, Nigel pressed the record button on the cassette player. Madonna would soon be history, but the whole conversation was now being taped. Nigel just prayed the cassette didn't run out and automatically click off too soon.

'What if we refuse to co-operate with you, Mr Price? We're doing nothing wrong. It's not us breaking the law. You're the one with the stolen goods, or at least you know their whereabouts. What if we just kick you out?' Nigel walked over to the refrigerator and got a can of beer for himself and Ian.

'If you ignore my request, if you attempt to continue using the System without me as a silent partner, as it were, then I'd be compelled to share your secret with everybody involved in horse racing. I know enough people, both honest and dishonest, who would kill for what you've got.' Nigel looked at Ian. Price had struck a raw nerve without knowing it. He continued. 'Reporters would snap up a story like yours. Your pictures would adorn the front pages of the sporting press. I know people within the industry who could distribute your photographs the length and breadth of Britain. Racecourses would recognise you and probably refuse admission. If you did get onto a racetrack, the bookies would recognise you, and you wouldn't get your bet on. Betting shops would have your picture, again preventing you from betting serious money. I could make your system useless nearly overnight.'

Nigel finished off his beer and belched. Staring at the ceiling, he cleared his throat. 'Rendering the System useless would benefit no-one—'

'On the contrary,' Price interrupted. 'My employers would be more than grateful to see a system such as yours destroyed. You see, they are in the industry too. Your system undermines the stability and profitability of the horseracing industry. I come out smelling of roses whatever the outcome, whatever you decide. I can't lose. Gentlemen, I'm on to a winner.' There was an air of arrogance in Price's voice, which needled Nigel.

Andy Wheildon

'No deal. We've got a system. It's ours, and you are not getting your hands on it. We'll just hibernate for a few months. Even for a few years. Anything you say to the press or your so-called friends will be forgotten by the time we step back into the ring.'

Without warning, the back door burst open, and Blundell walked in, holding a gun in his hand. 'Gentlemen.' Blundell looked at Nigel and then to Ian, both of whom had frozen when they saw the gun. He had their undivided attention. There was something wrong with the other man though, the one with his back to Blundell. The unknown man turned to look at him, shaking with fear.

'Good God. Price! It's been a long time. Eight years, at least.'

Price was just about to correct Blundell on the elapsed time since their last meeting when Blundell's gun coughed once. The bullet shattered Price's skull, and he was dead before he hit the kitchen floor, head leaking all over the linoleum.

Blood splattered over Nigel. Partially digested beer returned to the surface without hesitation. He turned to the sink and vomited over the dirty dishes. *Look at the mess I've made*, he thought. Ridiculous thought under the circumstances. At least he was still alive. *Sod the puke*, he decided.

Nigel slowly straightened and turned to review the scene. Nothing had changed. There was a body on the floor, a gunman by the cooker and a ghostly white friend rooted to the spot near the pantry.

Studying Form

Somewhat inadequately, Nigel pointed out the obvious. 'You've killed him!'

'Shut up and listen. That bullet was meant for you, and I've still got enough in the chamber to finish the job.' Ian sighed and fainted, falling to the floor. Blundell laughed, shaking his head in disbelief. Turning back to Nigel, he went on, 'I've been paid a considerable amount of money to kill you both. On the way here, however, I decided to disobey that order and give you a warning instead. There's someone out there who wants you both dead. Stop your exploits on the racetrack.'

'I don't understand.' Nigel looked down at Price who was still leaking blood all over the kitchen floor. Again, Nigel retched, but this time there was nothing in his stomach to throw up.

'Price was a man in the wrong place at the wrong time which, I might add, has always been a failing of the Price family in general. I'll be off now. I'm going to have to leave the body with you. I'm in a hurry, you understand.' Blundell took some rope from his pocket and asked Nigel to sit in the chair next to the one recently vacated by Price.

Nigel did as he was told. Blundell spent the next five minutes securing Nigel to the chair and ensuring Ian, who had a nasty bump on his head, would find it difficult to go anywhere in a hurry. Finally, Blundell stuffed some kitchen towel in Nigel's mouth and put heavy-duty sticking tape across his lips and eyes.

Andy Wheildon

'I'd be careful when you remove this, because it'll take your eyebrows and lashes. Don't say I didn't warn you.'

Nigel wasn't in a position to thank Blundell for his advice. He couldn't see anything, and he couldn't say anything. The way he was bound to the chair meant he couldn't move anything either.

'Right, I'll be off. Goodnight.' Blundell walked over to the door and, turning off the light, he left.

Nigel sat there, consumed by the silence.

It was impossible to struggle against the bindings that secured him to the chair, so he resigned himself to a long night of darkness, immobility and the stench of blood. He knew Price wasn't going anywhere. His only hope was Ian who had unfortunately banged his head on a counter when he crumpled to the floor. Nigel had been close to passing out too. His strength, he reasoned, came from the small amount of alcohol which had entered his bloodstream before the evening's catastrophic events had unfolded.

The cassette player clicked off.

*

Nigel was suddenly aware of another presence in the kitchen. He sat up straighter and concentrated on every sound. For the past few hours, his senses had been focused on his wrists and ankles. The twine securing them had become tight, and he was concerned by how numb they had become. Now, however, there was hope. *Please, be a friend*, he thought.

Studying Form

He was unable to say anything due to the tape across his lips and paper towel in his mouth. If he was perfectly honest, he didn't see the point in trying to say anything anyway. Until he was freed, his destiny lay entirely in the hands of others. It was pointless to mumble for help if the intruder had no intention of helping, pointless to plead for mercy if the intruder was merciless. If there were somebody there, in the kitchen, then he would either be freed or finished. He thought of Lucy and the tender moments they had shared together. He tried to smile, but the tape across his face made it difficult.

'Jesus Christ!'

'Mmmm.' Nigel recognised the voice as Zoë's. His heart missed a beat, and he rejoiced at the sound of her voice. Ian was the luckiest man alive, if he were still alive, to have a girl like Zoë. 'Mmmm.' He repeated, in an attempt to get her attention.

Nigel felt a hand against his face as Zoë took hold of the tape across his lips. Fortunately, she didn't yank the tape clear in one swift movement; she gently drew it back, easing it away from every whisker and hair.

'Jesus Christ,' she repeated, as she realised the tape had super-glue-like properties. She went towards the sink in the hope of finding a cloth to soak the tape off. Unfortunately, Price was in the way, staring up at her, motionless, dead now for three hours. Zoë screamed in shock and ran out of the kitchen. Nigel mumbled, but to no avail. Finding two people prostrate on the floor, one of them dead, and another sat, bound and gagged, on a chair, would be enough to render the most stable of characters momentarily unbalanced.

Zoë had seen enough. The man she loved was comatose on the floor, his best friend was tied up on a chair and a complete stranger lay on the kitchen floor with half his head missing. This was definitely a job for the police. She dialled 999 and had a hysterical conversation with an operator.

Within twenty-five minutes, Nigel had regained his sight and his capacity to speak, whilst Ian was nursing a large bump on his head, in no mood for conversation. He rested his head on Zoë's shoulder whilst he watched two ambulance men retreat from the kitchen. 'This is a crime scene. The police will call us back in when they're ready,' said one of the ambulance crew.

'I think it might be a good idea for you to go to the hospital,' Zoë suggested, looking at a dazed Ian.

He looked up and eventually focused on one of the detectives who had descended on their house.

'I'll come with you,' Zoë said reassuringly.

'What brought you over here so late at night?' Ian looked at Zoë, trying to focus properly.

'You asked me to call you last night, so I did. Three times. Initially, I thought you'd forgotten and nipped off to the pub. When I didn't get an answer at midnight... well, I wasn't going to get any sleep until I knew you were OK, so here I am.'

Ian got to his feet and felt a pounding in his head. The pain was unbearable for a couple of seconds, a thumping sensation inside his brain keeping time with his heartbeat. Eventually, his head got used to the new altitude and the pain subsided. *Next time, don't get up so quickly*, he thought, as Zoë guided him towards the front door and the waiting ambulance.

'So you don't know who the killer was?' Detective Constable Hicken turned his attention to Nigel who had remained seated amongst the human debris.

'Haven't a clue, I'm afraid. I reckon they knew each other though. The bloke said he was supposed to have killed *us*, me and Ian. This guy, Price, wasn't supposed to have been here. Even we didn't know Price before this evening. In walks Price, in walks a man with a gun and… bang.'

'Price. What did he want? Why was he visiting you, if you didn't know him?'

Nigel spent the next half-hour explaining to the detective how he and Ian had developed a seemingly unbeatable system that could predict the outcome of certain horse races. He described events leading up to the gun incident on the dual carriageway and the events of this evening.

A second detective walked into the kitchen and stared at Nigel.

'A bit of a mess, young man, don't you agree?'

'You could say that.'

'Yes, a bit of a mess.' The detective walked over to the sink and sniffed, turning up his nose at the stench. 'What happened here?' he asked, turning on the hot water tap.

Andy Wheildon

'My digestive system let me down when the bullet passed through Price's skull, I'm afraid.'

'Hmm, quite a graphic summary.' The detective smiled, turning off the tap and turning towards Nigel.

'Mr Price works, or rather he used to work, for one of the largest betting organisations in the country. I have been speaking to his superiors. Apparently, he's been a bit of a rascal over the years. Bending and breaking the rules along the way, though nothing bad enough to justify a red card. Just enough to ensure his employers kept a close watch on him.

'He's got a son, you know,' the detective went on.

Nigel shrugged his shoulders. 'No, I didn't know. I've told you: I didn't know Price before this evening.'

'Sorry. I was being rhetorical. Yes, a son named Gordon. Thirty-four years old, currently in Parkhurst prison, at Her Majesty's pleasure, having murdered a young investigator who was in pursuit of a dishonest bank manager.

'A strange case, according to my colleagues. The bank manager disappeared off the face of the Earth. According to the files of the unfortunate investigator, he was supposed to interview this bank manager on the night he was murdered. He went to the bank, got himself killed, and the manager... just vanished. When our lads got to the scene, they found a body, and a petty crook hiding behind a desk with the murder weapon in his hand.

'An open-and-shut case. Gordon Price admitted to the killing. His story was far from convincing. Unfortunately, the pressure was on us for a quick conviction, so Price took the rap. He was sent down indefinitely. And now look what happens. His dad takes a bullet in the head. It's all very strange.

'Oh, my name's Metcalf; I don't think I introduced myself. Have you been able to get us a description of the executioner?'

Detective Constable Hicken cleared his throat. 'Yes, sir. I have it here. I'm going to go down to the hospital to see if Mr Turner can add anything.'

'Very well, Hicken. I'd like a full report on my desk, first thing in the morning.' The detective walked towards the door of the kitchen and turned to look at Nigel. 'I'd get some sleep, if I were you. I need to see you at the station first thing too. Can you make it?'

Nigel said he'd be there at 9 a.m., sharp. Then all at once, he remembered the cassette tape. 'Hang on a moment,' he called to the detective who was making his way to the front door.

'What is it?'

Nigel moved across to the radio and rewound the cassette for a few seconds. With the volume turned up, it was possible to hear everything, every word, the single shot, even Ian falling to the floor.

'Bloody hell, sir. This is fantastic.' Hicken went to the radio and turned off the tape recorder, removing the cassette.

'Come on. Let's get that tape to the station and have a proper listen. Well done, Mr Green. I'm impressed.'

Nigel smiled weakly. 'I started the cassette recording so I could get evidence against Price, trying to get something on him to prove he was involved in the burglary in some way.'

The detectives left and the forensic team continued with their investigations. Nigel got a coat and was just about to go in search of somewhere else to stay for what was left of the night when the phone rang.

Saturday, 29 June 1991

Ian had spent the night at Zoë's after getting the all-clear and a packet of painkillers from the hospital. He hadn't been allowed to return to the house because it was still a crime scene, and forensics needed space to do their work. The doctor had taken a close look at him, paying particular attention to his eyes, then sent him for a routine X-ray.

'I'm going straight to Zoë's from here, and I'll be staying the night too,' he had informed Nigel from a payphone at 3.30 a.m.

'Oh, thanks. Don't mind me. I'll be fine.'

'You'll be all right. I'll see you in the morning. What time have they told you to be at the police station? Where are you staying tonight?'

'Nine o'clock, and I'm going to try Lucy's,' Nigel said.

'Me too. Nine o'clock not Lucy's. I'll see you there. I'm going to tell them everything they want to know. This is awful.'

'I know.' Nigel wanted nothing more than to get the whole mess cleared up. 'I'll see you later. Get some sleep. How's the head, by the way?'

'Bloody painful. My vision's a bit blurred, but apparently, it'll clear up in a couple of days. I've been told not to drink or drive.'

Andy Wheildon

'Every cloud.' Nigel said goodbye, hung up and set off for Lucy's, not caring about the late hour.

*

The following morning, Nigel took the bus to the police station, amused to see Ian and Zoë getting on the same bus some five or six stops along the way.

'My God, you look awful,' Nigel observed, by way of greeting.

'Thanks, and *hello* to you too.' It was true. Ian did look dreadful. He hadn't slept very well either. The slightest bit of pressure applied to the swelling on his head had caused a sharp pain to render him wide awake.

Nigel turned his attention to Zoë who also looked a bit pale. 'As beautiful as ever,' he said, trying to be sincere.

'Nice try. I look bloody awful too.' Zoë had her parents to thank for that. An interrogation from them both over the breakfast table had put Zoë in a dreadful mood.

Nigel noticed a slight hostility in her voice and decided silence, rather than idle talk, was the order of the day. He turned away and gazed out of the window, reflecting on the events of the past few months.

'Sorry, I didn't mean to snap.'

'Don't worry about it. I think we're all a bit tired.'

The bus reached the city centre and discharged its contents onto the street. They stood at the foot of the stairs waiting whilst a steady procession of early shoppers made their way from the upper deck.

'It must be a Tardis up there,' Nigel quipped, turning to Ian and Zoë. The procession turned to a trickle and Nigel was finally able to make his way to the front of the bus, thanking the driver as he got off.

He turned to watch Ian and Zoë say farewell with a tender, lingering kiss. Zoë smiled at Nigel and went off to work.

'Finished, have we?'

'Just,' replied Ian.

*

Detective Sergeant Stanley Metcalf had been at work since six o'clock. He had the enviable fortune of not needing much sleep to recharge his batteries. It was an attribute that allowed him to put more hours into the day when investigating serious or sensitive cases.

This murder intrigued him. The victim, James Price, was an unannounced guest who had a son currently serving a prison sentence for a murder committed some years earlier. He was aware of the Gordon Price case and the eventual outcome. He was aware of the rumours that had surrounded the case. Gordon and his family, it was rumoured, had been handsomely rewarded for taking a guilty plea to protect others.

Metcalf had put in a request to central records for authority to re-examine the Gordon Price case with a view to reopening it.

Andy Wheildon

The phone rang on Metcalf's desk. Stubbing out a cigarette and clearing his lungs of smoke, he picked up the receiver, 'Metcalf.'

'Stan, Jonathan here. Jonathan West.' A moment's silence inferred Metcalf didn't recognise the name. 'I worked on the Gordon Price case in the mid-eighties, and I've been asked if I have any objection to you reviewing our notes.'

'Jonathan, yes. I'm sorry. Your name had slipped my mind. I thought it was Kendrick who led the investigation, as senior officer.'

'Yes, sir. That's right. Unfortunately, Kendrick died three years ago.'

'Really, I didn't know.' Metcalf reached for a packet of cigarettes and took one out.

'The Big C, I'm afraid. Too many damn cigarettes.' Metcalf threw his cigarette into the bin, followed by the rest of the packet. 'Anyway, I'm interested to know your motives for looking at the files – it's no secret we thought the wrong person had been sent down. All water under the bridge now, though, I'd have thought.'

Metcalf spent the next thirty-five minutes describing the previous evening's events. '... and it's the first time I've investigated a crime that has actually been recorded on tape!'

'Quite astonishing. Do you mind if I come up? Purely in a support capacity, as an observer, we could say?'

'I don't see why not. I'll get my Chief Inspector to put in a request to yours. Could you pull the file for me, seeing as it's in your neck of the woods? ... I'll see you as soon as the paperwork's sorted then. Goodbye.' Replacing the receiver, Metcalf opened the drawer and started to write an internal memo to his boss. 'Bloody paperwork,' he muttered.

A few minutes later, he handed the memo to his secretary. 'Type this up and pass it to the Chief, there's a good girl,' he said.

'Certainly, sir.' Janice was well used to his patronising manner and ignored it. Her intercom buzzed. 'That's the Price witnesses here, by the looks of it.'

'Good. I'll see one of them with Jenkins now. Hicken and Lambert can have the other one.' Metcalf wandered over to the coffee machine and made himself a drink. 'Janice?'

'Not for me, thanks. I've just had one. Did you notice how low we are on coffee? It's your turn to buy,' Janice informed her boss.

Metcalf shook his head in disbelief and smiled. He dug deep into a trouser pocket and sorted out £3.50 in small change, pleased to be getting rid of the annoying five pence and ten pence pieces. 'You couldn't get it for me, could you? I'm a bit busy,' he said, handing over the money. It was a ritual they followed every time it was Metcalf's turn to buy anything. Janice often wondered if Metcalf knew what the inside of a grocery store looked like.

With his coffee in his hand, Metcalf walked out into the corridor. 'Ah, Mr Green.' Metcalf offered his hand in greeting.

Nigel took the offered hand and noticed Metcalf had a vice-like grip – *A sign of confidence and self-assurance or the sign of lessons in body language?* 'Good morning,' Nigel replied. 'But don't take "good" as the operative word. I've known better.'

'Indeed, Mr Green. Indeed. Come on through. I'll just fetch my colleague; we'd like to show you some photographs whilst we're having a chat. Janice will get you a coffee, if you want one.' Metcalf motioned Nigel towards an interview room and then went in search of his colleague.

Nigel turned to the only other person in the room and smiled.

'Quite right – I'm Janice. General dogsbody to his lordship, not that I'm complaining.'

'It doesn't do to complain, I suppose.'

'No. Not at work, anyway. There were two of you, weren't there? What's happened to your friend?'

'Oh, he went off to find a toilet. Whatever you do, don't offer him a coffee. He'll be backwards and forwards to the loo all morning.' Nigel relaxed for the first time in hours, warming to the casual conversation. Janice seemed nice.

Ian poked his head round the door. 'Excuse me, but does this building have any toilets? I've looked everywhere.'

Nigel laughed and opened the door to Interview Room 1, leaving Metcalf's secretary to deal with Ian. The room was cold, and the air smelled stale. Nigel walked over to a window and struggled to open it.

Studying Form

'Good idea,' said Metcalf, startling Nigel. 'Sorry, I didn't mean to make you jump. These places do tend to go off a bit. No direct sunlight and inadequate heating mean doors and windows are usually kept tightly closed and, as a result, the rooms get a bit stuffy.

'Anyway, Mr Green. Let's get on, shall we?' Metcalf and Nigel took a seat whilst a uniformed officer stood by the door.

For the next four hours or so, Ian and Nigel recounted to their respective interrogators the events of the previous few months. Nigel detailed the betting system he had developed and how he had got Ian to computerise it. Ian described, at length, the computer system he had developed for Nigel. Both described their successes and their movements from course to course. Ian was somewhat vague on the details of the murder and subsequent goings-on, since he'd fainted.

'Sorry, I can't tell you more,' Ian said to Hicken. 'I'm a bit squeamish when it comes to that sort of thing. The sight of blood, especially blood as fresh as that…'

'Yes, yes. Graphic detail is not required. Forensics have the pictures, don't worry.' Hicken too had a weak constitution. Fainting at the scene of three road traffic accidents and two post-mortems during his career had left him with a bit of a reputation with his colleagues. And he didn't like the nickname it had earned him either: Flopsie. He still had the occasional nightmare from his first post-mortem. On his own, guarding a body, waiting for a pathologist to arrive.

Andy Wheildon

The body had actually belched. Hicken could smell the corpse's last meal in that belch and had never eaten pickled onions again.

*

Parrot/Blundell had made good time back to London. As he had driven through the night, he had given his immediate future a great deal of thought. He knew, from friends, the police had always suspected the wrong person had gone to prison for killing the bank inspector. He also knew killing Price had been the only option available to him the previous evening. His only regret was that he hadn't killed Price years ago.

He reflected on the events of the fourth of October 1984 when he'd murdered a fellow employee from head office.

James Price had gratefully accepted, on his son's behalf, £25,000 in payment for Gordon Price taking the blame for a crime he did not commit, pleading guilty to manslaughter on the grounds of diminished responsibility. Gordon Price was already known to the police as a petty crook with a very low IQ. 'Something of a simpleton,' the judge had called him.

Price had known Blundell by reputation only. The bank manager had helped many in the underworld to launder money or secure funds when needed. Price had been approached by one of his underworld contacts and told he had to do a little favour, the kind of favour he couldn't refuse. His son had been shipped off to a bank one night, never to return. It had been quite comical really – Blundell had shot the bank's fraud investigator then said to Gordon Price, 'Here, hold this a moment,' passing him the murder weapon.

The plan had worked, to a point. The only problem had been James Price himself – his greed, pure and simple. The opportunity to realise a large quantity of cash at the expense of his son had proved too hard to resist.

During the final stages of negotiation, all those years ago, when Price had demanded more money for his son taking the blame, Blundell had made it clear he would kill Price should they ever meet again. Blundell now smiled to himself. No-one could say he wasn't a man of his word.

His thoughts returned to the present. He knew that Ian and Nigel would be able to identify him. He knew that they would describe the events on the dual carriageway the previous week. He had no choice now but to rid himself of his own identity and leave the shores of England once and for all. Australia was still the obvious choice since he had contacts in Sydney. If he delayed his escape, then the authorities would be on the lookout whichever border he tried to cross.

Pulling into a service station on the outskirts of London, Blundell decided to visit some friends in the capital in order to tie up a few loose ends and make the necessary arrangements to disappear.

Having ordered an all-day breakfast and been served with a mug of black coffee, he scanned the *Daily Express* to see if his actions of the previous few days had warranted attention from the national press.

Andy Wheildon

Forty-five minutes later, Blundell was in a branch of the National Westminster bank transferring funds to an account he had in Nantes, France. He had a soft spot for the city and had often spent time exploring the Loire Valley. Nantes, on the coast of the Bay of Biscay, was where his ex-wife had taken him on their final holiday together. He liked Nantes.

The money from Trist had been waiting for him so the transfer was quite a hefty one. Blundell also emptied a safety deposit box, returning his key to the manager, informing him he had no further use for it. In no time at all, Blundell was walking away from the bank, mingling with the mid-morning shoppers. The money, now in France would ultimately find its way to Australia.

As he walked along the pavement, he systematically disposed of his old passport, putting bits of it in each waste bin as he made his way to the nearest tube station. By the time he had reached the entrance to the Swiss Cottage underground station, Mr Rodney Blundell, bank manager, had changed his spots once more and become Peter Berwick, university lecturer. His new identity had been sitting in the safety deposit box waiting for an occasion such as this.

Changing at Green Park, Peter Berwick was on the way to Heathrow and, eventually, a new life down under.

*

'So, let me see if I've got this right,' Metcalf said, getting up from his chair to stretch his legs and straighten his back. 'You and your friend develop a system which can accurately predict the outcome of certain horse races. You are so confident in your system, when a horse fails to win, you actually question the integrity of the trainer rather than the accuracy of the system you've developed.' Metcalf looked to the ceiling in disbelief.

'Your own enquiries seem to confirm your suspicions. The trainer in question is rumoured to bend the rules under the instruction of one particular owner, a Mr'—Metcalf consults his colleague's notes—'Trist. You contact the trainer, Collier. You make him aware you know of his wrongdoing. Then you get shot at, burgled and are witness to a murder in your own kitchen. A murder committed by the same person, as far as you can tell, having given it some thought, who took a shot at you on the A1.'

'Correct.' Nigel nervously played with his cuticles.

With an abruptness that surprised Nigel, Metcalf walked across the interview room and opened the door. 'Right then, Mr Green, that'll do for now. We'll be in touch.'

*

Ian was waiting for Nigel outside the police station. It was a pleasant enough day, the sun shining brightly with only a slight breeze. Ian saw his friend approach and got up from the wall where he'd been sitting, wiping dust from his trousers.

Andy Wheildon

'Took your time, didn't you? I've been out here half an hour. What did you tell them, and have I got bird shit on my bum?'

Nigel checked for guano, perched himself on the wall where Ian had been sitting and sighed. 'I told them everything.' Squinting against the sun, Nigel looked up to his friend. 'The way it came out, it sounded like I was putting the blame on Collier and Trist.'

'That was the way I saw it too,' Ian agreed. 'They are the only people we've annoyed, or rather, *you've* annoyed. The only other time we've had any problems is when the bookie refused your bet, what seems like ages ago.'

Nigel thought for a moment. 'I'd forgotten about that. The manager of the betting shop, Fleming's on Mansfield Road, had photographs of us and a file detailing my betting in their chain of shops. We were turned away from a leading bookie, and then, lo and behold, a greedy so-and-so from the same organisation turns up on our doorstep and gets shot in our kitchen.'

'Metcalf told me Price was area manager in charge of fourteen shops. Thinking about it, we've ruffled the feathers of two people directly. Price the bookmaker and Collier the trainer.'

'It's got to be Collier who's behind the shooting. Or rather, it's more likely it's Trist. Collier just does as he's told. Back in Carlisle, he was of the opinion some misfortune would eventually come our way when you confronted him. You could see it in his eyes. He looked tired, distant. It seemed as though he no longer cared.' Ian looked back towards the police station. 'I wonder what they make of all this?'

'God only knows. Fancy a pint?'

*

Jonathan West had made good time from the north of London, pulling into the police station car park in the early evening. The security barrier lifted once his identity had been established over the intercom.

'Thank you, sir. Detective Sergeant Metcalf is expecting you. If you would park in bay sixty-eight and report directly to the control room. Just follow the signs.' With a click, the metallic voice was gone.

*

Metcalf wandered into the control room and walked up to the only person he didn't recognise. 'Hello, you must be West?' he said, hand outstretched.

'No. My name is Rhys. I'm a solicitor.' The offered hand was ignored.

'Sergeant West has just nipped out to spend a penny, sir.' The duty officer smiled to himself. He loved it when one of the suits made a fool of themselves.

Metcalf waited, making idle conversation with the solicitor. When West returned, the two made their way to Metcalf's office, and Metcalf gave a brief summary of the past twenty-four hours.

'Let's hear the tape then,' West said, having sat quietly, absorbing all Metcalf had to say.

Fifteen minutes later, West was shaking his head in disbelief. 'Amazing.'

'My sentiments exactly.'

'I have to ask myself the question: why would somebody turn so violently towards Price and leave the intended victims, now eye-witnesses, unharmed? Our assailant knows their evidence will identify him, eventually. So, why leave loose ends?' He watched Metcalf light a cigarette and take the smoke deep into his lungs. When the man gave no further response, West continued. 'After a few queries on the mainframe, I found Gordon Price, his son. I read the case notes and decided to take a closer look.'

West opened the file he'd brought with him. 'The bank manager who went missing after the investigator was killed – this is his picture.' He handed it to Metcalf. 'Obviously, it's a bit out of date.'

'I'll get our two young friends back to the station to see if they recognise him.' Metcalf stubbed out his half-finished cigarette in an ashtray, much to the relief of West, and went in search of his secretary to arrange a pickup after the weekend.

Monday, 1 July 1991

Trist had scanned numerous newspapers, both broadsheet and tabloid, and was somewhat perturbed not to find a story covering the death of two unfortunate youngsters. Most of the papers had a story about a betting shop area manager being shot dead. A pure coincidence, as far as Trist was concerned, until he read an article in one of the broadsheets.

'Mr James Price was known to the police, being the father of a Mr Gordon Price – found guilty of murder in 1984. It was rumoured, during the trial of Gordon Price, a substantial amount of money changed hands to ensure Price, of limited intellect, would plead guilty to the charge, thus shielding the actual perpetrator of the crime from prosecution.'

Trist knew all about Parrot's past. It was this knowledge that had ensured Parrot continued to do favours for Trist whenever the need arose. Picking up his phone, Trist called Parrot's number. After a long delay, the phone was answered.

'Yes!'

'Mr Parrot. I'd like to speak with Mr Parrot.'

'He's not here anymore.'

'I beg your pardon,' Trist became agitated.

'You heard me. He's gone, bags and all.'

'I don't suppose he's left any forwarding details, has he?'

'No, he bloody hasn't. He'd better not come back neither.'

The line went dead. Trist returned the phone to its cradle and went over to his drinks cabinet, deep in thought.

*

The police car arrived to ferry Nigel and Ian back to the station. The two friends sat in the back, but Nigel leaned forwards to look at all the gadgets on the dashboard and in the footwell of the front passenger seat. A monitor sat in a cradle, the screen blank. Nigel pointed to it. '*News at Ten*, when you're on the late shift?' he asked.

'Very funny,' the PC replied. 'This isn't your average taxi, you know. Not many people get to ride in one of these.' Stretching over to the passenger side, he flicked a switch bringing the screen to life. After a couple of seconds, the screen displayed the car in front through the lens of a camera. There were a series of figures scattered around the edge of the screen, detailing time, date and speed.

'So the guy in front is speeding,' Ian observed.

'If you say so. I'm watching the road. That apparatus should only be on when there are two officers in the car. And by the way, the guy in front is a woman.'

'Figures.' Nigel had always been something of a chauvinist when it came to female drivers.

The police officer laughed. 'Women are the safest drivers. But I must admit, it's great when we pull them over to caution them. They flirt like mad. With some, it's the uniform; with others, they just don't want to get into trouble.'

'Oh well, there she goes,' Nigel observed. The car in front indicated left and pulled into a petrol station. As the police car drove past, all three occupants glanced towards the driver they'd been following.

At the police station, Ian and Nigel were ushered into separate rooms once more. On the table in each room was an unopened folder containing a large number of photographs.

Metcalf turned away from Nigel, leaving him to peruse the photographs at his leisure. 'Take your time, Mr Green. But try to find me a killer, if you would. I'll be in my office.'

Twenty minutes later, both Ian and Nigel had identified Rodney Blundell as the man behind the gun in their kitchen and the man behind the gun on the dual carriageway. Nigel also told Metcalf about James Frederick Collier and Derek Trist whilst, in the other room, Ian described events at Carlisle where Collier had threatened Nigel.

Metcalf took West to the station canteen. 'We can't do much about Trist, can we?' West poured himself a coffee.

'This is a murder enquiry, so we can do whatever we want. We'll visit Trist first thing in the morning. Routine enquiries. Establish links with Collier, his relationship with him, that sort of thing. See if he's the aggressive sort. We'll play it by ear initially. But I agree, we've very little to go on.'

Andy Wheildon

'What we need to do is circulate the picture of Blundell to all forces and all ports. It should be only a matter of time before he's seen.'

Metcalf wasn't convinced. Blundell would have gone to ground. Therefore, circulating his details was not really a priority – beans on toast, however, was.

Monday, 1 July 1991
– Afternoon

Rebecca spent the weekend reviewing the code that had appeared when the FORTUNE.EXE file had been decompiled for a second time. Finally, she was confident she knew how the program worked – from the EXE file referencing a large database to the large database receiving updates from a remote company called RLDS. She took this information to her dad who was thrilled since his gambling on Saturday had seen the System fail twice.

'So the System is failing because we are not keeping the database up-to-date,' Rebecca concluded. 'If we can get the database up-to-date—'

'The what?' asked Griffiths.

'Sorry, Dad. There are a load of race results stored on the computer in something called a database. The most recent race result in the database is from three weeks ago. The system needs up-to-date information to work properly, I'm guessing. As time passes, if we don't keep the race results current then the System becomes less effective. Eventually, it will be worthless.'

'So what do we do to get the info we need?'

'*Really*? You really want to take this on?'

'Too right I do. We are looking at a potential goldmine here. I have seen two young blokes picking up thousands of pounds. Why not me... us?'

'Well, I suppose so. How exciting... apart from the fact that it's stolen.'

'OK, I appreciate this isn't totally above board, but nothing ventured...' Griffiths was a little uncomfortable he was now involving his daughter in his wrongdoing.

'I've found a phone number that the computer uses to get race results via a modem,' Rebecca said.

'A what?'

'Blimey, Dad. Just forget it for the time being. I've found a file on the computer which automatically connects this computer to another computer to get the race results. I would think we need to get permission to access the external computer. Anyway, we need a modem. You need to give me fifty quid, and don't worry, you'll get some change.'

*

A few hours later, the early evening news was on in the background whilst Rebecca prepared tea. She looked up at the screen and saw a picture of the man she knew as being a friend of her fathers. She stopped what she was doing to listen to the newscast. 'Dad!' she shouted. 'Dad, come here quickly.'

Griffiths ambled into the kitchen and saw Rebecca staring at a small TV on the counter. The reporter announced the man who had been murdered the previous Thursday here in Nottingham, had been identified as Mr James Price, area manager of local turf accountants, Flemings.

Griffiths and his daughter watched the report together, open-mouthed.

'Bloody hell.' Griffiths was stunned. 'Murdered?' He looked towards his daughter. 'The System?'

'I don't know. He's your mate... was your mate.'

'He was never a mate. More a blackmailer, really.'

'Oh dear.'

'Don't worry, nothing heavy and nothing to worry about.' Griffiths turned to the TV. 'Not now, anyway.'

'But the System, Dad? I know you stole the computer. I know you know who created the System. You told me you've seen them gamble and win big money. You and Price stole a computer, and now Price is dead. For fucks' sake, Dad. Are you next?' Rebecca was distraught.

Emotionally, Griffiths wasn't far behind her.

'I had a gun pointing at my stomach a few weeks ago,' Griffiths admitted. He was ashen-faced and had to sit down.

Rebecca also sat down and stared at her father, waiting for him to continue. A few minutes later, Rebecca was fully up to speed. She sat back in her chair and looked towards the ceiling, noticing some cobwebs around the kitchen light. 'If you were to go to the police, can you remember what the guy looked like?'

'I'm not going to the police. I've no friends there anymore. In fact, I probably still have a few enemies. It's only been eight years.' Griffiths thought for a moment. 'Actually, I'll make a couple of phone calls to see what's happening. I might be able to get something. I tell you what, buy the thingy you mentioned earlier. Let's see if we can get the System up-to-date and have a play.'

Rebecca sighed, got up from the table and went back to preparing the tea. She had lost her appetite, but ten minutes later, neither of them let any of the food go to waste.

*

Within a couple of weeks, Rebecca had succeeded in purchasing a modem, opening an account with RLDS and updating the database. Griffiths had been able to establish Price's murderer had intended to kill Nigel Green and Ian Turner, and Price had been *unfortunate* in being in the wrong place at the wrong time.

The word *unfortunate* brought a wry smile to Griffiths' face. 'How fortunate for me,' he reflected.

'So, it looks as though we are in the clear.' Griffiths had concluded. Price's demise was not connected to him in any way so he could relax.

'How reassuring,' Rebecca said in a somewhat unconvincing voice. 'So, what now?'

'Now we have a go with the System of course. Let's nip down to Colwick Park and give it a go, shall we?'

Studying Form

'Really, there's a race meeting here in Nottingham?' Rebecca knew racing took place in Nottingham but had no idea when the meetings took place.

'Yep, Monday twenty-second. First race at 6.15. It's an evening meeting. Are you going to join me?'

'Twenty-second? That's Mum's birthday.'

'I know.' Griffiths sighed and turned away.

Tuesday, 2 July 1991

DS Metcalf and DC West drove south to the heart of London, making slow progress once they reached the Capital. 'This is ridiculous,' Metcalf observed. 'I thought the traffic was bad in my neck of the woods, but this is unbearable.' Even though it was a hot day, he kept his window closed to prevent exhaust fumes filtering into the car. 'Is it like this all the time?'

'Nearly. It settles down a bit after eight in the evening, unless there's something happening. But when that's the case, congestion is only localised. Don't worry, we should do the next two miles in about twenty minutes.' West grinned as Metcalf looked skywards, shaking his head in disbelief.

'Six miles an hour, I ask you!'

Twenty-three minutes later, the two detectives were in the company of Trist's secretary. 'He'll see you now, gentlemen. Walk this way.' They followed her and were shown into an elegant office with expensive-looking paintings on three of the walls.

'Thank you, Katie. Hold my calls, would you? But buzz me at a quarter to.' Trist turned his attention to his visitors, offering his hand in welcome. 'Gentlemen, Derek Trist. But I assume you already know that.'

Studying Form

'Indeed, we do, sir.' Metcalf shook Trist's hand then walked to the window, admiring the view. 'Is that the Tower of London in the distance?' Metcalf asked.

'Yes, it is, and over there to your right, you can see the Post Office Tower. I'm quite fortunate to have this view. It's one of the best in this building. High enough to lose the drone of the traffic, but not too high to lose the clarity of detail whilst watching the world go by below. Give it twenty years or so, and I'm sure the views will disappear. High-rise offices would be my guess. Anyway, how can I help you?'

'Purely routine, sir. What is your relationship with Mr James Frederick Collier?'

'Jim? He trains my horses, over in Lambourn. Why? Nothing's happened to him, has it?'

'No, sir. Nothing has happened to him. It's just his name, and yours incidentally, has been mentioned in a murder inquiry.'

'Me? Murder! You're joking.'

'I seldom joke, sir. Especially when I'm on duty. You may have seen it in the papers. A betting shop manager was murdered three days ago.'

'Yes, I did. But what on earth has that got to do with me and Jim?'

'I'm not able to disclose details of our enquiries. Suffice to say, names have been mentioned, and we are here.' Metcalf reached into his jacket pocket and pulled out a picture of Blundell. He passed it to Trist. 'Have you ever seen this man?'

Trist immediately recognised it as a younger version of the man he knew as Parrot. 'No, sorry. I've never seen him before.' Handing the picture back to Metcalf, he hoped his shaking hand went unnoticed. 'Who is he?'

'Somebody we would like to speak to, to eliminate him from our enquiries. Are you sure you've never seen him before?'

The intercom emitted a short burst. Trist walked over to his table and pushed a button on the console, 'Thank you, Katie.' He turned to Metcalf. 'Positive. I'm quite sure I haven't seen him before. I have an urgent appointment; you'll have to forgive me. My secretary will show you to the lift.'

In the lift, West mentioned a slight shaking of the hand when Trist returned the photograph to Metcalf.

'Yes, I noticed too. It's nice when the old tricks of the trade provide an insight into a substantial lead you were hoping for.'

*

A few days later, Metcalf made the long journey to Lambourn in the knowledge that Collier would be at his stables. En route, he had picked up a colleague from Thames Valley Police in Newbury. Discussing the case as he drove along the winding roads of Royal Berkshire, he was thankful for his colleague giving directions.

'Where are we, exactly?' asked Metcalf as they left the M4 at junction 14.

'We are approaching Hungerford Hill. I'm taking you the scenic route to show you where Collier lives. We'll pass his house near East Garston. His stables are about five minutes further on, in Lambourn itself.'

Metcalf's car pulled into the stable courtyard, and he decided to park next to a Range Rover which was in front of, what looked like, an office door. The two policemen got out of the car, and being in plain clothes, only raised slight curiosity from a stable-girl who walked past smiling.

'Hello, there. Where would we find Mr Collier?' Metcalf asked.

'Hi Through the door and turn left. Straight on to another door which will probably be closed because he's having his morning meeting with the senior lads.' The stable-girl strode off without waiting for thanks.

'Thank you,' Metcalf said, more to himself than the girl.

The second door was, as predicted, closed.

'We'll wait,' said Metcalf.

It was a sunny day, so they returned outside and rested against the bonnet of their car, watching as stable life continued uninterrupted.

Eventually, a couple of men walked out of the building. Metcalf was quite taken aback by their height. He estimated 5'3" or thereabouts. The two looked very strong and fit. Lifting himself off the car and unfolding his arms, Metcalf straightened himself up to tower over them.

'Has Mr Collier finished his meeting, do you know?' Metcalf asked.

'Yes, just. Go on through – the door's open.'

'How very friendly,' Metcalf said, leading the way and, on reaching the second door, knocked once before walking into a large office which was bursting at the seams with paperwork.

A tired old man looked up from his desk and, on seeing them, rose to his feet.

'Can I help you?' Collier asked.

Metcalf took his warrant card from his pocket and passed it to Collier who studied it closely.

'My name is Metcalf, Detective Sergeant Metcalf, and this is Detective Sergeant Lester from Thames Valley CID, Newbury. I am investigating the murder of a turf accountant named James Price. My enquiries have linked a person of interest to you, Mr Collier.' Metcalf retrieved his warrant card from Collier.

Collier busied himself moving papers from chairs and inviting his visitors to sit down. He apologised for not being able to offer them a drink and then, whilst returning to his chair, asked, 'So how can I help?'

Metcalf spent the next forty-five minutes questioning Collier about his business contacts, the owners he trained for and whether anything out of the ordinary had happened during the previous six to eight months. Lester took notes whilst Collier answered all the questions.

At the end of the interview, Collier asked for the identity of the person who had been specifically linked to him. Metcalf passed a picture of Blundell to Collier.

Studying Form

'I am good with faces, gentlemen. But the man in that picture? I have not seen him before. This man is not known to me, sorry,' Collier said.

'No need to apologise. Thank you for giving us a bit of your time and answering my questions.' Metcalf got to his feet and, waiting for Lester to finish off some notes, shook Collier's hand and bade him farewell. 'I'll be in touch.'

As the two detectives drove away, Metcalf knew he was no nearer connecting Blundell to Collier or Trist. In fact, having seen and talked to Collier, he was even further from establishing a connection. Investigations would continue in the morning.

*

A few days later, Nigel and Ian were back in their own home with all traces of what had gone on in the kitchen removed. Nigel decided a relaxing evening in front of the telly would be a good idea. He was exhausted and in no mood to socialise. Smiling to himself, he reflected on his current social situation and how socialising would be difficult anyway.

Ian popped his head round the door. 'We're off to the Arboretum if you fancy a pint.'

'No, thanks. I'm not in the mood for a busman's holiday. I'm going to relax in front of the telly. You two go and have fun.'

'OK, thanks. See you later.'

'Bye-ee,' Zoë called out, fighting her way into a heavy leather jacket Ian had bought her.

'Bye-ee,' Nigel mimicked, in a high-pitched voice.

As the front door slammed shut, Nigel pointed the remote control at the TV and video. The news was on BBC One and the tape in the VCR carried a random selection of races from a few years ago.

Nigel switched between news items and horse racing, not paying particular attention to either. Then all of a sudden, the hairs on the back of his neck stood on end, a shot of adrenaline coursed through his veins, and his finger hit the pause button on the remote control.

In the centre of the parade ring amongst the crowd of jockeys, trainers and owners stood Trist, Collier and Blundell obviously sharing a joke together.

Nigel ran to the front door to call his friend back then thought better of it. He turned to the phone and called the police station.

The duty sergeant on the other end of the line was less than helpful and sounded most unimpressed when Nigel tried to convince him that he, Nigel, had solved a murder.

'Congratulations,' said the duty sergeant.

Nigel insisted he needed to speak to Detective Sergeant Metcalf as a matter of urgency concerning the murder of James Price. The duty sergeant assured Nigel the message would be passed on and thanked him for the call before terminating the call.

Nigel replaced the receiver and returned to the television. Trist, Collier and Blundell remained glued to the spot, exactly where Nigel had left them a few moments earlier. He switched off both the TV and the video. *Evidence*, he thought, *which connected a murderer with a trainer and an owner*. Metcalf had informed Nigel there was no connection between Trist and Blundell, so that line of enquiry had hit a dead end. Nigel's video would surely change all that.

The front door burst open. 'We missed the bloody bus and it's started to rain.'

Ian and Zoë walked into the front room laughing. Zoë struggled out of the coat she had recently struggled to get into whilst Ian pulled his pullover over his head, his glasses falling off in the process.

'Look at this,' Nigel said, pushing buttons on remote controls and settling himself back into his chair. 'Recognise anyone?'

Everyone's attention turned to the television. Ian watched a few horses circling a parade ring and then, disbelief in his eyes, he turned to Nigel. 'Stop, stop! Look at that. It's him. Stop the video. Go back!'

'Who? Where? What?' Zoë was puzzled at Ian's reaction, the abject fear in his face. 'What's going on? Will someone explain?'

Nigel rewound the video and paused it once more on the 'three amigos'.

Ian walked over to the television screen and pointed to Blundell. 'That's the killer, isn't it?' Nigel nodded his agreement. 'And that one is the trainer, Collier. And this one? I don't recognise him.' Ian turned to Nigel, eyebrows raised.

'Trist.'

'No, really?' Ian was aghast. 'That means Trist *did* know Blundell. Does that mean…?' Ian tailed off. *What* did *this mean?*

The phone rang, and Nigel got up to answer it. As he passed Ian, he looked towards the television and said, 'I think we've got Trist. He'll go down for this.'

*

Metcalf had phoned Nigel back as soon as he got the message and was in the car on the way to Nigel's house just as soon as he had persuaded his wife it was necessary and very important. The drive took less than an hour, and sitting in Nigel's living room, Metcalf was all ears… or eyes, to be more accurate.

'There!' Nigel pointed to the television screen which showed a band of interference running along the bottom and three men smiling. The video recorder complained at being put on pause for so long whilst the interference danced at the bottom of the screen.

'So let me get this right. The gentleman on the left is definitely the person who entered your home and shot Price? I must admit the resemblance to the man in the photograph is striking.'

'Correct. And the other two are Trist, the racehorse owner, and Collier, the trainer.'

'Thank you, Mr Green. Yes, I have interviewed both Trist and Collier, so I agree with your observation. I might even go as far as saying "your powers of observation do you credit" but that would be a tad flippant. This is a very important development which I will investigate fully. However, I must also consider your welfare. The killer knows you witnessed the killing, yet he left you alive. I am finding it difficult to understand why he left this very loose end. Why would he let you live? I can only imagine he thinks he's untraceable, in which case, he has probably left the country already. Anyway, I'm thinking out loud. I'll leave you in peace now, but there will be an officer outside for the next few weeks as a precaution.' Metcalf got to his feet and went across to the VCR then realised he had no idea what knob to press. 'Could I have the cassette please?'

Nigel ejected the video tape and handed it to Metcalf.

As he drove to the local police station, Metcalf put a call through to Hicken asking him to find out all he could about Trist and Collier.

*

The evening before the anniversary of Rebecca's mum's birth had both Rebecca and Griffiths looking at the race card for the next day and typing race information into Henry. For some reason, Rebecca had christened the System 'Henry'. In eager anticipation, Griffiths said, 'Okay, let's see what Henry's got for us.'

Rebecca hit the return key on the keyboard, and the result of the 8:20 was known. Griffiths shrugged his shoulders and said a monkey could have chosen that horse. 'It'll start favourite and the odds will be naff,' he observed, more to himself than his daughter.

'So, it's a cert. then!' Rebecca reasoned. 'We'll be putting money on a dead cert which, incidentally, I still don't believe exists.'

'Let's take a look at the other handicap race on the card.' Griffiths returned to the paper to see how many runners were in the first race. 'Fancy typing in another eleven runners?'

Rebecca sighed. 'Nothing ventured...'

Ten minutes later, both Griffiths and his daughter had agreed on their tactics for laying a bet the following evening. They would split their money in half. The first half would go on Sir Danik in the first race, and any winnings would be added to the stake for their second race, the fifth race on the card, which would go on the probable favourite Merton Mill.

Monday, 22 July 1991

'It'll be nice to get back into the swing of things,' Nigel said to Ian as they got on the bus in the city centre. The bus was packed since it was one put on as a *special* for the race meeting on the outskirts of the city. 'We'll have some time to spare before the fifth race so we can soak up the atmosphere and have a beer as usual, like normal punters. It's been ages since I've been to Nottingham races. Crazy really. It's like living in Brighton and never going to the beach.'

'Or Cleethorpes?' Ian suggested.

'Yeah, OK. Brighton, Cleethorpes, Skegness, Mablethorpe or wherever you come from.'

'Cleethorpes.'

'A bit nippy though, I would imagine? Wind coming in off the North Sea.'

'True. Brighton would probably be a bit warmer. Anyway, the fifth race and not the first?'

'Absolutely,' said Nigel. 'Let's just see how it goes. The first race could see a bit of an upset, according to our little system, so I don't want us to suffer if the System has got it wrong. It is, after all, the first time we've used it for nearly a month. Race five I am confident in, so let's just stick with that. How's

Zoë, by the way? She hasn't been around for a few days.'

'I know.' Ian turned and looked out of the window as the bus ambled along Huntingdon Street, his stomach churning a little. 'The past few weeks have taken their toll. I'm not sure whether it's Zoë or her parents causing friction, but it's gone a bit cold. Immediately after the incident in the kitchen, everything seemed fine; she was so strong for me and supportive, but recently, her enthusiasm has waned. I reckon she would prefer a boyfriend with a steady job. Maybe she's decided horse racing and the occasional murder are just not her cup of tea.'

'Good point,' Nigel stared towards the front of the bus, allowing Ian to wallow in his self-pity.

After a few minutes, Ian turned to Nigel and asked about Lucy. 'I heard you talking to her on the phone a couple of days ago. You sounded quite up-beat, quite enthusiastic.'

'Yeah, we'll see. It would be nice if we got back together. Lucy and I met up in town a couple of days ago and enjoyed discussing old times. Well, the best bits anyway. We parted on excellent terms, and she said, "Let's do it again". Why not invite Zoë round, and I'll invite Lucy. It could be like sitting in the kind of atmosphere you could cut with a knife, or it might turn out to be a nice evening. Who knows?'

'I'll think about it.' Ian already didn't think much of the idea but decided he would give it some further thought.

Studying Form

Eventually, the double-decker arrived at Colwick Park, and everyone disembarked, snaking their way to the turnstile entrances for Nottingham Racecourse. Ian bought a race card though he had no idea why. Maybe he was just trying to take his mind off Zoë. He was actually feeling pain in the pit of his stomach at the thought of losing her. Nigel could see the distress in Ian's eyes and offered a few words of encouragement.

'You'll be fine. Things will work out over time. It hurts now. Eventually, it won't.'

Ian gave himself a shake. *Just snap out of it,* he told himself. He quickened his pace towards the turnstiles in an attempt to strengthen his resolve.

The place was buzzing, and the glorious weather put broad smiles on the faces of the mingling crowd. Ian and Nigel made their way to a beer tent, four-deep at the bar. The two split up and, after about ten minutes, were back together again, both having secured a couple of pints each. They stayed in the bar and found somewhere to sit once the place began to empty for the first race.

Looking at his race card, Ian absentmindedly went through the first race, trying to remember which horse was going to win if the System was still working.

'Sir Danik,' Nigel said, without being asked.

'Oh, yeah. That's the one. So, no bet on this race then?'

'Well, there's no reason why you can't tip your toe in the water if you want to.'

'The term is "dip your toe"…'

'What did *I* say?'

'You said tip rather than dip, or at least that's what I heard.'

'Pardon?'

'Very funny... OK, I think I'll go and have a wander around the bookies. Are you staying here?'

'Yes. I'll look after the beers, the seats and'— looking hopefully towards Ian's pocket—'the race card, if that's OK?'

'Be my guest.' Ian handed over the race card, picked up one of his beers and turned away. 'See you in a bit.'

Nigel flipped through the pages of the race card, oblivious to his surroundings and Griffiths and his daughter walking into the beer tent and up to the bar. He started to regret letting Ian nip out to watch the first race whilst he stayed in the tent with nothing more than a few beers and a race card to keep him company. Nigel took a look around and appreciatively noticed a nice pair of legs at the bar.

With drinks in hand, Griffiths turned from the bar with Rebecca and saw Nigel almost immediately. 'Shit, keep walking and don't look towards the exit, whatever you do. We'll take the table over there.' Griffiths motioned with the pint of Guinness in his left hand.

'What's up, Dad?'

'Hold on.' Griffiths sat down with his back to where Nigel was sitting next to the exit. 'The bloke behind me. At the table with three pints on it.'

Studying Form

Rebecca looked over. 'Good-looking! What about him?'

'We've stolen his system.'

'*WE*!' exclaimed Rebecca.

Nigel looked up, disturbed by some outburst near the bar. Not seeing its source, he went straight back to his race card, taking another large sip of his beer and not giving the interruption another thought.

'Keep it down, for Christ's sake. OK, so we are *using* his system. He's the bloke who Price got me to watch when he kept picking winners in his shops, and he's got a friend who—'

'Who's just walked into the tent?' Rebecca asked her father as Ian returned to the table, picking up one of the three pints.

Griffiths glanced over his shoulder then back to Rebecca. 'Yep, that's him. Now let me think.' Griffiths relived the past five or six weeks in his mind's eye and replayed the scenarios where he had got too close for comfort. 'I don't think either of them know me. I think we'll be alright. It's a pity we got stuck in traffic and missed the first race. I wonder how our horse got on.'

Rebecca got up, winked at her dad and ambled across to the exit, pausing at Nigel and Ian's table. 'I don't suppose you know the result of the first, do you? We got here too late.'

Ian looked towards Rebecca and smiled. 'Sir Danik came first, a couple of lengths ahead of Keen Vision. I can't remember who was third.' Ian paused. 'So, did you save some money by missing the race, or are you now going to be annoyed for the rest of the meeting because you missed out on a winner?'

'Money saved, I think. Thanks.' Rebecca returned to her dad and sat at the table, quite amused that both Ian and Nigel were looking over. 'Damn it, Dad. The horse only went and won.'

'Blimey, what were the odds?'

Rebecca gave her best pained expression. 'I didn't ask.'

'Well, never mind. That just gives us loads of confidence for the next race. We've got a couple of hours to kill before the race at 8.15. Let's have a wander and find something to eat.' Griffiths drained his glass of Guinness and licked his lips free of froth, sighing appreciatively.

Walking past Ian and Nigel, Rebecca smiled at the two lads, whilst Griffiths looked straight ahead. The smile was returned by both recipients.

Nigel raised a glass. 'To Zoë and Lucy,' he toasted.

'Indeed,' Ian said resignedly, as he followed Rebecca and Griffiths with his gaze.

*

The following morning, Nigel and Ian sat at the kitchen table and toasted Zoë and Lucy again. Ian had, eventually, agreed they should all go out for a meal together. Nigel had suggested a carvery, whilst Ian had thought an Indian meal would be better, so they had decided the four of them would hit the city centre on Thursday evening and see what they could find. Ian knew of a couple of restaurants near the ABC cinema at the top of Angel Row but couldn't remember what they were called.

At the same time, Griffiths and his daughter sat at their kitchen table munching on toast. Griffiths was enjoying his toast with a thin layer of marmite whilst Rebecca lavishly spread seedless strawberry jam on her two pieces. Coffee was percolating on the stove; they were both extremely happy with how things had worked out the previous evening.

'I'll update Henry in a minute, Dad. What on earth are we going to do with him? Could he be worth a lot of money?'

'It certainly looks that way. We've got Henry; Green and Turner have got their system. One and the same. They travel to race meetings to put bets on because Price warned them off his shops and threatened to expose them both to all the betting shops in the chain. As far as I know, that never happened and now Price is out of the way. I can travel to race meetings and put bets on, just the same as them. I would think it's going to be highly unlikely we pick the same race meetings so we will probably never cross paths. There is room for *our* 'Enry and their system – just so long as word doesn't get out.'

'Okay, fine. But just as a matter of interest, how much of the two grand we picked up last night will find its way into my bank account, hey Dad?'

'Reckon you could find something to do with a thousand pounds?'

'Really? Wow.' Rebecca got up from her chair and gave her dad a hug in a brief, rare moment of affection. Regaining her composure and sitting down, she took a mouthful of toast and, whilst chewing, said, 'Clothes.'

'Now, why does that not surprise me?' Griffiths quipped. 'One can never have enough sweaters, jackets, jeans, shoes, et cetera, et cetera.'

Rebecca gave a sarcastic smile and took herself off to the computer to update data from RLDS.

*

Ian looked across to Nigel, took a deep breath and nervously asked him whether he wanted the good news first or the bad news. Nigel smiled, for a moment. He then saw the expression on his friend's face and realised this was something serious.

'You have my undivided attention. Let me hear the good news first.'

'Well, the good news is we have a system which looks to work perfectly. The winner of the first race and the fifth last night should remove all doubt that it's robust enough to miss a few weeks.'

'This, I knew already. So, what's the bad news?'

'I've been meaning to broach the subject for ages, but I've never quite found the right moment. Now, for some reason, seems to be the right time to get this off my chest. The System is going to break soon.'

Studying Form

Nigel stared at Ian, head to one side with a worried expression. 'What makes you say that? When will it break? *Why* will it break?'

'I programmed it to break. I programmed it to break after a certain date. Buried in the code, there is a routine which takes a look at the date every time it launches. The code looks for a file and, normally, leaves the file alone. After a certain date, the code will delete the file. Every time you log in after that, the code won't be able to find the file, and the program will just abort.'

Nigel looked confused. 'Why? Well, make that two "why"s actually. Why did you do that, and why are you telling me?'

'I did it really early on when I first started writing the code for you. If things had gone pear-shaped between the two of us, and you had shut me out, then it gave me the comfort of having some sort of leverage, if I needed it. That's why I did it.'

'And?'

'And – what was the second why?'

'Why are—'

'Oh yes, why am I telling you now? That, I suppose becomes part of the good news! We haven't gone pear-shaped, we're still buddies—'

'That's debatable—'

'I'm telling you now because it's time to update the System with a new 'lockout' date. But this time, we'll both know about it. I've come clean. I trust you implicitly and have done for as long as I can remember, even though I couldn't admit that to myself before.'

'How reassuring.'

'Yes, so there's no deceit on my part, and we're all above board. The other thing it gives us is a safeguard in case someone steals the System and starts to use it. After a period of time, the program will just stop working. When we were burgled and lost the computer, if whoever stole the computer has somehow got it working—'

'It'll soon stop working!'

'Exactly. Pretty clever, huh?' Ian tailed off.

'Thanks for sharing. No, really. Thanks a lot.' Nigel got up from the table and walked out. Out of the kitchen and out of the house.

'Well, that went well,' Ian said to his cup of tea.

*

Griffiths walked into a betting office in Aspley, one he'd never visited before. Pages from the *Sporting Life* were being pinned to the walls as he entered, and Griffiths acknowledged the shop manager whilst the man got on with the task. Griffiths took a betting slip out of a dispenser and reached for a pen. He perched himself on a stool. Initially, the pen didn't work, so he scribbled across the betting slip until a line of ink appeared. The betting slip was ruined due to the scribble marks having transferred to the pink. Reaching for another betting slip, he looked up to the board in front of him and aimlessly studied a race card.

He was keen to try the System out again following the success of the previous evening. Rebecca had been given £950 cash. Money, the likes of which she'd never seen before. Griffiths had stuffed £700 in a drawer in his bedroom, and he had £300 in his back pocket.

The meeting Griffiths was interested in had four handicap races and two stakes races. Henry (he liked the nickname) had provided the name of the predicted winning horse for three of the handicaps, the fourth handicap having been rejected by the System. Griffiths was not sure why but was undeterred. Of the three races where the System had predicted a winner, there had been one race where the winner was far better than the opposition as far as the point allocation from the System was concerned. So that was the race he chose to gamble on.

Griffiths wrote out the betting slip and walked up to the counter.

'Give me two ticks,' the shop manager called over.

'No hurry, take your time. Any time between now and half past two will be fine,' Griffiths joked.

The manager smiled, unlocked the security door and made his way behind the counter, reaching for the betting slip Griffiths offered under the bandit screen.

'Blimey, that's quite a wager,' the manager observed. 'I'm going to have to phone it through. I'll only be able to give you SP though.'

'Yeah, that's fine,' Griffiths said resignedly.

Four hours later, Griffiths was £1,350 better off: Jackson Flint having prevailed at Redcar.

Andy Wheildon

*

Later that day, the phone rang. Ian skipped down the stairs and answered it. It was Nigel.

'You know what, I'd probably have done the same thing. This morning, I overreacted, storming out. Sorry. I'm at work right now, but I'll be finished by six. We're stocktaking, and I don't have a shift behind the bar this evening, so I can meet you in the Bell if you want, say, six thirty?'

'Six thirty sounds great. See you then.' Ian put the phone down and smiled to himself – all was well.

*

Metcalf had been making progress with his investigations, having now established a link, thanks to Nigel, between Collier, Trist and Rodney Blundell – the missing bank manager. Collier's career, both as a jockey and trainer, was now fresh in his mind. Trist's education, career path and current position in a high-profile firm of stockbrokers was also now known to Metcalf. He was scratching his head, however, over Blundell. There was no information anywhere about Rodney Blundell. He looked at the picture he now had of the three at the racetrack, taken from Nigel's video recording. 'Disappeared is right,' he muttered to himself. 'In!' he bellowed, following a knock on his door.

'We've got Mr Collier for you, sir, in Interview Room 4.'

'Solicitor?'

'No, sir, Mr Collier has volunteered to attend, all informal, as you requested.'

'Good, thank you.' Metcalf got up from his chair and walked past the uniformed constable standing at the office door. In passing, he asked his secretary to come along to see if their guest wanted a drink.

'Mr Collier, good afternoon. Nice to see you again. Thanks for coming to the station. Quite a coincidence you're in Nottingham. Can I offer you a drink?'

'Coffee, white no sugar, would be nice.'

'Make that two, would you please, Janice?'

'I stayed over following last night's race meeting here. You were lucky to catch me. I don't normally phone the stables whilst I'm away, but this morning I needed to check something with one of my lads and heard you had been looking for me. So, here I am.'

'Excellent, Mr Collier, thank you again. Now, this is just an informal conversation, but I will be asking you direct questions about your relationship with Mr Trist and others.'

'Others?' enquired Collier. 'I take it you're going to elaborate?'

Metcalf ignored the question. 'How long have you known Trist, and what does your work for him involve?'

For the next ten minutes, Collier summarised their relationship, starting with his first meeting with Trist some six years ago, having been introduced by an owner Collier already had on his books. Since that time, Trist had placed four horses in Collier's stable, their relationship a purely professional one, pretty…' Collier paused, looking for the right word. 'Well, dull, I suppose.'

'Dull?'

'I have eight owners. I am not close friends with any of them. I meet them from time to time, and we discuss their horses and the races their horses will run in. They pay their bills. It is, to all intents and purposes, dull.' Collier shrugged his shoulders.

'I would never describe *my* job as dull,' Metcalf observed.

'The owners are dull. The job is… well, it's my life. Training horses, planning their racing career, getting the best out of them and the jockeys. Winning. There's always the adrenaline rush when you get a winner.'

'I take it Trist likes winning?'

'Obviously. All the owners like winning.'

'Have you ever been asked by Trist to stop a horse from winning, in order to improve its potential odds in a future race?' Metcalf leaned forwards and stared deep into Collier's eyes.

There was a knock at the interview room door, and Janice walked in with two coffees and some Hobnobs. She placed the tray on the table and made a hasty retreat. She'd seen that stare before.

Once the door was closed, Collier sighed and reached for one of the coffees. 'How long does this conversation remain informal?' he asked.

Studying Form

*

'So, when is the System due to fall over?' Nigel asked, that evening in the Bell, watching Ian sink most of his pint in one go. 'Steady on, there. It won't evaporate, you know.'

'I'm thirsty, and a week on Thursday. Thursday, first of August, to be precise. There's nothing significant about the date. I picked it at random as far as I can remember. As I said this morning, I did it ages ago, and it seemed a good idea at the time.'

'An *excellent* idea, seeing as we've had it stolen. Do you think anyone could have cracked your code? I know it's password protected, but someone at work mentioned "brute force attacks" which can find passwords.'

Ian considered his answer before answering. 'I am no expert, and my code is not impregnable. The code can be reverse-engineered and stripped back to the bare bones. It would take a while to read through the code and understand it though, because I didn't document it as I wrote it.'

'What do you mean, you didn't document it?' Nigel asked.

'Anyone worth his salt as a programmer should write lines inside the code explaining what is going on. It's called "commenting". The comments help the programmer to remember what they are doing or, more importantly, what they *were* doing if they need to review the code years later. It also helps other programmers who have legitimate cause to be looking at, and potentially changing, the code.'

'So, whoever stole the computer could potentially access the System?'

'Excellent choice of word: *access* is exactly right,' Ian said. 'The risk is out there. I'm thinking of getting a tattoo, by the way.'

'Really? Where?'

'There's a place on the outskirts of town, over in Arnold.'

'No, I meant whereabouts on your body.' Nigel sighed.

'I know! Not sure yet. Probably a half-sleeve on the right arm and shoulder.'

'OK. What are you thinking of getting done?'

'Again, I'm not sure, maybe a dawn sunrise. So far, I've got as far as wanting a tattoo, or at least thinking about it. There's no hurry.'

'Can we get back to discussing the System?'

'Yeah, sorry. If the person who stole the computer has unlocked the program, then hopefully, they'll not find the bit of code which references an external file. But, having said that...' Ian sighed. 'If they are good enough to *get in*, they are probably good enough to *stay in*.'

'Bollocks. Another pint?' Nigel got up and set off for the bar, returning with two pints of Murphy's and two packets of Smiths crisps. 'Cheese and onion or salt and vinegar?'

Ian gratefully accepted the green packet and devoured its contents with some speed.

Studying Form

'How are you fixed for Friday, by the way?' Nigel asked. 'I want to drive up to Carlisle again.'

Ian thought for a moment then said, 'I can't see any problem with that. It was an easy drive last time. Quite pleasant, really. Friday is the day after our night out with Lucy and Zoë though. If we're driving the next day, I don't think I'll be drinking Thursday evening.'

'Good point. I still think we should go ahead with the evening though.'

Thursday, 25 July 1991

Ian was really nervous at the prospect of going out with his girlfriend. Struggling to decide what to wear reminded him of how he'd felt before their first date, just a couple of months ago. The butterflies in his stomach had returned, and he was annoyed with himself. This was how it should feel if he were going on a first date with a girl he loved... Well, he thought he still loved Zoë, but her recent reluctance to meet had resulted in his feelings beginning to wane. Would tonight rekindle a mutual love? Or would tonight prove beyond doubt things could never be the same, and to all intents and purposes, it was over?

Nigel poked his head around the door. 'Are you still up for driving?'

'Yeah, not a problem. I said I'd pick Zoë up at 7.15. The table is booked for eight o'clock. I suppose you want me to pick up Lucy too? There should be time, shouldn't there?'

'Yes, it's actually not too far out of our way. We can park at the multi-storey just off Maid Marion Way.'

'Cool, what time is it now?' Ian asked.

'It's just gone six, plenty of time. Good luck, by the way. I know what you're going through. Hopefully everything will be civil and friendly.'

Studying Form

'Of course. There's no reason for any friction. I'd like to get a good night's sleep though, since we're off to Carlisle again.'

'Noted. We don't have to leave too early tomorrow morning. We know the lay of the land, don't we?'

'Absolutely. I'll be down in a tick.'

Nigel's head disappeared from around the door, and Ian was alone with his thoughts once more. He turned on the radio and let Nottingham's commercial radio fill his mind. Bryan Adams was at the top of the charts. 'That'll do,' Ian muttered to himself.

With Nigel sat in the back of the car, Ian and Zoë were deep in conversation as they approached Lucy's house. 'The red Volvo on the left, that's where Lucy lives. Just pull up behind it.'

Ian drove past the car then pulled up.

'Or in front... I won't be a moment.' Nigel jumped out of the car, walked up to the front door of number nineteen and rang the doorbell.

'Yes, she's nice,' Ian said, answering Zoë's question about Lucy. 'I must admit though I'm not too keen on a late night tonight. We're off to Carlisle tomorrow.'

'Does Lucy know about the System?'

'Yes. After the murder, Nigel went round to Lucy's and told her everything. I haven't seen her since she found out, so it will be interesting to see how the conversation goes. Oh, here they come.'

The back door opened, and Lucy climbed in. 'Hi there, Ian, and hello, Zoë – nice to meet you.'

Once Nigel was in and the door was closed, Ian started the car and pulled off. The four engaged in idle chit-chat whilst Ian negotiated getting onto a busy Maid Marion Way and then getting off it again within about a mile.

'NCP?' Lucy enquired.

'Yes, any particular level take your fancy?'

Lucy chuckled. 'Not too far away from the stairwell if at all possible.'

Within twenty-five minutes, the four were seated at the back of a small, intimate Indian restaurant with their noses in four substantial menus.

'This is going to take forever,' Zoë observed. 'Are we having a starter and a pudding?'

'I'm up for three courses,' said Ian. Lucy and Nigel smiled at each other and nodded in agreement.

'In that case, I know what I'm having,' Zoë announced.

'I thought you were going to take forever?' Ian smiled in surprise.

'Nothing's forever,' Zoë reasoned lightly, wiping the smile from Ian's face.

The waiter came over and took their orders. He suggested poppadoms whilst their first course was being prepared. The decision was unanimous, and the appetiser duly arrived to be consumed with relish... literally. And chutney.

'So, you have a son, Nigel tells me.'

'Yes, Jason. My parents are looking after him just now. He's coming up to his first birthday in a couple of weeks. He's already getting a personality, though my mum doesn't think so. He seems to frown every time he wants a number two.'

Ian and Nigel frowned without realising it, and Zoë and Lucy laughed at the sight.

'So, do you work, Lucy? Ian hasn't told me anything about you,' Zoë asked.

'Yes, I do work. I'm a scientist.' Lucy paused for dramatic effect... and got it.

'Wow,' said Zoë. 'Er... what field?'

'Excellent, well done. I am a research scientist at Nottingham Uni., and I spend a lot of time at the Queens Medical Centre.'

'That place is huge,' Zoë said, warming to the topic.

'It's the largest in the country.'

'Wow,' Zoë repeated, and then realised she was wowing too much.

The starters arrived, interrupting the conversation.

'Wow,' Ian said, somewhat sarcastically, admiring a marvellous looking Seekh kebab.

'Absolutely, let's tuck in,' Nigel said, somewhat redundantly.

The conversation turned, inevitably, to racing.

'Yes, we're off to Carlisle tomorrow. We'll be setting off at about ten, let the rush-hour traffic die down a bit. It'll be a nice drive. No need for me to navigate, since we've been there before.'

'Hold on,' Ian interjected. 'Just because we've made the journey once doesn't mean I can remember every twist and turn. I will still be relying on you to get us there. We need petrol, by the way, so maybe a few minutes before ten?'

'We can call in at the twenty-four-hour garage on the way home tonight if you want?' Nigel suggested.

Zoë looked at Lucy and then back at Ian. 'Riveting,' she said, with a smile.

'Yeah, sorry.' Ian realised their companions were not finding the petrol conversation the least bit interesting. 'What have you got to tell us about Carlisle?' Ian turned to Nigel.

'I thought you'd never ask,' Nigel joked. He was in his element, and his audience werc all ears.

The waiter interrupted him, removing plates and busying himself by removing the poppadom crumbs from the immaculately white tablecloth.

As the waiter walked away, Ian chuckled to himself.

'What's so funny,' Lucy asked.

Ian shook his head as if to say don't ask. 'The waiter walking away reminded me of something at school.'

Nigel sighed – he had lost his audience.

'Go on, tell us,' Zoë said, with an air of resignation in her voice. Fortunately, she was smiling though.

'Well, you did ask. It was an English lesson, and our teacher, Mrs Radford, handed out strips of paper to everyone. The strips of paper were all the same with a single sentence and the teacher said absolutely nothing. No-one knew what was going on.

Studying Form

'Anyway, a couple of minutes later, the teacher handed out another strip of paper with a second sentence, and it was obvious the second sentence followed on from the first. So gradually, we all started to discuss what was in front of us, since a story was unfolding, and more importantly for the English lesson, we discussed what *might* come next. We started to look forward to the next bit of paper to see if the class discussion proved right.

'After a while, we had, I don't know, ten to fifteen bits of paper in front of us, and one kid in the class said, "The waiter is sixty-five." Well, there was uproar in the classroom. No-one knew what this kid was on about. We all looked through the bits of paper, and no-one could figure out where that snippet of information had come from. We were all scratching our heads, so to speak. So, the kid said, "It says here – The waiter served the drinks and then retired."'

Zoë and Lucy laughed, and Nigel tutted, shaking his head.

'It will stay with me forever, even the teacher had a belly laugh. Mark Wetherby was the boy's name, and he was the spitting image of Starsky out of *Starsky and Hutch.*'

'Anyway. Nigel, you were saying,' Lucy turned her attention to her on-off boyfriend.

'Carlisle, tomorrow, five o'clock. Duggan.'

'Is that it?' Zoë quizzed. 'No drama, no excited anticipation for your audience?'

'There's no following the *school* tale. I can't compete,' Nigel said.

317

Andy Wheildon

The Indian waiter came out of retirement, not sure why everyone around the table was grinning at him as he served the main course. 'More drinks?' he enquired.

As they drove home after an enjoyable, relaxing meal, Ian approached number nineteen once more, from the opposite direction. He pulled up opposite the red Volvo and both Nigel and Lucy got out. 'I'll see you in the morning,' Nigel said, poking his head through the back door of the car. The door banged shut, and both he and Lucy were gone. Ian watched as the two walked towards the front door. He turned to Zoë. 'Where to now?'

'Can you drive me home, please,' Zoë said. There was sadness in her voice.

Ian took a deep breath and pulled away from the curb. Over the next five miles, there were tears and deep discussion – no-one else was involved, but for Zoë, it was over. She cried and she apologised. She had to think about Jason, herself and her parents. She needed security and safety. Being with Ian, there was neither. It was too dangerous. The murderer had not been captured. The relationship had to end. It was for the best. Ian pulled up outside her house and switched off the engine. He turned to Zoë and tried to smile.

'Thank you for everything,' he said. 'Nearly every day for the past few months I have woken up with a smile on my face, and it's you who put that smile there. It's only been a couple of months, but I've now got memories which will stay with me forever. I hope you find what you're looking for, and I wish only the best for you in the future. You *and* Jason.'

Ian stared out of the car, looking straight ahead. 'One day, I might even get myself an allotment, you never know.'

Zoë laughed and sniffed back a tear. 'Goodbye, Ian. And thank you.'

She got out of the car and walked up the driveway. Ian never saw her again.

Friday, 26 July 1991

Nigel walked through the front door a few minutes past 9 a.m. Simon Mayo had just handed over to Simon Bates on Radio One, and Ian had just put the kettle on in the kitchen. Whilst Simon Bates prepared the nation for the Radio 1 Roadshow at Southsea later that morning, Ian busied himself with tea and toast.

'Hi there.' Nigel made his presence known and sat at the kitchen table. 'How did it go last night?'

'Not good. She ended it. With a killer still at large, she has concerns for herself and her child. There were a few tears as I drove her home, but the last words were *goodbye and thanks.*'

'Oh dear, sorry to hear that. I suppose, all things considered, she has a point.'

'I know.'

'Did you offer to change? Did you apologise for the mistakes, if you made any mistakes?'

'Sounds a bit desperate. No, I did none of that.'

'Like I said: sorry, mate.' Nigel reflected for a moment. 'There's nothing more to be said then. She was nice. Right now? A cup of tea will help. Two cups of tea, I mean.' Nigel smiled and shrugged his shoulders.

'Tea and a trip to Carlisle.'

'I'm off for a quick shower. Did you get petrol last night?'

Studying Form

'No, the mood didn't take me.'

'Course not, silly me.'

Nigel scampered up the stairs whilst Ian buttered his toast and added milk to his tea. He left a teabag in a cup for Nigel but didn't bother with any hot water because the tea would only stew.

'Forget the tea,' Nigel shouted down, before slamming the bathroom door shut.

*

Carlisle was again bathed in sunshine. Nigel and Ian went about their business with an element of routine. The two distributed £2,000 amongst the bookmakers whilst mingling with punters from all walks of life. The racecourse was packed.

Back in the car, they played their *who-won-the-most-money* game – again, now a matter of routine – and Ian was the victor by a mere £87. Their journey home was uneventful, but when they found themselves on Maid Marion Way, Ian got a pang of sadness. Nigel was, of course, totally oblivious.

*

Metcalf was discussing his case with a superior. 'I'm not sure holding back a horse is actually a crime, as far as common law goes. Obviously, it is a crime in racing circles, and anyone found guilty of doing so would be banned from the industry, as has happened before. But it's not the kind of crime anyone would end up in court for.'

'Indeed. I agree with you. Also, I agree with what you say about the trainer. I think Collier… Is that his name?'

'Yes, sir'

'I think Collier is just an unfortunate bystander in all of this. He may have grounds for making a complaint against Trist for blackmail, but I don't think he wants any trouble. He will be keen for us to be discreet and ensure he isn't implicated in anything. So, what's your next step?'

'Trist has denied ever seeing Rodney Blundell, but we have photographic evidence to the contrary. He is, therefore, lying. I don't want to barge in and present this evidence to him without having more to go on. With your permission, sir, I'd like to take a look at his finances. If Trist employed someone to kill Green and Turner, then he must have paid a hefty sum. I'm sure that sort of thing doesn't come cheap'

'Yes, I agree. I'll oversee the process for getting hold of the necessary information. These things take about three weeks though. Have you any leads on Blundell? Finding the killer would go a long way towards nailing Trist as an accomplice.'

'Nothing, I'm afraid, sir. There is an international warrant out on him. The photograph we got from Nigel Green has been fully circulated, but it's a few years out of date. He's vanished.'

'Hmm, like an old oak table.'

'Pardon, sir?

Studying Form

'Nothing. That's all, Metcalf. Keep me informed. I want to know the moment you get a lead on Blundell.'

'Yes, sir. Thank you.' Metcalf got up from the table and left the office, pleased to be able to get out for a cigarette.

*

At the same moment, Parrot/Blundell/Berwick was walking out of a newsagent in Sydney, taking in the breath-taking view of the Sydney Opera House and the harbour bridge behind. It was gloriously sunny, but there was a nip in the air when in the shade. He crossed the road, so he could walk in direct sunlight. Lovely but cool, now the sun was on his back.

As he walked away from the newsagent with the harbour pier behind him, going towards his private lodge, he wondered how long he would be in Australia. Would he ever be truly free to go anywhere he wanted? Probably not. He was, however, working on a new identity. He had many cemeteries to visit in this neck of the woods.

*

A couple of days later, there was a knock at the door, and Griffiths got up from his kitchen table. He called to Rebecca, upstairs, 'I'll get it.'

He opened the front door and was greeted by a warrant card and, 'Detective Sergeant Metcalf. Can I have a word?'

'Come in,' Griffiths said, moving away from the threshold to allow Metcalf to pass. 'Head on into the kitchen, straight on. Just follow the smell of fish – I'm preparing tea.'

Metcalf found himself in a small kitchen furnished with a small kitchen table and a stove with three pots simmering away and a glowing grill overcooking some white fish.

'Cooking not your strong point, I take it,' Metcalf quipped, somewhat rudely.

'Yeah, you could say that, DS Metcalf. It's been a while… and a promotion – Congratulations.'

'Frank, how long has it been? Four years, at least.'

'I've been out of the force four years, so probably five. How can I help you?'

'I'll come straight to the point; I don't want to see the fish incinerated. I'm investigating the murder of a certain Mr James Price, and it would appear you knew him. I have a few witnesses who have said you and he have been seen together *recently*. I want to know about you and Price, and what *exactly* you were doing in the company of a man who has since been murdered.'

'I was horrified when I heard Price had been murdered. I knew about his past and his involvement in the Bank Manager case. The papers have been suggesting his death was something to do with that.'

'Don't tell me what I already know, Frank. How about telling me what you've been up to in the past… I don't know… the past six months? What have you done this year? How has your private investigator work been going? Have you been privately investigating anything that would interest me, involving Price?'

'Let me make you a drink, and then I'll tell you about a system that beats the bookies. You'll be amazed at what I've got to tell you.' Griffiths had no idea Green and Turner had told Metcalf about the System already. Griffiths had no idea Metcalf was also investigating a burglary connected to the killing.

Metcalf sat back and let Griffiths talk for over an hour. After about fifteen minutes, Metcalf realised Griffiths was going into too much detail. Experience had taught him that it was what was *not* being said in such circumstances that would prove important. 'Carry on,' Metcalf said encouragingly, every now and again.

'How often did you follow them to a race meeting?' Metcalf asked.

'Three.'

'So, you witnessed them winning considerable amounts of money at three racecourses?'

'Well, no. Only two. I was warned off on the last occasion.'

'What do you mean, warned off?'

Griffiths knew he was now walking on thin ice, but he decided honesty, during a murder investigation, was the best policy. So, he went on to describe the moment a gun was used to dissuade him from following Green and Turner. He chose not to tell Metcalf about committing burglary later the same day.

'Interesting,' said Metcalf, referring to his notes. 'That same day, well the evening actually, Green and Turner were burgled. Any idea about that?'

'No idea.' Griffiths hoped he sounded convincing.

'Could you come down to the station tomorrow, Frank? I want to show you some photos. Hopefully, you can remember what the guy with the gun looked like, and hopefully, you'll be able to point him out. The station tomorrow, about 10 a.m.?'

'No problem.'

'Good. I'll get off then. Sorry if I've ruined your tea. Good job you turned the grill down.'

'I'll see you out.'

Once Metcalf had gone, Griffiths raced up the stairs and knocked on Rebecca's door. 'We need to lose the computer downstairs, like fast. Go out and buy a computer tomorrow, and do what needs to be done to get Henry working on the new computer. It's urgent. Remember Metcalf from work some years back?'

'Yes, what of it? Why the sudden urgency?'

'Well, Metcalf is now Detective Sergeant Metcalf, and he was downstairs just now. He's investigating Price's murder, and I let on I had seen the wrong end of a gun recently. The burglary came up in discussion. The computer has to go. How much will it cost to replace it?'

'I don't know, Dad,' Rebecca said, shrugging her shoulders. 'I suppose I've got some money from the Nottingham trip and from the nice little earner last Monday. I'll sort it out. Tomorrow is going to be tricky though.' Rebecca paused for thought. 'No, tomorrow's fine. Priorities and all that!'

'Thanks, you do your mum proud.'

Griffiths closed Rebecca's bedroom door and, going back downstairs, wished his beautiful wife was still alive.

Thursday, 1 August 1991

'Dad, there's something wrong with *Henry*. He's stopped working.' Rebecca called her dad in from the garden where he was harvesting some runner beans.

Putting the beans on the kitchen table, he followed Rebecca into the front room and sat down next to her as she showed him what was wrong.

'So, as normal, I turned the computer on. I put my own operating system password in, and the computer booted up as normal. Now, at the DOS prompt, I typed in FORTUNE, again as normal. The program asks for a password which we know. So, I typed it in and... nothing. Straight back to the DOS prompt.'

'The what?'

'That thing on the screen.' Rebecca pointed to three characters to the left of the screen. 'C colon backslash, followed by the greater than sign. It's called the DOS prompt, but that's not important. What is important is the System isn't working.'

'OK, let's not panic, and let's think for a moment. What's changed? We have a new computer. Is that the only thing that's changed? Have we done something wrong moving Henry from the old computer to this new one? Surely, that's the answer,' said Griffiths, sounding rather smug.

Studying Form

'That's what I thought initially, but only for a moment. We've had this new computer for two days. Henry was fine two days ago; Henry was fine yesterday. The only thing to have changed, as far as I am concerned, is July has changed to August. So, I put the System clock back to July 30, and it still doesn't work.'

'The system clock? Does that mean you've fooled the computer to believe it's yesterday? Blimey, clever. And, er, oh dear.' Griffiths sat down and looked at the blank computer screen, thinking about the fortune he was about to lose. 'Remind me, what did you do to get the password? Something to do with decomposing, wasn't it?'

'Decompiling. I was able to decompile the code and then recompile it. You're right though. I will need to decompile the application again and try to find what is happening. But I don't understand the code fully. I'm not a programmer in this language. I would need to give it to someone else. Then we would either be sharing our goldmine with someone else, or we would be saying goodbye to it if they decide to take it from us. I'm being a half empty kind of person here. Worst case scenario, and all that…'

Griffiths sighed. 'What now then? Do you want to retrain as a programmer in a new language?'

'Not really, Dad, thanks all the same.' Rebecca stared out of the window and idly watched a double-decker bus drive past, the upstairs deck packed with passengers. As always, she was thankful for the net curtains. 'We could ask the authors, I suppose?'

Griffiths laughed out loud and shook his head. 'You've got to be joking.'

'Not really, Dad. Let's give it some thought. Obviously, we would have to approach them with caution. Your friend, Price, didn't do too well when he met them.'

'He was never a friend, Rebecca.'

'Yeah, OK, sorry. We would need to be cautious, that's all I'm saying. If you talk to them, tell them you have the program, tell them you can decompile it, tell them you can publish the program so everyone can use it and tell them that would result in their system becoming useless.'

Griffiths thought for a few moments. 'So, what exactly do I have to say?'

Rebecca went back to staring out of the window. 'I don't know, yet! Maybe what *I* just said.'

*

Nigel answered the front door, slightly annoyed – having just sat down to read an article in the *Sporting Life* from a few months ago. The article featured Frankie Dettori and his winning one hundred races in the 1990 season when still only a teenager.

'Hello?' Nigel said, looking at two familiar faces though recognising neither. Looking quizzically at them, he asked, 'Can I help you?'

Griffiths was somewhat uneasy but decided to take the bull by the horns. 'We've got a copy of your racing system.'

Studying Form

Nigel stared at Griffiths for some time then glanced at the young woman by his side. Turning back to Griffiths. 'And you are?'

'I am... we are here to discuss keeping the System alive and successful. If that interests you at all?'

'Why do I feel like I know you but have absolutely no idea who you are? Both of you?' This time he stared at Rebecca. Nigel repeated, 'Who the hell are you?'

'My name is Rebecca, and this is my dad, Frank. We have your system; we have used your system. Quite successfully, I might add. We have updated the System with data from RLDS. Unfortunately, the System has stopped working... Do we really need to do this on the doorstep?'

Nigel just stood and stared.

Ian popped his head over Nigel's shoulder. 'What's going on? Oh, hello again!'

'You know these people?' Nigel asked in an agitated voice. 'You actually know these people?'

'No.' Ian smiled, not realising what was going on. 'I do, however, recognise a pretty face,' he said, looking directly into Rebecca's gorgeous green eyes. 'We saw you at Nottingham races, didn't we? You missed the first race.'

'Blimey, that's right,' Nigel said. 'You asked us if we knew the result of the first race in the beer tent!' He turned to Ian. 'They have a copy of our system.'

Ian's smile disappeared immediately. 'What? How?'

Rebecca said again, 'Do we have to do this on the doorstep?' She smiled at Ian, seeking an ally.

Nigel led them both into the kitchen and invited them to sit at the kitchen table.

'Where's the radio cassette recorder?' Griffiths asked.

Ian and Nigel exchanged worried glances which were not lost on Griffiths.

Resignedly, Griffiths gave an explanation. 'I was working for James Price at the time he was murdered... in this very kitchen,' he said, looking around and giving a shudder. 'I know people in the police force, and I hear you taped the event. Ah, on that very machine?' Griffiths pointed at the radio cassette recorder on top of the fridge.

Without saying anything, Nigel walked over to the fridge and unplugged the radio. He opened the fridge door, put the radio inside and slammed the door shut. He turned back to Griffiths and Rebecca and said simply, 'We're listening.'

Twenty minutes later, Ian and Nigel knew exactly where they stood. The choice was simple. Either they lost the System completely, when Griffiths and his daughter managed to reverse-engineer it and share it far and wide, or they retained the System and took on a couple of eager partners.

'I quite like the name Henry,' Ian said, smiling at Rebecca. She smiled back, and Ian was surprised to get a feeling in the pit of his stomach similar to when he first saw Zoë.

Studying Form

'So,' summarised Ian. 'you're prepared to keep the System a total secret, scout's honour. You agree not to share the application. Actually, why don't you destroy your copy? No, on second thoughts, forget that. Keeping the System is your bit of security. You keep the copy as an insurance policy! I don't believe this. You agree not to share the System, and we agree to tell you what's going to win. We do all the work, and you get free money. This doesn't sound right. No, this is totally wrong. How about you pay us for the information?'

Ian looked at Nigel with a Eureka moment flashing in his head.

Nigel had an identical Eureka moment.

Griffiths didn't see the enlightened glance between the two.

'That's reasonable, Dad,' Rebecca said to Griffiths. 'We now have an investment in the System. We want the System to be successful, and we want the System to remain secret. We keep the secret; we pay for the knowledge in the knowledge that the knowledge we have—'

Everyone laughed. The mood was lightening amongst the four in the kitchen. 'Far too much knowledge, for my liking,' Ian said.

'Agreed,' said Nigel.

The next couple of hours saw Ian warming to Rebecca, and the four discussing how they were going to share information and travel to different racetracks around the country. The System was due to go into hibernation from the second of November when the

Flat season saw its final fixture at Folkestone, so they would all have a busy couple of months ahead of them.

It was Ian who showed Frank and Rebecca out when the discussions had finished. He was feeling a bit dizzy because he hadn't eaten for a while. As the two visitors walked away, Ian called after them. 'Fancy a drink tonight, Rebecca?'

She turned and smiled. 'Sure, I'd like that. I'll pick you up at seven, if you want?'

'Wow, you have a car?' Ian was surprised, which on reflection was a bit chauvinistic. 'That would be great, thanks. Seven would be perfect.'

Ian closed the front door and went back to Nigel in the kitchen.

'You know what?' Nigel asked his friend.

'We could sell the information?'

'Exactly. Well, a slightly modified version making sure it isn't 100% accurate. Just enough to keep customers satisfied. Let's give it some thought.'

'Absolutely. I'm off out with Rebecca this evening,' Ian said matter-of-factly, as he went to put the kettle on. 'She's picking me up at seven.'

'Good for you. She seems nice. In that case, can I ask a favour?'

'Go on,' Ian turned to face Nigel.

'If you get anywhere with her, could you steal back our system?'

Ian smiled. 'The thought had crossed my mind.' He made tea for two.

Studying Form

*

In the weeks that followed, Griffiths found himself driving all over the country, successfully placing bets on horses given to him by Nigel and Ian. The price for the information they gave varied. If the odds were shorter, the cost of the information was low. If the odds were longer, the cost was higher. Griffiths was happy with the arrangement, and his bank balance was improving at a fair rate of knots as a result.

Ian and Rebecca became an item rather quickly and began talking about finding a place to live together within a couple of months.

Nigel, with Ian, continued to visit racecourses other than those being frequented by Griffiths, and they too improved the standing of their respective bank balances. Nigel was able to buy the property he lived in from his parents and planned on having Lucy move in. *That will probably be the catalyst for Ian to move out*, he thought.

Once the 'relationship' between the Griffiths, Nigel and Ian had settled down, Nigel decided to dip his toe in the water and advertised in the *Sporting Life*. He offered to provide detailed information, for a fee, on potential winners for handicap races. He put, in his advert, some of the previous winners he had successfully predicted and waited for customers to take the bait.

They did, in huge numbers. Financially, Ian and Nigel were secure, and their *Studying Form* publication became everybody's must-have source of information and the talk of the racing industry.

Acknowledgements

My gratitude goes to the following people who have helped me on this somewhat long journey to becoming an author. Thanks for your honest feedback and support which kept me motivated throughout and apologies for dragging my heels for so long. The novel took quite a while to finish.

My wife, Dawn, who employed the patience of a saint in response to my years of mumbling, 'I should get the novel done.' Her attention to detail whilst undertaking a final proof read has me thinking she's in the wrong job.

Jodie Wentworth, who read the novel in its first iteration and came all the way to Reading from London, one Sunday afternoon, laden with wine, pudding and superb feedback.

Karl Sharp, for suggesting I pass the novel to a highly rated film director. A truly motivating suggestion. Maybe – one day.

Ann Hoar, for suggesting I go easy on the chauvinism (as did my editor!).

Mark O'Sullivan, for buying the odd beer or two whilst appraising the manuscript in the early days.

Andy Wheildon

Latterly, my thanks must also go to Chris Kellett who cajoled me into putting pen to paper for one final flourish to get the novel across the line. Maybe I should buy him a pint.

Also, I owe a huge debt of thanks to my editor Kat Harvey for improving the read beyond measure and showing patience when the all too frequent typo or syntax error raised its ugly head. I am truly grateful.

Throughout the novel, reference is made to places around the UK and actual horse races that took place. I am indebted to Adrian Buttery for advising me of the existence of the *Raceform Flat Annual 1991*, and also to *eBay* for helping me find a copy.

About the Author

Andy Wheildon has been something of a nomad throughout his life, living in Birmingham, Nottingham, Grimsby, Nottingham (again), Brighton, Reading and, latterly, Stirling, Scotland.

Having finished an engineering degree in Nottingham, he decided that engineering was not for him, so he took a few part-time jobs on the south coast before finding work for a credit card company in Brighton. He then moved to Reading and subsequently Stirling whilst working for a large insurance company for a period of twenty-nine years.

Recently Mr Wheildon retired. Now, he busies himself on his allotment or can be found with a guitar in his hand, having decided to learn the instrument at the ripe old age of fifty-seven and three quarters.

Married with two adult children, Andy looks forward to a long retirement helped by a few cruises in the coming years, having recently discovered that cruising is the way forwards for truly relaxing holidays.

Thanks for reading this far!

andywheildonbooks.co.uk

Printed in Great Britain
by Amazon

45199959R00195